TARA HUDSON was born and raised in Oklahoma. She graduated with a degree in law, mostly because she believed all the horror stories about English majors and their careers in the food-service industry. Luckily she soon remembered how much she loved telling ghost stories, particularly to her girlfriends, who liked visiting abandoned cemeteries as much as she did.

Tara currently lives in Oklahoma with her husband, son, and a menagerie of ill-behaved pets.

Visit her at www.tarahudson.com.

ARISE

✢TARA HUDSON✢

HarperCollins*Publishers*

First published in the USA by
HarperCollins*Publishers* Inc. in 2012
First published in paperback in Great Britain by
HarperCollins *Children's Books* in 2012
HarperCollins *Children's Books* is a division of HarperCollins*Publishers* Ltd,
77-85 Fulham Palace Road,
Hammersmith,
London, W6 8JB.

www.harpercollins.co.uk

ARISE
Copyright © Tara Hudson 2012
All rights reserved

Tara Hudson asserts the moral right to be identified as the author of the work.

ISBN 978-0-00-743727-6

Printed and bound in England by Clays Ltd, St Ives plc.
Typography by Erin Fitzsimmons

1

MIX
Paper from
responsible sources
FSC
www.fsc.org **FSC® C007454**

FSC™ is a non-profit international organisation established to promote
the responsible management of the world's forests. Products carrying the
FSC label are independently certified to assure consumers that they come
from forests that are managed to meet the social, economic and
ecological needs of present and future generations,
and other controlled sources.

Find out more about HarperCollins and the environment at
www.harpercollins.co.uk/green

To my new son, Wyatt –
you are my greatest challenge, and my biggest reward.

ARISE

Chapter
ONE

The entire world had gone dark, and I had no idea why.

No matter how widely I opened my eyes, no matter how many times I craned my neck or spun around in search of even one speck of light, I found none. There was nothing but thick, impenetrable darkness.

Before I'd opened my eyes to all this pitch-black, I had the vague impression that I'd just been someplace warm, familiar. Someplace safe.

But wherever I was now, I didn't feel safe at all. I felt

sightless and trapped. Like I was on the verge of being consumed by the darkness . . . like it was trying to eat me whole.

Although I couldn't see, I could still hear things: the swish of my long dress as I whirled in useless, searching circles; the hiss of my increasingly panicked breath.

I heard something else, too—some sound I couldn't quite identify. Not at first.

It started softly, almost muffled. A strange noise echoing out from beneath layers and layers of cotton. But as the sound grew in volume, it also deepened. Slowly, it transformed into something stronger. Something that more closely resembled a continuous thudding.

When the thudding gained a certain steadiness—a rhythm—I sucked in one sharp breath.

I recognized the sound now, and it made me want to scream.

If I were anyone else—any*thing* else—I probably wouldn't have reacted that way. After all, the rhythmic thudding of a heartbeat usually meant something positive. It meant life.

But for me, an audible heartbeat meant only one thing: someone nearby was dying.

It wouldn't be me, of course. I hadn't felt a genuine heartbeat in my chest since the day I drowned, on the night of my eighteenth birthday more than ten years ago.

The sound I heard now was definitely made by a *living* heart. And I couldn't fight the horrible suspicion that it belonged to someone I loved.

Joshua Mayhew, for instance. Or even his little sister, Jillian. Both very much alive, and both of whose heartbeats I monitored carefully after I'd worked so hard to protect them.

Hearing that terrible thudding now, I forced myself to calm down and focus more intently on the darkness. I strained and squinted, peering into the dark until, blessedly, weak light began to shimmer along the edges of my vision. I watched each new sliver closely, silently praying that it would reveal the owner of that heart. Selfishly praying that it wouldn't be Joshua. As I waited impatiently, another realization struck me: I could rely on senses other than sight and hearing. This was strange, considering the fact that ghosts can't smell, taste, or feel anything outside themselves. At least not very often.

Yet I could smell a sweet, musty decay all around me. It overlay the scent of damp air. Combined, the scents had an almost disorienting effect. The smells, the heartbeat, the shifting darkness—all of it made me dizzy and uncomfortable.

Thankfully, the light grew brighter, and I could finally see that I stood in a dim room. Across from me, heavily slatted shutters ran from a wood-planked floor up to a beamed ceiling. The shutters blocked most of the light from what could only be the sun, shining outside a wall of windows.

Furniture filled the room: randomly placed chairs and end tables, as well as a low coffee table that flanked a couch. Flung across the couch, in some sort of make-shift slipcover, was a white bedsheet. And flung across the sheet was a person.

At first I thought she might be a child. On closer inspection, I realized the tiny figure was actually closer to my own age. She had curled into a protective ball on the couch, spine pressed to the back cushions and sharp hip bone jutting up in the air. Her head lolled sideways onto one of the couch's arms, and her dark brown hair cascaded in a tangle to the floor.

Even in the darkness of the room I could see the unhealthy sheen of her skin. Sweat glistened upon her sunken cheeks, and her eyes fluttered behind their closed lids.

Something about the girl's face gave me an actual chill. Something about her features . . .

I leaned closer for a better look, and, at that moment, the girl opened her eyes to stare blankly into the room. Her eyes were red rimmed and unfocused, addled by either sleep or some kind of chemical. Probably the lat-ter, judging by the overturned prescription bottle that had spilled a rainbow of pills across the table in front of her.

Under normal circumstances—if anything about this scene could be classified as normal—I would have been worried about this girl. However ineffectively, I would have tried to find someone to help her. I would have grasped at her with my dead, incapable hands.

But these were not normal circumstances.

Because just one sight of the girl's eyes rooted me to the floor. Those eyes, though bloodshot and bleary, were still a luminous green, shining out from a face I knew very well.

My own.

Chapter
TWO

Death, a voice rasped in my head. *It always starts with death.*

I bolted upright with a shriek.

Immediately, I felt the press of a hand upon mine. My adrenaline surged at the unexpected touch, and I moved to jerk away from it. Whoever had pressed against my hand grabbed it more tightly and held me firmly in place. It took a few more seconds of struggling before I calmed down enough to look at the face of my captor.

He stared back at me, his eyebrows furrowed above

dark blue eyes. With one of his hands grasping mine, he ran the other through his black hair and then rested his palm upon the back of his neck—a nervous, worried gesture.

Without warning, I threw my free arm around my captor's neck and pressed my lips to his.

At that moment I didn't care that I was dead and shouldn't have been sleeping, much less dreaming; I didn't care that I'd dreamed about myself in some unfamiliar, near-death state; nor did I care that I should behave more carefully around the boy I now kissed since I was invisible and he wasn't.

All I cared was that Joshua kissed me back.

Wherever his hands clutched at my bare skin—my arms, my shoulders, my exposed thigh—they ignited a shower of fiery sparks. Even my lips burned from their contact with his.

This minor miracle happened every time we touched. At each press of my ghostly flesh to his living, Joshua and I both experienced waves of sensation that, with prolonged contact, turned into the actual feel of each other's skin.

Maybe this was unique to me and Joshua, maybe not. For all I knew, every ghost-to-spiritually-aware-human interaction happened this way. Whatever the case, I knew one thing for sure: I never grew tired of it.

I sighed quietly when Joshua pulled his lips from mine. Although I sighed in disappointment that our kiss had ended, I also sighed in relief. As Joshua leaned away from me, I could see we were alone in his bedroom, lying on his bed. No one had seen us kiss.

But my relief turned into embarrassment when I realized that, during our kiss, I must have rolled on top of him. Joshua was now beneath me, with my thighs pressed against either side of his hips. My filmy white dress—the one in which I'd died and was now cursed to wear forever—had crept up to a seriously inappropriate height on my thighs.

Gape mouthed, I stared down at Joshua. His mussed hair and his lack of a T-shirt told me that my post-nightmare shriek had woken him up, too. And his broad grin told me he wasn't even slightly embarrassed by our current position.

"Yikes," I murmured. I moved to roll myself off, but he pinned me to him by wrapping one arm around my waist.

"Aw," Joshua protested. "No 'yikes,' Amelia. Why don't you make yourself comfortable up there?" His grin turned wolfish as he secured his other arm around me.

I scowled. "Joshua Mayhew, even if I'm in your bed every night, I'm not . . . *cheap*."

Although his bedside clock read 3 a.m., Joshua laughed so loudly his entire family could have heard him, if they were awake.

"Amelia Ashley," Joshua teased. "The fact that you're in my bed every night means I don't think you're cheap. And, for the record, I think it's adorable that you used the word 'cheap.' You *are* aware it's the twenty-first century, right?"

"What can I say? I'm a twentieth-century kind of girl," I grumbled; but I let him tug me closer, until I had to drop my arms on either side of him to keep myself upright.

Hovering there, I studied Joshua's face for a moment: his midnight-sky colored eyes, his full mouth, his high cheekbones. Then I peeked at the nearly bare body extending beneath that face. And beneath me.

"Well," I murmured, "since I'm already here . . ."

Then I dipped down and pressed my lips to his again.

Beneath my kiss, I felt Joshua smile triumphantly. As he moved his mouth against mine, he placed his fingertips on the delicate skin beneath my jaw. Then he ran them down my throat to my collarbone, where he traced them lightly back and forth.

I moaned quietly, and, in an instant, Joshua rolled us over so that he stretched out above me. I closed my eyes and placed my hands on his bare back, anticipating the moment I would feel his skin, smooth and warm and real. In my excitement, I hitched one leg up and wrapped it around Joshua's hip.

And with that gesture, I stopped feeling anything at all.

I opened my eyes and sighed, not really surprised by what I now saw above me. Instead of the ceiling of Joshua's bedroom, a maze of trees branches—bare except for a heavy layer of frost—tangled together. A mix of rain and sleet now fell noisily around me. Luckily, I couldn't feel the sting of ice as it battered my shoulders.

As I pushed myself into a seated position and took in the rest of my surroundings, however, I didn't feel very lucky. To my right, a squat brick structure—a chimney, I think—rose up toward the sky. Beneath me, row upon row of shingles sloped precariously down toward a very familiar backyard.

Excellent. I always wanted to know what the Mayhews' roof looked like.

At that dry thought, I pulled my legs into my chest, wrapped my arms around them, and lay my head on my knees. Then I puffed out a big, angry sigh.

I guess I should have been grateful, considering how short a distance I materialized tonight. The last time this happened, I'd opened my eyes to what I'm pretty sure was an entirely different county.

Before materializations like this one started occurring, I honestly thought I'd learned to control them—learned how to prevent the ghostly vanishings that transported me, unwilling, to someplace else, sometime else.

I was wrong, obviously.

It wasn't that I *wanted* to materialize away from Joshua tonight. Far from it. But over the past few months, I'd come to the sad realization that we couldn't go much further than we already had, physically, without me disappearing into thin air. Every time we kissed too long, or held each other too closely, I'd vanish. If Joshua's fingers strayed too far below my collarbone—*zap*, to a deserted car lot. If I loosened just one of his buttons—*poof*, to the top of a picnic table at some rest stop on the side of the highway.

Each time I vanished, I could materialize back instantly, free from ice or any other kind of harm. But the mood was always dampened, to say the least.

And each time I vanished, I slowly learned my lesson: unless I kept a tighter guard on my emotions, and my actions with Joshua, I had no control over what happened to my body.

I guess I hadn't learned the lesson well enough. Not yet.

I couldn't help but sigh loudly. This situation was so unfair I could almost taste it, tart and bitter on my tongue. After all, my desire wasn't so crazy, so outrageous, that it needed to be denied in such a harsh way. What I wanted—what Joshua and I both wanted—was simple, and normal, and genuine.

And obviously impossible.

I lifted my head from my knees and sighed again. There was nothing I could do about the problem now except get back to Joshua and try to make things right. As right as they could be anyway.

I closed my eyes and focused on the house beneath me. I heard a soft whoosh of air, and when I opened my eyes, I found myself sitting on a bed, staring into the familiar glow of Joshua's bedside lamp.

If only *all* my materializations could be this controlled.

Behind me I heard the shifting sound of bedsprings. I threw a wary glance over my shoulder and saw Joshua. He'd propped himself against his headboard and faced forward, frowning in deep thought.

I'd expected to find him frustrated, or angry, or maybe even a little sad. Instead, Joshua simply looked . . . intent. Like he was trying to solve some difficult problem.

Sensing my presence, he stirred and caught my eye. Without leaning away from the headboard, he stretched his arm across the bed to me.

"Hey, stranger," he said with a slight smile.

I groaned, turning more fully toward him before I took

his offered hand. "How long was I gone this time?"

"Not too long—only a few minutes. Getting better, I think."

I snorted. "Better? Seriously? It's hardly getting better if it just keeps happening."

Joshua shook his head and smiled wider, undeterred. "You're wrong, Amelia. The disappearances are getting shorter and shorter. I bet they stop happening altogether soon. It's going to get easier—I promise."

In the face of his perpetual optimism, I bit my lip to keep my mouth shut. Or to keep my response locked inside, more like it.

How could I tell Joshua the truth about what I'd really been thinking lately: that our relationship would *never* get easier? That if things were this difficult now, when we were both young, they would grow insurmountable as Joshua aged.

Because, inevitably, Joshua *would* age. Very soon he would graduate from Wilburton High School and move away to college. At some point he would probably want a girl he could introduce to his family, one whom all of them could see and half of them wouldn't want to exorcise. A girl he could make out with for more than ten minutes. A girl with whom, maybe someday, he'd start a family.

A girl I could never be.

Still biting my lip, I looked at Joshua more closely. The soft, hopeful look in his eyes told me that he didn't share my troubled thoughts. At least, not at the moment.

"So, where'd you go this time?" he asked, taking his hand from mine and brushing a strand of hair off my face.

I pulled my lip from my teeth and tilted my head to one side. "Your roof, actually."

Joshua's eyes widened. After a long, stunned pause, he cleared his throat. In an intentionally calm voice, he asked, "Oh? And how was it up there?"

"Icy. Probably freezing."

Joshua grimaced, from either the idea of the storm outside or the thought of me sitting in it. "This one wasn't like any of your old nightmares, was it?"

"No, thank God for that," I said, shuddering.

I hadn't had a real nightmare in several months, at least not in the way I defined the word "nightmare."

Before I'd met Joshua, before I'd saved him from drowning in the same river I had, a series of waking nightmares controlled my afterlife. In daylight as well as darkness, I would sometimes lose consciousness and then relive part of my death. Upon waking, I would find myself someplace other than where I'd been just before the nightmare occurred. I'd learned these nightmares were involuntary materializations, much like the ones I experienced now, but worse.

I still wasn't entirely sure why the nightmares had ended. I suspected it had something to do with the fact that I now remembered the details of my death. Or maybe because I'd fought back against the dark spirits who had engineered that death.

Whichever the case, the end of the nightmares meant the beginning of an entirely new set of troubles. These new—but still unwanted—materializations, for example. And then there were the weird dreams, like the one I'd had tonight.

I didn't like thinking about the dreams, but after one occurred, I just couldn't stop. I obsessed over their details, trying—without much success—to find a pattern in them, or a reason for them.

So far each dream differed in content from the previous one. But they all shared a pretty common theme. All of them happened at night, when I *shouldn't* have been sleeping, and all of them were incredibly disturbing.

In each dream I saw people for whom I cared but couldn't speak to them, couldn't touch them. Sometimes I saw Joshua, watching me with a cold, impassive expression while I begged him for help. Sometimes I saw Jillian drop to her knees in pain as Eli—the cruel ghost who had tried to acquire my soul for his demonic masters— tore the life from her.

Or sometimes I saw my father's ghost, wandering lost beneath the ruins of the bridge I'd destroyed several months ago in an effort to protect Joshua and Jillian from Eli. In those dreams my father called out to me. He asked, in a broken voice, why I hadn't yet freed him from the dark netherworld that waited just outside the living boundaries of High Bridge.

I hated those dreams the most.

Tonight's dream, however, was a new one. Never before had I watched myself like some outside observer; never before had I seen myself hurting, maybe even dying, in a setting I didn't recognize.

I didn't exactly have the clearest memories of my life before death, but most things I recalled had at least a touch of familiarity to them. Nothing about tonight's dream, however, seemed familiar—not the dark room or the shabby furniture. The only aspect of the room I recognized was the girl on the couch. Me, maybe.

So . . . what on earth was I supposed to make of *that*?

I shook my head and curled up beside Joshua without touching him. Joshua mirrored my position, facing me. My long silence didn't seem to bother him, probably because I'd had so many of them lately.

"Well," he finally said. "At least tonight's materialization wasn't a nightmare. But you did sit up screaming earlier. Do you want to tell me what *that* was about?"

My eyes darted down to the pillow beneath my head, away from Joshua's intent gaze. I shrugged. "Another one of those weird dreams I keep having. This one was different, though. Weirder."

I felt Joshua twitch beside me. "How so?" he asked.

I continued to study the pillow while I described the dream's eerie details. When I finished, Joshua blew out a puff of air.

"That's . . . well, that's creepy, Amelia."

"Very. And the even bigger issue is that I don't sleep. The fact I'm dreaming at all makes me think these dreams are—I don't know—important maybe? Tonight's dream *really* makes me wonder. Everything seemed so real: the sounds, the smells."

"And you're sure you saw yourself alive in this one?"

"Well . . . not completely sure. The girl looked a lot like me, but there was something else about her. Something I can't put my finger on."

Joshua frowned, thoughtful. "Maybe the girl was just some, you know, manifestation. Of your worries."

Despite my apprehensive mood, I couldn't help but laugh. "Wow, Dr. Mayhew. Someone's been doing his psychology homework."

"My favorite elective." Joshua chuckled good-naturedly. Then he yawned.

I propped myself up on my elbow, glanced over his

shoulder at his bedside clock, and fell back onto the bed beside him.

"We can talk more about this later," I said. "It's past four already, and you've got a calculus final today."

"Don't remind me." He groaned, pulling his own pillow around his ears in a U shape. "Why sleep at all? I'll probably get a better score if I just try to hallucinate the answers."

"I'm not going to let you hallucinate your way through your last final. We've been studying for weeks. So . . . *sleep.*"

With the pillow still pressed to his ears, Joshua shook his head. But even through the fabric, I heard the muffled sound of another yawn.

I guess I didn't need to give him any more commands or warnings because soon, without further protest, he began to drift off. Eventually, his breath deepened enough that I knew he'd fallen asleep again.

With an enormous sigh, I rolled over to stare blankly at the ceiling. For a while I tried to stay calm and restful. To run through a few of the calculus equations Joshua had struggled with the most. But soon, instead of numbers, my head started to spin with all the lingering questions that still plagued me.

Several months ago I thought I'd finally solved my greatest problems. I'd begun to piece together the sketchy details of my past and gain control of my ghostly powers. I'd prevented Eli from trapping me in the dark netherworld and forcing me to become a sort of grim reaper like him. Even Joshua's grandmother Ruth and her coven of ghost hunters had left me alone as some sort of repayment for saving Jillian's life.

So I'd *earned* a chance to enjoy whatever time I had left with Joshua, right?

Wrong.

Instead, my new, Eli- and Ruth-free existence had only become peaceful enough to allow another mess of problems into it. There were too many things to think about, too many issues I couldn't resolve. Like the haunting image of my doppelgänger languishing in that dank room. Or my total inability to kiss my boyfriend for more than a few minutes. Or . . . or . . .

"Ugh," I muttered in disgust, but then clamped my lips shut when I heard a small hitch in Joshua's breath.

When he began to breathe evenly again, I carefully slipped off the bed and tiptoed to the broad window seat on the other side of the room. I curled up on the seat's thick blue cushions, tucking my feet beneath me and pressing my forehead to the windowpane.

Right now I'd give just about anything to feel the glass, cold and soothing against my skin. No such luck, though. I felt only the numb pressure of the pane in front of me and the cushion beneath me.

Just two more objects in the living world I couldn't really touch.

Forehead still pressed against the window, hair hanging around my face so I couldn't see anything but the dark, icy view outside, I shook my head. Then I burrowed more fully into the cushions, settling in for another troubled night spent obsessing over the things I would never be able to change.

Chapter
THREE

A sharp *clunk* rang out beneath me as someone's foot connected with the wooden leg of the chair in which I now sat. I looked up in time to see Jillian's eyes dart guiltily down to her bowl of cereal.

I spared a quick glance at Joshua. He must have heard the sound too, because he glared at his sister across the breakfast table. I, however, just shook my head and pulled my elbows off the table. Obviously, I wouldn't get to spend the morning sulking with my head in my hands as I'd originally planned. Instead, I would once again have to play peacemaker between the unwilling and the unreceptive. And these days I didn't know which Mayhew sibling was which.

I placed what I hoped was a calming hand on Joshua's arm, but he'd already begun to growl a warning at his little sister.

"Jillian, I swear . . ."

"Don't swear, Joshie," she taunted, the corner of her lips twitching. "Mom and Dad don't like it when you swear."

Joshua's scowl deepened. "Seriously, if you don't stop it—"

"Stop what?" she interrupted, raising her eyebrows innocently. She turned from one side to the other as if to solicit support from their parents. The older Mayhews, however, couldn't have been more disinterested in their children's fight. Joshua's dad stayed buried behind his newspaper, and Joshua's mom focused intently on her breakfast—almost too intently, as if deliberately avoiding any involvement in her son and daughter's endless bickering.

So Joshua could have—should have—let the incident blow over. He could have ignored Jillian, like the mature older brother he was supposed to be. Unfortunately, our rough night had made Joshua as cranky as I was, and he decided to react.

Before I could utter the words *Let it go, Joshua,* I heard another sharp crack from under the table. When Jillian immediately yelped and bent down to grab her shin, Joshua grinned in triumph. Obviously *his* kick, unlike Jillian's, had met its mark.

Upon seeing her brother's grin, Jillian howled.

The howl echoed throughout the kitchen, nearly rattling the silverware and cereal bowls with its force. The sound was so piercing, Jillian's parents had no choice but to pay attention. Newspapers and coffee cups dropped to the table as the older Mayhews let out almost identical, frustrated groans.

Rebecca focused upon Joshua first, fixing him in a gaze that could have frozen lava.

"One morning," she said, shoving her mug farther away from her. "Just one morning I'd like to eat breakfast without having to break up a fight."

I looked over at Jillian, who continued to moan in pain, albeit with a hint of glee in her hazel eyes.

"Sorry we bothered you, Mom," she whimpered, intentionally quivering her bottom lip. "But Joshua just won't leave me alone."

"Are you sure, Jillian?" Rebecca asked. "Because I could have sworn I heard the first kick come from your direction."

I had to choke back a laugh. Jillian, however, was less

amused by her mother's ability to simultaneously ignore and monitor her children. Jillian began to sputter wordlessly, a faint pink flushing across her cheeks as she came to the realization that her howls hadn't fooled anyone. While she floundered for a response, her father tapped his fingers impatiently upon his discarded newspaper. He caught his wife's eye and then shrugged.

"What do you think?" he asked her. "Ignore this stupidity or ground them both from the party?"

"Ignore?" Joshua offered, but not loudly enough to rival Jillian's shriek of protest.

Her blush darkened to a livid red at the suggestion that she couldn't attend tonight's party, which promised to be the biggest of the semester. Worse, this was the first party that her parents had finally given her permission to attend—permission they'd only granted after Joshua and Jillian had both sworn, on penalty of military school or a nunnery, to stay far away from High Bridge.

This punishment was tantamount to social homicide, and Jillian knew it. So she blurted out what must have been the first defense that came to mind.

"I don't know why you're punishing me for anything," she shouted. "Joshua's the one who made Grandma Ruth leave—he deserves a lot worse than I do."

The moment the words left her mouth, all the livid red drained from Jillian's face. Just as quickly, an uncomfortable silence fell over the table. Each pair of eyes turned slowly, incredulously, toward Jillian.

To Jeremiah and Rebecca, such an accusation must have sounded outrageous, not to mention completely unfair. As far as they knew, Joshua hadn't caused his grandmother to abruptly pack up her few possessions last month and move to New Orleans to live with Jeremiah's sister and her family.

But Jillian and Joshua both knew the truth about what had really driven Ruth from this house.

Me.

Only a few months ago I'd inadvertently cost Ruth Mayhew almost everything she held dear. In doing so, I'd apparently taken away any reason she had for staying in Oklahoma.

Like Joshua, Jillian, and a surprisingly large number of people in Wilburton, Ruth was a Seer—a living person who, after some life-altering, "triggering" event, could see ghosts. But unlike Joshua (and, so far, Jillian), Ruth made it her mission in life to exorcise the dead. To banish them from the living world forever.

Ruth, and many other Seers, had moved to Wilburton expressly for that purpose, since High Bridge and the river beneath were such hotbeds of ghostly activity. Over time Ruth had earned her place as the cold, unrelenting leader of the Seer community, a role that she happily filled.

Until I came along and ruined everything.

Prior to my showdown with Eli on High Bridge, Ruth was constantly busy. Constantly surrounded by a mass of friends and obedient followers. But when she called off my exorcism so that I could save her granddaughter, things changed, in a way that made me think her mercy hadn't sat well with her fellow Seers.

Soon after, Ruth spent most of her days sitting sullenly at the Mayhews' kitchen table and most of her nights sulking in her bedroom. She almost never left the house, and the phone never rang for her. In fact, she hardly even spoke anymore. Sometimes she would toss a resentful glare in my direction; but, for the most part, she suffered her apparent banishment from the supernatural community in an angry, restless silence.

She only broke that silence last month when she announced her desire to move to New Orleans. Ruth packed all her possessions into a handful of cardboard boxes and hired a troop of professional movers. She claimed that boredom with Oklahoma had inspired the sudden move. But like I'd said, Joshua, Jillian, and I knew better.

Within a matter of days she left with nothing but a perfunctory good-bye to her son and his family.

The Mayhews' initial reaction was one of disbelief. Even amusement. But shortly after the moving van disappeared into the thick line of trees at the end of the Mayhews' driveway, a sort of hollowness began to echo through the house. Like something was missing.

No, not "like." Something *was* missing. However badly Ruth might have treated me, she was still an essential part of this family, one whose absence had a profound effect on its remaining members. For Jillian to make such an accusation—that her brother had caused a dramatic rift in their family—was pretty serious stuff. Not something you just blurted out at the breakfast table in a last-ditch effort to avoid being grounded. Especially when the entire family would spend ten hours cramped in one car tomorrow, driving to the French Quarter to spend Christmas with Ruth.

So if anyone got the chance to respond to Jillian's accusation, tomorrow would probably give new meaning to the phrase "road trip from hell." Wisely, Joshua chose this, the tensest moment of an already-tense morning, to act civil. He cleared his throat and gave his parents a tight smile.

"Look, let's just forget it." He shot his sister a pointed look—one that said, *Stop acting like an idiot or we're both screwed.* Aloud he said, "Sorry for the kick, Jill. Okay?"

In her first intelligent move of the day, Jillian caught the look and nodded. "Okay," she answered and then, reluctantly, added, "I'm sorry, too."

The apology lacked sincerity, but the fact that she'd delivered one at all bought her and Joshua a few moments to escape.

Joshua hiked his heavy winter coat off the chair and onto his shoulders with one hand. After sweeping his book bag off the floor with the other, he practically bolted from the table. Jillian scurried to follow. Jeremiah and Rebecca hadn't even had the chance to reprimand Jillian for her combative comment by the time both of their children—and I—were out the back door.

Outside, Joshua and Jillian gave each other only the briefest of glares before dashing to their respective cars. I said a silent prayer of thanks that the brutal cold kept the two of them from lingering to fight some more. Within a matter of minutes, Jillian started her tiny yellow car and tore recklessly down the icy driveway without bothering to let her windshield defrost completely.

Joshua had already unlocked his driver's side door and ducked into it to start the heater before he realized that I hadn't followed him off the back porch. He looked up at me in momentary confusion, but then his face fell in recognition: he knew from my expression that I wouldn't be joining him at school today.

He sighed and placed one hand on top of the roof of his truck. "Again, Amelia? Really?"

"I have to, Joshua. You know I have to."

"No, I don't," he said, frowning heavily. "Besides, it's freezing today."

I shrugged. "So? It's not like I can feel it."

This time I heard a note of defeat in Joshua's sigh. "Fine. But just be careful out there, okay? Don't get too close to it."

I smiled, but not very widely. "I never do."

Pulling his door fully open, Joshua just shook his head. He didn't even try to mask his disappointment as he slipped into the cab of the truck.

Just before he slammed the door and started the engine, I called out, "See you back here this afternoon."

Through the frost on the windshield, I caught one last glimpse of his face—still wearing that disappointed expression—before he backed the truck down the driveway and disappeared onto the main road.

Late that afternoon I stamped my feet on the ice-encrusted grass and rubbed my fists along my bare arms a few times. Then I made a little cave of my hands and placed them in front of my mouth so that I could puff air into them as if I could warm them with my breath. As if I even needed to warm them in the first place. Still, the gestures made me feel more normal. And normal was a feeling I desperately needed right now.

In front of me the river moved more quickly than

usual, its waters swelled and muddied by all the sleet last night. The river, however, wasn't the ugliest part of this scene. That honor went to the remains of High Bridge, only a few hundred feet downriver from me.

The ruined bridge stretched across the muddy water as bleak and stripped as the forest surrounding it. From here I could see the mangled girders and places where large chunks of concrete had fallen, leaving gaping holes around which someone had placed sawhorses and criss-crossed ribbons of yellow tape. More sawhorses guarded each end of the bridge, warning drivers to find some other route if they didn't want their cars to become aquatic. Along the edges of the bridge, the metal railings tilted at crazy angles as if some enormous force had knocked the entire structure off-kilter. Which, in essence, it had.

At that thought I smirked. I didn't feel one ounce of regret for wrecking the bridge. I hoped a strong wind sent the whole thing crumbling down into the water below.

I gave it a final scowl and then turned my attention to the barren trees across the river from me. Something about their skeletal branches, clawing at the gray sky, suited my current mood. And my current task.

I closed my eyes and began to breathe heavily, slowly, in an effort to calm myself. To focus. Against the black canvas of my eyelids, I pictured a scene similar to that of the living world today but even colder. A place much darker, too, and more menacing. An otherworldly place where rogue ghosts, enslaved wraiths, and demons waited.

Eli's netherworld.

I squeezed my eyes tighter, concentrating on the things I remembered about it: the violent purple sky; the gnarled, glittering trees; the river of tar moving toward the dark abyss underneath the netherworld version of High Bridge. Then I pictured the black shadows—dead souls trapped there by Eli under order of his masters—as they shifted among the netherworld trees.

I wanted them to reappear so badly I could almost hear them whispering in the darkness. Begging, in hushed but urgent voices, to be set free. I kept my eyes shut for a few more moments, wishing, praying.

But when I opened my eyes, my heart sank. Nothing around me had changed—not the cold gray sky, not the icy grass, not the muddied river.

I sank to the ground, letting my dress puddle around me. I didn't want to admit defeat, but I'd started to run out of excuses for myself. Every day I tried to reopen the netherworld, and every day I failed. Why should today be any different?

When I'd decided to pursue this task several months

ago, Joshua thought I'd lost my mind. After all, I'd only narrowly escaped an eternity spent trapped in the netherworld. So he had no idea why I would want to waste even a second trying to get back into it.

Even now a small part of me wondered whether Joshua had a point: maybe what I'd spent months doing at this bridge *was* crazy or, at the very best, in total disregard for my own safety. Honestly, though, I didn't care about my safety, and I certainly didn't care about crazy. Not where my father was concerned.

It broke my heart when I learned that my father had died not long after I had. But not knowing what had happened to his ghost hurt far worse, mostly because I knew what waited for him after death.

If my experience as a ghost was any indication, my father was now spending his afterlife in one of two ways: either lost like I'd been or trapped by Eli in the darkness of the netherworld. Since I'd never run into my father during my years of wandering, I had to assume he'd fallen victim to Eli—a fate I obviously couldn't allow him to suffer.

But none of my attempts to help him had worked.

At this point I couldn't deny my strongest suspicion: that I'd lost whatever ghostly powers I had discovered the night I overcame Eli and his dark masters. Sure, I could still touch Joshua, and I could still (sometimes) control my materializations in the living world. But I could no longer create that supernatural glow upon my skin or feel its surge of power, and I couldn't materialize into the netherworld.

Arguably, what I did at the river this afternoon was no more productive than what I'd done every few mornings for the last two months: sit on the front porch of my childhood home and watch, unseen, as my mother prepared for her day.

Though my visits were sporadic, I'd easily memorized her daily routine. Each morning she drank two cups of coffee in the front room, staring blankly at either the steam rising from her mug or at photos of my father and me; I couldn't tell which. After that she left—usually forgetting to lock the front door—and drove off to work in her creaking brown sedan.

Every time I saw her she looked tired and lonely; every time, the sight of her flooded me with angry, impotent guilt. Which was why I couldn't bring myself to visit her every day. I just didn't have the strength.

But today I did.

This morning, after I'd left Joshua, I followed my mother to work and watched unseen as she worked a punishing job as the stockroom clerk for the local hardware store. When her shift finally ended at 3 p.m., I materialized to the river, determined to do something—anything—for at least one of my parents.

Now, standing uselessly beside the river, I sighed. However much I wasn't helping my mother, I certainly wasn't helping my father, either. This afternoon's activities had proven as much.

I ran one hand through my hair, tugging at its dark brown ends as if the pressure might force me to concentrate harder. Assuming my concentration had anything to do with my ability to reopen the netherworld. Assuming I hadn't been barred from it entirely.

I released the poor strand of hair, which I'd twisted fiercely around my index finger, and groaned in frustration. The groan echoed back from the barren tree line, mocking me.

I pushed myself up off the ground and brushed my skirt smooth, although the ice hadn't actually wrinkled it. Then I turned my back on the river and walked toward the tree line. There, on the trunk of the largest cottonwood, hung a wristwatch. Joshua had nailed it there a few weeks ago, after I'd come home late one too many times.

I leaned in close enough to see both the little and big hands resting near the dayglow five.

"Crap," I murmured. Late again.

I could try to blame it on the blank gray sky—much darker, I realized, than it looked when I usually left.

But what was the point? No matter what my excuse, I'd probably still find Joshua disappointed but unsurprised when I materialized back to the Mayhews' house. On the plus side, he'd have almost no time to obsess over his calculus final, and even less time to argue his way out of the party I'd finally convinced him to attend.

I cast another brief glance at the watch, and a thought struck me. What if each second ticking away on the watch's little face *meant* something? What if those seconds, blending together into minutes then hours then days, had started to create something?

Like a rift. A growing distance between Joshua and me, lengthened by each second that we lived separately—me haunting my parents, and Joshua living his life, as he should.

The rift had already begun to form, I was sure of it. But when would it become too wide to cross? Maybe sooner than I thought . . .

Suddenly, a blast of frozen December air hit me. I felt the cold along my bare shoulders, and the chilly silk of my skirt raised goose bumps wherever it touched my legs. Before I could react, I heard a soft snap somewhere inside the forest.

I immediately dropped into a protective stance, shoulders hunched and fists clenched. The sudden chill, the mysterious noises . . . past experience had taught me what—or who—they preceded.

"Eli?" I whispered, staring into the darkness of the forest.

Then I blinked back in surprise at myself.

Because, upon saying his name, my voice had sounded *hopeful*. Was I so desperate to rekindle my powers, so intent on reentering the netherworld, that I would welcome the reappearance of my enemy? My murderer?

I *had* to be crazy to want to see him again.

Fortunately or not, nothing answered my whisper. I waited, motionless, but I saw no movement in the woods except the occasional stir of a branch in the wind.

In all likelihood I was probably freaked out over something as benign as a squirrel running across a twig. That explanation made far more sense than the return of my ghostly nemesis who, for all I knew, was trapped somewhere darker than I could imagine. Besides, the cold sensation had disappeared almost as soon as it had arrived, even before I spoke Eli's name.

But still, I shivered—whether from the memory of the chill, or from the dark thoughts buzzing around my pessimistic brain, I didn't know. All I knew for sure was that I wanted to leave, now. So I closed my eyes, thought of Joshua, and prayed that this materialization took me where I really wanted to go.

Of all the things I didn't trust, a tall bonfire in the middle of an enclosed structure ranked pretty high on the list. And yet I found myself huddled near one that night, desperately trying to maintain a wide smile.

To the right, an unfamiliar couple had practically melted into each other on top the hay bale next to ours. To the left, near the entrance of the barn, a group of guys threw mock punches at one another. They looked playful right now, but probably wouldn't after everyone had knocked back a few more drinks.

With his eyes still locked on the flames in front of us, Joshua took another swig from his bottle of beer. He gulped and then wiped his mouth with the back of his hand. "If one more person pukes in a horse stall, we're leaving."

I forced a laugh. "At least they're aiming for the stalls and not the bonfire."

Joshua arched one eyebrow and looked at me from the corner of his eye. I sighed and raised both my hands in defeat.

"I know, I know. But you said you were going to try to have fun tonight. And all you've done for the past two hours is drink and talk to me."

"Talking to you *is* fun." He flashed me that charming grin, the one that made my chest ache. Tonight, however, I wasn't buying it.

"No dice, buddy," I warned. "I'm not going to sit here and watch you lose friends because of me."

Joshua's grin shifted from sly to sweet. He stretched one hand across the hay and laid it on top of mine. "You're worth it," he said. Even over the roar of the fire and the noise of the party, his voice sounded quiet, sincere.

I could feel the ache in my chest tighten when, as if on cue, Joshua's best friend, David O'Reilly, stumbled over to us. With an enormous belch, O'Reilly collapsed onto the hay next to Joshua, forcing Joshua to scoot so close to me I nearly dropped to the ground.

"Make yourself comfortable, O'Reilly," I grumbled, but then I bit my lip. I reminded myself that I couldn't really blame either boy: O'Reilly had no idea there were two people on the hay, and Joshua could hardly tell O'Reilly to make room for me since O'Reilly didn't even know I existed.

Sighing, I pushed myself up off of the hay and turned to face them. What I saw didn't surprise me, unfortunately.

Joshua and O'Reilly sat beside each other, not moving or speaking. Both stared intently into the bonfire as if it might do their talking for them.

Joshua's eyes caught mine. He looked like he wanted to be anywhere but here.

"What are you waiting for?" I asked him, putting on what I hoped was an encouraging smile. "He's your best friend, and this is his party, in his barn. Say something."

Joshua nodded slightly. Then he spoke, keeping his eyes fixed on the fire.

"Hey, O'Reilly."

"Hey, Mayhew."

Their greetings hung in the air like balloons waiting for something to tether them. But as the seconds ticked by without any follow-up, I realized that a conversation between these boys obviously wouldn't happen without help.

I sighed, this time in genuine irritation. I couldn't believe Joshua had let it go this far. O'Reilly was Joshua's oldest friend in the world. And they hadn't spoken to each other in *weeks*.

Their awkward exchange tonight was just one example of why I'd practically forced Joshua to stay at this party far longer than he wanted to. Because, for as much as my daily activities worried Joshua, his worried me, too. Or, more accurately, his lack of activities.

Over the course of just three short months, Joshua went from the friendliest person at Wilburton High to the most reclusive. Like his grandmother Ruth, Joshua had lost his social life; but unlike her loss, his was self-inflicted.

At first I thought he just needed some time away from his friends. After all, he'd watched those same friends try to kill his sister while under Eli's dark spell. Who *wouldn't* need to recoup after something like that?

Joshua, however, recovered from the shock faster than anyone, including Jillian. Only a few days later, he seemed as sunny and doggedly optimistic as ever.

Yet he kept avoiding his friends, long after I laid waste to High Bridge. No more eating lunch with them, no more answering their calls. When one of them tried to talk to him at school, he would take one look at me and politely excuse himself, putting as much distance between them and us as possible.

Every time I brought up this strange behavior with him, he simply shrugged and flashed me that charming grin. "Nothing's wrong," he would reassure me.

But I wasn't fooled, nor was I the only one who noticed the change. In October his buddies had teased him about his new reputation as a loner. In November they'd call a few times a day, leaving concerned messages on his cell phone. By early December they'd stopped bothering to do even that.

If Joshua kept this up, he'd have no friends left by graduation.

I watched him continue to squirm uncomfortably on the hay for a few more seconds. Then I folded my arms across my chest, squared my shoulders, and gave him my most commanding look.

"'Hey, O'Reilly' isn't good enough, Joshua. *Talk* to him. Please. For my sake."

Joshua squirmed a bit more but nodded again. He cleared his throat, like anything more than a casual greeting would take serious effort, and asked, "So . . . a beard, huh?"

O'Reilly ran a hand over the thick red stubble on his

cheeks. "Yeah. I had to celebrate No-Shave November."

"And now you're celebrating . . . what? Don't-Get-Any-Play December?"

"Dude," O'Reilly protested, "like you have any room to talk. You haven't had a girlfriend in, like, forever."

Joshua's eyes met mine for just a second. Then he looked back at the fire. "Whatever, Grizzly Adams. You look like a bear died on your face."

O'Reilly boomed out a deep guffaw and, before he had time to remember how distant they'd been, punched Joshua roughly on the shoulder. Joshua laughed, too, the sound gusting out of him like a sigh of relief.

Boys, I thought, shaking my head. *An insult and a punch, and all is forgiven.*

Then I grinned broadly, feeling no small amount of relief myself when they began to talk as if the past few months hadn't even happened. Maybe, if the two of them kept this up, I wouldn't have to worry about Joshua being lonely.

Because you are *going to leave him, aren't you?*

Another voice broke into that dark thought, calling out to Joshua.

"Thank God, man. I thought we were gonna have to hold an intervention. I was afraid you were becoming one of those guys who moves into the attic and starts collecting toenails or something."

A figure came strolling toward us, his face obscured by shadows and shaggy, light-brown hair. I knew what I'd find if I could see him fully: a genuine smile, warm brown eyes. Scott, Joshua's second closest friend, was a good guy. Someone I normally welcomed. My smile faltered, however, when I saw who had followed him across the barn.

Jillian and her friend Kaylen walked behind Scott, both swaying unevenly in the firelight. When they grew closer, I could see that Kaylen had thrown one arm over Jillian's shoulder. In her free hand, Kaylen held a brown bottle, which tilted toward the barn floor and spilled its foamy contents onto the dust and hay.

Both of Jillian's arms were occupied by the effort of keeping Kaylen upright. Once they got close enough to the hay, I saw Jillian's frustrated expression, the one she often wore around Kaylen. It made me wonder why Jillian spent any time at all with her supposed best friend.

Still struggling to hold Kaylen steady, Jillian accidentally bumped her knees against O'Reilly's.

"Little help here?" she complained.

"Any time, Jilly-bean," O'Reilly said, drawling the "any" suggestively. He reached up to grab Kaylen's waist; but at the last moment, Kaylen seemed to regain some of her composure. Just as Jillian released her, Kaylen slipped almost gracefully onto the bale between Joshua and O'Reilly.

She made a small noise—a cross between a hiccup and a giggle, I think—and somehow, annoyingly, managed to sound more adorable than drunk. Even her thick blond hair still looked good, tousled in all the right places. She shifted backward, propping her arms behind her and letting her impossibly short jean skirt ride higher up her thigh.

"Blech," I murmured. In a rare moment of recognition, Jillian's eyes met mine and she snorted softly in agreement. Quickly, she looked away, back at the crowd on the hay.

"She's all yours, boys," Jillian said. "Come get me when she's ready to go home. Or when you get tired of her, too."

With a quick nod at Scott (who so obviously had an enormous crush on her), Jillian turned and walked back into the darkness of the barn. From the corner of my eye, I saw Scott sigh heavily, no doubt pining after her.

The three figures on the bale, however, captured more of my attention. Well, two of the three figures anyway.

By now Kaylen had leaned forward again and placed one hand on each of the boys' knees. But only her left hand, which clasped Joshua, moved. She ran it up his thigh and back down to his knee, talking rapidly as if to distract him from the uninvited touch.

"Josh, honey," she slurred. "Does this mean we're friends again?"

An involuntary growl escaped my lips.

Joshua shot me a worried look and tried to move farther away from her without falling completely off the bale. "Yeah, we're all friends again. Aren't we, O'Reilly? Why don't you tell Kaylen how much you missed me?"

O'Reilly was more than happy to take over the conversation. He leaned around Kaylen, grinning widely at her. "Yeah, dude. I missed him so much, I couldn't eat, couldn't sleep . . . couldn't shave."

"Bah-da-dum-dum-ching," Joshua sang, crashing his hand in the air against an imaginary cymbal.

Unfortunately for O'Reilly, Kaylen clearly wasn't interested in the performance. She didn't spare him so much as a glance. Instead, she pressed herself more firmly against Joshua's side.

"Well, I know *I* missed you," she said. Then she lowered her voice for just Joshua—and, unintentionally, me—to hear. "Can I show you how much?"

I felt an abrupt wave of heat from the bonfire, sharp and stinging against my back. The sensation was so strong I arched my neck against it. It quickly spread across my whole body until my cheeks flushed and I had to fan my face rapidly with one hand.

When Joshua grabbed Kaylen's hand—to take it off of him, I'm sure—the heat intensified. Without thinking, I stepped away from the fire and closer to the hay bale. Close enough to hear Kaylen whisper, "Kiss me, Josh."

My hands clenched, and I readied myself to shake the barn rafters, or maybe even cause an earthquake directly beneath Kaylen's feet.

Kaylen, however, beat me to the punch. Joshua had just placed her hand back in her own lap when she darted in like a snake and planted her lips on his. She tangled her fingers in his hair so quickly I almost didn't see her move, and she pulled him close to her.

Joshua made a small noise, in pleasure or protest I wasn't sure. I didn't have time to ask. At that incredibly inconvenient moment, the barn disappeared from sight.

Chapter
FIVE

For the second time that day I found myself gazing up at the ruins of High Bridge.

In the moonless dark it seemed creepier than it had this afternoon. More broken and hollow, like the skeleton of some giant, mythical creature. Above me the ribbons of caution tape fluttered in the wind. Otherwise the place was so quiet I could almost hear my nonexistent blood pumping from the surge of emotion I'd just experienced.

I'd accidentally materialized here the moment I

saw Joshua kissing Kaylen. Or Kaylen kissing Joshua. Whichever. I didn't exactly care about the specifics right now.

Gnawing furiously at my lip, I turned to stare at the darkened river. But instead of the water I could only see a wild blur of mental images.

Her hand on his leg. His hand on hers. Their lips pressed together.

Was I angry? Oh, yes. Angry, and jealous.

But the longer I stared at the river, the more quickly I realized my jealousy didn't resemble that of a normal living girl. Not by a long shot.

After all, a living girl wouldn't be jealous that her competitor could actually *feel* what she touched. A living girl wouldn't be jealous that her competitor didn't disappear when she kissed a boy. And a living girl wouldn't worry that her boyfriend might—in fact, probably would have to—choose someone else because at least someone else could grow with him. Change with him.

A millennium could pass and I wouldn't change with Joshua. I would never change, never again.

I felt my breath speed up, but I couldn't seem to slow it. I couldn't stop thinking these thoughts. Because, however much I disliked her, Kaylen was a normal, living girl. In fact, she probably wasn't even that annoying once you got to know her. It's not like she was *intentionally* going after someone else's boyfriend, either. As far as she knew, Joshua was very available.

And however much Joshua might deny Kaylen now, she or someone like her would eventually break through his defenses. How could she not? Girls like Kaylen could touch him for longer than ten minutes, attend school with him, meet his family, laugh with his friends. . . .

Girls like me couldn't do any of those things. Girls like me just screwed things up for the living people we loved. One look at Joshua's current social life proved it.

The evidence was everywhere: the way Joshua looked at me before telling someone "Sorry, I can't talk right now"; the frequency with which he walked away from his friends, like he was afraid that even a minute spent around them might reveal my presence.

Joshua had intentionally limited our exposure to the living world. To keep himself from looking like he was crazy in case anyone caught him holding hands with thin air. To keep me safe from any unfamiliar Seers.

By turning away from the living people he cared about, Joshua thought he could protect us. And in the process he'd hurt himself.

I guess I should have felt grateful he hadn't taken this mission so far as to start avoiding his family too. But would that day come? Would Joshua discover in five, ten years that he could no longer explain to his parents why they couldn't meet his girlfriend? Why he couldn't marry her and start a family?

Such questions didn't matter, not today. I knew that's what Joshua would say if he could have heard my thoughts.

But those questions would become reality soon enough. When you had a ghost for a girlfriend, you eventually had to choose between the living and the dead. Between a normal life and a haunted one.

He'd already started to make this choice with his friends. And I suspected he'd keep making that choice—with his family and his future—if I let him.

Which I couldn't. I wouldn't.

In the end I would have to do something to make Joshua stop choosing me.

I suddenly felt the ache in my chest pull into itself, smothering-tight. I had to stop thinking about this. I had to focus on something else, fast. Trying to distract myself, I looked up at my surroundings for the first time since I materialized here. Then I blinked back in surprise.

High Bridge stood directly in front of me, so close I could almost touch it.

Without meaning to, I must have climbed up the steep embankment and stopped at the edge of High Bridge Road. Now my toes rested on the asphalt while my heels stayed on the grass, as if they knew well enough to keep me away from this place.

Up close, any sane person would see the bridge for what it was: dangerous. I had every reason to fear it now as much as I did in the past.

But suddenly I didn't. I didn't fear this place at all.

As I continued to stare, I felt my eyes narrow. My feet began to pull themselves completely off the shoulder and onto the road. Slowly, mechanically, my legs carried me forward until I was walking across the bridge. Just taking a calm little stroll.

Inside, however, I was anything but calm. With each step I took my anger grew. Anger at Kaylen, at Eli, even at Joshua. Anger at my whole stupid existence. But especially anger at High Bridge. It had ruined my life, and the lives of countless others.

"You know what?" I said aloud, addressing the bridge, a hysterical smile twitching at one corner of my mouth. "You really piss me off."

"Still?"

The word drifted toward me no louder than a breath. Yet the moment I heard it, I nearly jumped out of my skin. I spun around frantically, searching for the speaker; but as far as I could see, I was the only one there.

Except . . .

I squinted, peering at the path I'd just walked.

Something about the look of a particular spot seemed . . . off. As I watched, the air began to shimmer and shift until, floating above what had been an empty road only seconds before, something took shape. At first it hovered like a mist: pale and not quite translucent. But soon it solidified, and I could make out the contours of a human figure.

A man, sitting hunched, close to the railed edge of the bridge. His arms lay across his knees, and his hands and head hung limp, lifeless. His long, curly hair had fallen forward, hiding his face.

But I didn't have to see it. I didn't even need him to whisper another word. Because I knew exactly who had just appeared less than four feet away from me.

"Eli," I gasped, taking a jerky step backward.

"Wait," he said in that same choked whisper. "Wait."

I didn't want to wait; I wanted to get out of here. But I stood transfixed as Eli turned his head toward me and, with horrific slowness, rolled his eyes up to meet mine.

A small, strangled noise escaped my lips.

The mist blurred the rest of his features, but Eli's eyes blazed an electric blue, like centers of impossibly hot flames. Bright, and ghastly.

I felt a surge of phantom adrenaline telling me to run. But I couldn't look away.

"Eli?" I repeated. "Is . . . is that you?"

When he nodded, the gesture looked labored. Painful.

My mind began to race. Eli should still be somewhere in the darkness beyond the netherworld, imprisoned there by the demons he once called masters. If he was here now, in the living world with me, then that meant his masters were . . .

My head swiveled frantically, searching the bridge around us.

"Where are they?" I gasped. "Tell me."

"No." From the corner of my eye, I saw him shake his head. "No, Amelia, not here."

"Tell me," I demanded, my voice jumping an octave. "Tell me now, Eli."

"Not here," he said. The words seemed to crawl their way out of him. *"There."*

"'There'?" I repeated, still hunting for any other sign of movement on the bridge. "Where's 'there,' Eli?"

"The netherworld."

I whipped my head back around to face him. "If that's true, then how are *you* here?"

"I'm not here, either," he said, still struggling to speak but gaining a little momentum with each word. "Not really."

I twisted one corner of my mouth into a frown, confused. "What are you saying? That you're . . . what? Still in the netherworld right now?"

"Yes. I'm projecting."

"Projecting?"

He shook his head. "No time. They'll find me soon, and—"

"So they *are* on their way?" I interrupted. "Then I guess you won't mind if I don't stick around to catch up. See ya, Eli."

"Amelia, no! Please, wait—listen!"

I rocked forward, ready to jog, run, *fly* away from here if I had to. But the urgency in Eli's plea made me hesitate. I paused long enough to see a glint of real fear in those unnatural blue eyes. Then I swore under my breath.

"Fine," I said aloud. "Whatever you have to say, say it fast."

He let slip a gravelly sigh that sounded almost relieved. "I'm here to warn you, Amelia."

"About what?"

Eli's eyes darted around, searching the bridge as I had. Then he met my gaze and lowered his voice even further.

"They're weak right now, without a spirit like me to build their ranks. But they *are* coming, Amelia; and they're coming for you."

Something inside me clenched. "All the more reason to get the hell out of here, right?"

Eli nodded again. "Exactly what I wanted to tell you.

It's not going to happen tonight, but it will happen. Soon. I've heard them talking. They want you. And this time they're willing to do their own dirty work to get you."

"'Dirty work'?"

"Killing," he said. "They'll murder everyone in this town if that's what it takes to make you help them."

I heard my own terrified whisper before I had time to think it.

"Joshua."

Even through the shifting mist, I thought I saw Eli scowl. "Yes, him. And everyone else you care about. The more of your loved ones they take, the better. Think of them as hostages, to force your hand."

Faces flashed across my mind: Joshua, my mother, Jillian, even Joshua's parents and his friends. As easy to find in this small town as a Baptist church.

"Oh, God," I moaned, and Eli responded with a coughing sort of laugh.

"God has nothing to do with these creatures, Amelia. At least, not anymore."

A panicky sensation began to twitch along my neckline like a quickening pulse. "Then what do I do? What exactly am I supposed to do?"

"You have to get out of here," Eli urged. "Tonight, if possible."

"Away from the bridge?" I asked, my voice rising in

pitch. "Just stay away from this place?"

I felt a slight twist in my core as I pictured my father's face. How could I leave him here? But how could I *not*, if that meant protecting everyone else?

Slowly, reluctantly, I nodded. "I . . . I could do that. I could stay away. For a little while, at least."

"No, Amelia, that's not good enough," Eli said. "You have to get away from Wilburton. From Oklahoma."

"Okay. Okay." I continued to nod mechanically, my mind racing. "I can do that too. We're leaving tomorrow for Christmas break. That should buy me a few more days."

"Still not good enough, Amelia. You have to stay away *forever*, especially from the people you care about. Otherwise, their association with you might get them killed."

"'Association'? I . . . I don't understand."

"My old masters aren't omniscient, Amelia. They don't know your every move, or every detail about your history. All they can do is follow you, study you, and then act accordingly. Whatever—whoever—they see with you, they will attack. But if you don't give them anyone to hunt, then . . . well . . ."

My stomach dropped. "So you mean I have to leave everyone . . . permanently? Leave Joshua?"

"If you want him to survive this. If you want his

freedom, and yours . . ."

As Eli spoke, he trailed off, distracted. After a moment of silence, his head jerked to the right. He stared intently behind us, at the empty bridge, as if there was something approaching that only he could see.

Which, I realized, was probably the case.

When he whipped back around to face me, his eerie blue eyes had widened. "I have to go. For your sake, Amelia, I hope I never see you again."

Maybe I imagined it, but I thought I saw a trace of sadness in all that unnerving blue. "What about you, Eli?" I asked softly.

"Too late for me, I'm afraid," he whispered. Then his eyes darted once more to the right; and, without another word or glance, he vanished like a puff of smoke in the wind.

Chapter
SIX

I didn't wait to act. As soon as Eli disappeared, I did,
too, materializing back to Joshua's house instantly.

The next breath I took was a gasp, gulped noisily into my lungs while I hunched, doubled over, in the
Mayhews' backyard. I wrapped my arms tightly around
me, but the gesture brought no comfort, no warmth. It
just made me feel smaller, and more alone.

What if Eli had lied to me? Tried to trick me into
doing something I didn't want to do? It wouldn't be the
first time.

The difference was, now I didn't doubt him. Not even for a second. Because everything he'd said made a perfect, horrible kind of sense.

How naive, how absolutely *stupid* I'd been to think that I'd managed to stay off the evil spirits' radar. I'm not sure why—too much exposure to Joshua's blind optimism, maybe—but I'd thought that, with Eli gone, the spirits would stay anchored to High Bridge until another servant willingly joined them.

If Eli told the truth, then I'd thought wrong. Very wrong.

By doing so I'd put everyone in terrible danger. Not that they hadn't already been just by living in proximity to that horrible place. But now, thanks to me, they were potential targets in some demonic hunting expedition.

It made me sick, the idea that one of them might get hurt because of me. And the idea that I'd have to do as Eli suggested and leave? That idea terrified me almost as much.

Is that really what I have to do? I asked myself. *Leave all the reminders of my old life, like this town and my childhood home? Leave the people I love?*

Like my mother. Like Joshua.

"No," I moaned quietly, fighting my newest wave of nausea.

How could I do it? How could I actually desert them?

And how could I not, if it meant keeping them safe? My protective glow, my poltergeist powers had vanished. If I stayed, if I tried to fight the netherworld creatures again, I would surely lose. The only defense I could provide them would be to stay as far away as possible.

But still: leaving? I couldn't even imagine it. Not really.

It was one thing to wonder whether I might one day have to leave Joshua. To anticipate some dark day, at some indeterminate time in the future, when I couldn't see him anymore. It was quite another thing to think that day might come tomorrow.

I tried to imagine it: a voluntary return to my old existence. Indistinguishable days and nights spent wandering in unfamiliar places. Never laughing with Joshua, never seeing his face. I tried to picture his midnight blue–colored eyes when I told him I had to leave and never come back. Doing so just made me nauseated all over again.

I forced myself to straighten up and breathe slowly. After a few even, methodical breaths I could think more clearly. More rationally.

What if I didn't *have* to do it tomorrow? I could go with the Mayhew family to New Orleans, get myself and them far away from the bridge. No matter what Eli said, that would gain me at least a few days to figure out where to go next.

And give me time to figure out what to say to Joshua. What words to craft that would break his heart, and keep him safe.

I'd just brushed that thought aside to deal with it later when another one took its place

My mother.

My stomach clenched again when I thought of her, alone and unprotected, living so close to the bridge. How long after I'd gone would the dark spirits find her?

She had to leave too, obviously. At least for a while. But I had no idea how to make that happen. I could hardly tell her myself, and I doubted she would listen to Joshua—an eighteen-year-old stranger—if I asked him to warn her.

Near tears, I marched up the wooden steps to the Mayhews' back porch and began to pace, stomping noiselessly across the floorboards. Around me, fat snowflakes fell, undisturbed by my movements. As I continued to pace, I batted uselessly at them. There had to be another solution for my mother; there just *had* to be.

Suddenly I remembered something Eli said on the bridge: although powerful, the demons weren't omniscient. They didn't know everything about me. In fact, they may not know *anything* about me, not yet. So maybe they didn't know my mother existed. Maybe Eli was right—by leaving this town and the people I cared about,

I *could* keep them safe. Without my presence to give away their identities, my mother, Joshua—everyone—would stay anonymous, hidden from the dark spirits.

And all it would take was a gigantic sacrifice on my part.

I shook my head forcefully. I didn't have time to feel sorry for myself; I needed to spend every second I had left either enjoying my last moments with Joshua or planning how to end them.

Most of all, I couldn't let Joshua know what I intended to do. He would stay away from High Bridge on his own after I'd gone, so I had no worries there. But if he knew that I planned to leave—or where I planned to go—he might try to stop me, or follow me.

"God forbid," I murmured, even though my brain knew this was the only way. The right way.

"God forbid what?"

The sound of Joshua's voice, nervous and unsure, drifted toward me.

I looked up and found him leaning against the frame of the back door and silhouetted by the hallway light. Through the darkness, I could only see a few of his features: a crease of worry between his eyebrows, a strained twist at the corner of his full lips. God, I loved that face. I didn't want to think how much I'd miss it.

He was obviously still worried about what had

happened tonight between him and Kaylen. Despite everything, a tiny laugh passed my lips. In a matter of hours my problem with Kaylen had gone from mountainous to fly sized. Insignificant, compared to everything else.

"What's so funny?" Joshua asked quietly.

Knowing that Joshua could see me clearly, I forced a smile.

"Actually," I said in an offhanded tone, "I was laughing at myself."

"You were?"

I widened my smile until it ached. "Absolutely. Just laughing about how much I overreacted earlier. How was the rest of the party?"

"Overreacted?" he said, ignoring my question. "About Kaylen? Hardly. You have every right to be mad that she kissed me. It was totally—"

"Not your fault," I finished, swiping my arms across each other in the "safe" signal.

In the dark, I saw him shake his head. "But I've known Kaylen for years. I should have guessed what she was up to."

I laughed lightly. "I expect certain things from you, but the ability to read Kaylen's twisted little mind isn't one of them."

"Are you . . . sure, Amelia? You don't want to scream

at me for an hour or two?"

I pushed my lips out into a fake pout. "Wow, Joshua. I may be a little jealous, but I'm not crazy."

I could hear the smile in his words when he replied, "Huh. Well, in my experience, jealous sometimes equals crazy."

"Oh, does it?" I teased. "In your vast experience?"

"Hey," he protested, pushing himself away from the doorway and walking toward me. He came close and hesitated, just a moment, before pulling me into his arms. When I melted against him, he gave a low laugh. "Don't knock all seven of those dates I had last year. They taught me a lot about the female mind."

"More than you've learned in the past three months?" I said, nuzzling into his chest, wishing desperately that I could feel his warmth right now. Just a little physical sensation to help me keep up the happy charade, to prevent me from revealing to him how I really felt inside: scared, defeated, sad.

Lucky for me, Joshua couldn't read my thoughts. His hand moved to my back and started to trace circles there. Slowly, the places where his fingertips touched began to burn.

"I hope you know," he whispered, "that there's only one girl I want to kiss. And she's never smelled like stale beer."

"Not in the past decade anyway," I whispered back, smiling weakly. When I burrowed closer to him, Joshua laid his chin on top of my head.

"You have no idea how relieved I am. I seriously thought we were going to have a huge fight tonight."

I leaned back and looked up into his eyes. In the shadows, their dark blue seemed almost black. "You weren't *planning* on fighting with me, were you?" I asked, still smiling.

"Nope. I planned on keeping my mouth shut while you did all the talking."

"Wise. Very wise, indeed."

He grinned back at me for a moment, but the expression unexpectedly faltered. All at once he looked like he wanted to say something . . . something I probably wouldn't like.

I tilted my head to one side. "What's wrong?"

He grimaced, clearly deciding whether or not to speak his mind. "Nothing's wrong, really," he said hesitantly. "It's just that, well . . ."

When he trailed off awkwardly, I frowned. "It's just *what,* Joshua?"

He released a jittery puff of air and then launched into a dizzying rush of words.

"It's just that you've been acting really weird lately, Amelia. All depressed and quiet. I keep thinking that sometimes I do stuff to make you mad, but you never really say anything one way or another. Then tonight happened, and I wondered whether you were going to explode. Because that's what people do when they keep everything inside for a long time: they explode. So I've just been . . . waiting, I guess. For the nuclear meltdown."

Once finished he panted, as if exhausted from the effort.

As for me, I simply stared at him, motionless, speechless. I didn't really know what to make of his confession, except that he obviously read me better than I'd expected.

Distract him, I thought. *Otherwise he'll have you figured out before you get within two miles of New Orleans. He'll know you're trying to leave. And then how will you protect him?*

I pushed him away, crossed my arms over my chest, and forced my mouth into a scowl. "Are you saying that I'm the only one acting weird, Joshua? What about you?"

"What *about* me?" he asked, taken aback by my cold tone.

"Last time I checked, Mr. Popularity just had his first real conversation with his friends in months. And I basically *made* you do it."

Joshua crossed his arms too, suddenly defensive. "Yeah, so?"

"So I know what you've been doing."

"And what exactly is that?"

"Avoiding the living, Joshua. Choosing the dead."

His arms dropped. Even in the dark I could see his pained expression. "Don't call yourself that, Amelia. Please."

"But that's what I am," I pressed, my tone softening a bit. "I'm dead. There's really no point in calling me by any other name, is there?"

He shook his head. "Doesn't matter. Living, dead—I don't care. I'm with you. And I'm going to do whatever needs to be done."

I sighed. "That's one of the things that's been bothering me lately, Joshua. I understand why you think you need to do it, but just . . . *don't,* okay? Don't let go of your friends because you think it will benefit me."

"Benefit us," he corrected.

"'Us' is okay," I said, fighting the cruel little voice that reminded me of what a lie I'd just told. "We're going to be all right. In fact, we'll be even *better* if you just go back to living your life the way you did before we met. Except, you know . . . with me in it."

Joshua's eyebrows drew together in doubt. "Are you sure, Amelia?"

I threw my hands up in the air. "You keep asking me that like you have some reason to think it isn't true."

"Are you saying I don't . . . ?" He cracked a small, questioning smile.

"I'm saying you don't."

In my head, I added, *Actually, I'm saying it'd be better if you started living your life like I wasn't even in it. But whatever.*

"How about I make you a deal, then?" Joshua said. "I'll make an effort to spend time with my friends, and you'll try to be—"

"Happier?" I offered.

"Happier works."

"Good," I said, nodding. "Happier works for me, too."

Joshua laughed. "And here I thought we weren't going to have a big fight."

I drew closer to him. "I can think of a few ways we could make it up to each other. I mean, you weren't planning on sleeping tonight, were you?"

"Absolutely not. That's what tomorrow's car ride is for."

His smile broadened into the one I loved so much, and I paused, just for a second, to memorize every detail of it. Then I melted into him again.

Chapter
SEVEN

By hour six of our drive to New Orleans, I wished I *had* slept last night. Nightmares, involuntary materializations—any number of unpleasant things would have been preferable to this car ride.

With bleary eyes I surveyed the interior of the Mayhews' SUV. Though it looked spacious enough, the vehicle had already proved too small to handle this particular grouping of people.

In the front, Jeremiah and Rebecca continued to trade positions between the driver and passenger seats.

Despite this split of duties, the two couldn't seem to stop bickering over who had the best set of directions. As a result, we'd spent half the drive on the highway and the other half on a disconcerting maze of back roads. So instead of four remaining hours in the car, we had at least six more ahead of us.

To no one's surprise, Joshua and Jillian weren't handling the endless claustrophobia well, either. Like young children, they'd occupied *hours* of this drive with snide remarks, kicked seats, and passive-aggressive sighs. Now, in a rare but nearly blissful period of silence, Jillian stretched across the first row of bench seats, listening quietly to her iPod while Joshua napped beside me in the back row.

While he slept, his head rolled backward on the top of the seat, affording me a good view of his profile. I watched it for a moment and then sighed. If only I could find a way to sleep without nightmares, I might forget how little time I had left to look at him.

I turned to stare out the window, at the other problem plaguing our drive. Apparently, the winter storm had decided to follow us south. Although we'd driven hundreds of miles away from Wilburton, the snow continued to fall, piling up in the ditches alongside the highway and shifting like thin, insubstantial ghosts upon the surface of the road. Flurries swirled against the windows, distorting the landscape that moved past us.

Without the responsibility of navigating through this storm, I might have found the scenery peaceful. But my mind still reeled as much as it had last night. In fact, it hadn't stopped reeling. For many hours I'd alternated between trying to find a way out of my exile and reminding myself that, by evading the dark spirits, I would keep them from hurting anyone else.

I'd also spent a great deal of time wondering where I'd materialize to once the Mayhews returned home. I couldn't decide whether I should pick the location in advance, in case I was too upset to make a decision when the time came, or whether I should just vanish to somewhere unknown. Somewhere so far from Wilburton I could never find my way home again.

As I stared out the window, with my mind jumping from one bad option to another, my eyes occasionally caught on an individual snowflake. I mindlessly followed one's progress until the wind whisked it away and another flake took its place. The longer I watched the flakes, the more they mesmerized me, like a thousand tiny hypnotists intent on distracting me from the problems at hand.

While the storm held my attention, another part of my mind caught glimpses of the landscape behind it. White hills and valleys—indistinguishable from one another in the heavy snow—rushed past us. I started to suspect that an empty world waited just beyond this vehicle. A world untouched and blank: not for me to write my story upon, but to disappear into. To fade against, finally, like the ghost I was.

I shook my head lightly, trying to focus, but I couldn't make anything out in all that infinite white. Soon my eyes glazed over and my vision blurred until I'd had far more of the bright emptiness than I could take. I turned back to the dark interior of the SUV for some relief.

And then I gasped.

The upholstered seats, the low ceiling of the SUV—everything was gone. Replaced by the bright, blinding snow.

I looked down to find that my legs, instead of being curled beneath me in the back row of the SUV, were buried ankle-deep in the snow. Inexplicably, I'd gone from the safety of the vehicle to the center of the blizzard. From what I could see—which wasn't much—the SUV had disappeared, wiped from existence by the storm.

Upon realizing this, I could actually *feel* the blizzard: the cold wind gusting around me, battering my shoulders and whipping my dark hair into tangles in the air; the frozen ground stinging the soles of my bare feet; the snow soaking the hem of my dress until it clung, wet and uncomfortable, against my legs.

But just as abruptly as I'd entered it, the storm ended.

I watched, stunned, as the dark clouds broke apart to reveal a soft, summery blue sky. The last shriek of the winter gale died in the air, and a warm breeze took its place. Then, like the grand finale of some fantastic play, the heavy layer of snow melted into lush, green grass— grass that should have died months ago and shouldn't now sprout a blanket of wildflowers.

Within seconds I'd gone from the Arctic Circle to some prairie paradise.

I lifted one foot and marveled at the daisy that had just popped up beneath it. "What the . . . ?" I murmured aloud.

"More like 'where the,' actually," a pleasant voice chirped from somewhere behind me.

I spun around, sending an impossibly thick cluster of dandelion seeds into the air. For a moment I didn't see anything but their wispy cotton strands. Only when they drifted up, toward the clear sky, could I see her.

She stood only a few feet from me, with her hands clasped in front of her. Her feet were bare like mine, and she rocked back and forth on her heels as if she had news she couldn't wait to share. Her green eyes seemed to sparkle with that same exciting secret. She ran one hand through her wild auburn hair and then, unbelievably, *waved* at me.

"Hi, Am—a."

Her voice crackled like radio static in the middle of my name. The weird noise obviously didn't bother her, though, because she broke into a warm smile.

Too baffled to do much else, I smiled back.

"Um . . . hi," I said. "And you are? And I'm where?"

Her smile turned dimpled, and mischievous. "Not—lat—someone wants—talk to you."

Again her words crackled, as if she were trying to speak over a broken connection. She shook her head, auburn curls bouncing against her shoulders. Then, without so much as another staticky word, she vanished.

I stared openmouthed at the empty space she'd left. There was no evidence that she'd been there at all except maybe the wildflowers now seemed a little thicker, a little wilder where she'd stood.

"No, really." I spoke to the vacant field, feeling dizzy from all this weirdness. "Where am I?"

"Don't you know?" another unfamiliar voice teased, not much louder than the breeze.

I spun around again, searching for the new speaker. This time, however, I found no one watching me. Nothing surrounded me but the flowers, the ankle-high grass, the cloudless blue sky.

"Who's there?" I called out, still spinning, still finding nothing.

"Me," the voice whispered again.

"Me, who?" I demanded, my own voice sharp and impatient. Another second of this eerie place, these cryptic visitors, and I'd have to reevaluate my sanity.

"You know who, darlin'."

My mouth twitched and then pulled itself down into a disbelieving frown.

Darlin'.

The way the disembodied voice dropped its *g* and drawled out the word with affection . . . only one person in the world had called me darlin', and had said it in that way.

My father.

The voice sounded like it had in all my nightmares about him. But here, in this beautiful place, it also sounded richer. Clearer. Which shouldn't be the case since my father was trapped in the dark netherworld.

I felt the muscles in my neck tense. "No, really," I almost growled, defensive for reasons I didn't fully understand. "Who are you?"

"There's not much time," the voice cautioned. "I need you to listen. I need you to uncross your eyes, darlin'."

I froze. No part of my body moved, except perhaps for the frown, which released its hold on my mouth.

The image sprung into my mind before I had time to think. A flash of memory. I hadn't had one in months, not since the struggle this fall on High Bridge. But suddenly, without warning, I could picture my hands clasped around a math textbook. Calculus, judging by all the letters and numbers dancing impossibly around one another on the page.

"Ugh," the flash-me groaned. "This stuff is making my eyes cross."

I heard my father speak from somewhere to my right: "Then you've gotta uncross them, darlin'."

He'd said that at least a thousand times before, and who knows how many times after. This was our routine, our own goofy comedy bit. Whenever a problem bothered me, I'd say it made my eyes cross; and every time, my father would suggest I uncross them, as if the problem was that simple to solve.

Just uncross your eyes, darlin'. Nothing to it.

Silly. Meaningless, really. But it always made me laugh, even helped me to focus, because the phrase was *ours*.

Besides than my mother and me, only one other person knew that phrase, knew what it meant to me.

"Dad?"

I breathed the word like a prayer. I received one quiet word in acknowledgment:

"Amelia."

Maybe I should have been more skeptical, demanded more proof. Instead, I started to cry. Because I knew how my father's voice sounded when he spoke the name he'd helped give me.

"Dad," I called again, frantic. "Dad, where are you? I've been trying to find you. I've been trying to—"

"There's no time, Amelia," he interrupted. "You have to listen to me. They're coming."

Immediately I knew whom he meant. And the warning chilled me just as much as when Eli delivered it last night. But this time I steeled myself against the fear and drew my head up so my father would see—if he could see me at all right now—that his daughter's backbone had survived her death.

"I know, Dad. That's why I'm leaving Oklahoma."

"That's not enough," he said. "You have to—but not without—"

The same static interference that had broken up the girl's voice now distorted my father's. Like the two of them were speaking on the same radio frequency.

"They want—but it's hard to—the rivers—mustn't rise."

"What? Dad, I can't hear you. 'The rivers mustn't rise'?"

I moved to the right and then the left as I'd seen Joshua do when he wanted to get better cell phone reception. Then I craned my neck up, my face pointed to the sky as if my father's face might appear there.

No such luck. My father continued to speak, but infuriatingly, I could only catch a few words at a time. Worse, his voice began to fade, the volume lowering until I could barely hear him at all.

"Darlin', you need to—please—not soon eno—"

His last word faded entirely and, after a long silence, I realized he was gone.

I stood perfectly still, staring at the field of wildflowers without seeing them. My father had tried to warn me about something, that much I knew. Something to do with the demons of High Bridge. Something urgent.

A thin shiver of fear ran through my heart. I'd wanted to contact my father so badly, for so long. But his visit—if that's what just happened—brought me no comfort. Still, I wanted it to, very much. So for a brief moment, before I tried to analyze what few words he'd given me, I closed my eyes. In the quiet of my own mind, I replayed his warning, if just to hear his voice.

When I opened my eyes, I had the second shock of my already-strange day.

Without any effort on my part, I'd moved again. Instead of a flowering prairie, the window of the SUV faced me. Through it I could see other cars, so close to the SUV that I could touch them if someone opened the window. But these cars weren't passing us on the highway. They were parked in line outside a long stretch of ancient-looking, cramped-together buildings. I leaned closer to the window, just enough to see the tops of the buildings reaching up to a dark, starry sky.

The cars, the buildings, the night sky—all things that shouldn't be there, if you considered the fact that the last time I sat in this vehicle there had been nothing to see outside but a midafternoon snowstorm raging over the middle of Nowhere, Texas.

I frowned and then turned toward the interior of the SUV. There, two astonished faces stared back: Jillian, sitting openmouthed and wide-eyed in front of me; and Joshua, looking basically the same, beside me.

Another uncontrolled materialization, I supposed.

I sighed wearily and met his eyes. "How long was I gone this time?" I asked him.

"Gone?" he whispered, frowning. "Amelia, you've been right beside me for the last twelve hours."

Chapter
EIGHT

I opened my mouth to respond to Joshua but then popped it shut. What did he mean, I hadn't left his side? That wasn't *possible*. Not after everything I'd just seen and heard.

I tilted my head to one side, studying Joshua's confused expression. "Did I . . . was I sleeping again?"

Still staring at me intently, he nodded. "Yeah, for a couple hours, actually. But in the last few minutes, you were . . . shouting."

"Huh?"

"Shouting. Loudly." His eyes darted to the front of the car and then back to mine. "Even my dad said he thought he heard something. That whole inactive-Seer thing, I guess?"

"Oh." My voice sounded flat. "Sorry. I didn't know. I must have been . . . talking in my sleep."

Or screaming out to my dead father.

Across from me, Jillian whipped her head from side to side, obviously trying to shake away the fact that I'd frightened her. Then she rolled her eyes, composed her face into its far more common look of disapproval, and dropped back down into her seat. Before she sunk out of sight, I heard her mutter, "God, you're creepy."

Before yesterday her words would have bothered me. Hurt me, like they always did. Tonight, however, I didn't really have the energy to care what Jillian thought I was.

I glanced back up at Joshua. He still watched me with that slightly unnerved expression.

"Sorry," I repeated in the same emotionless tone I'd used earlier.

He gave me a small, uncertain smile. "No biggie. It was just a little, you know . . ."

"Creepy." I sighed.

Then, with a shrug, I turned away from him to scrutinize the fabric of the headrest in front of me. At this moment, all I wanted to do was bury myself in my own thoughts. But Joshua leaned forward, trying to recapture my gaze.

"Want to talk about it?" he offered quietly.

"Not really." After a beat I added, "No offense."

From the corner of my eye, I saw him shake his head as if to say *None taken*. Which probably wasn't entirely true.

I felt a twinge of regret, so sharp it actually hurt. I didn't *want* to hurt Joshua. In fact, I wanted to tell him everything I'd just seen. But I shouldn't. Couldn't. Not now, when our expiration date loomed so close. Besides, I could hardly force more than a few words past the bitter taste of disappointment in my mouth.

I just couldn't believe it: the whole thing had been another useless, haunting dream? Standing in the field, seeing the girl, talking to my father—all an illusion? It seemed impossible.

But if Joshua said I hadn't left, then I suppose I hadn't. Instead, my brain had created everything in some sort of frenzied, tantalizing fit of wish fulfillment. After ten years apart, and after months of searching for him, I guess it made a cruel sort of sense that I would imagine some mystical interaction between my father and me.

I wanted to shout aloud, to protest how unfair it all was. And more than anything, I wanted to confide in Joshua. I didn't want to spend my last days with him locked in some secretive prison of my own making.

Screw it, I thought and turned to him, mouth open. But Rebecca's voice interrupted me.

"Holy crap, hallelujah," she sang out from the front seat. "Ursulines Avenue. We made it."

"Truer words were never spoken," Jeremiah agreed, and then pulled the car to a stop outside a redbrick building. "Troops," he commanded, "prepare to disembark."

"Gladly," Jillian groaned as her father killed the engine.

I heard the clicking of seat belts and then the snap of someone's door handle. Immediately, the overhead lights flooded the SUV. In the darkness, I hadn't seen Jillian sit up again. Now, for just a moment, her gaze caught mine as we both blinked against the sudden brightness. Maybe I imagined it, but I thought I saw something strange there, in the depths of her eyes. Curiosity? Anticipation? She looked away too quickly for me to decide.

"Ready?"

Joshua's whisper in my ear made me jump.

"Y-yeah," I stammered. "Sorry."

"For what?" He laughed and then leaned around me to push part of Jillian's seat forward so that we could get out of the back row.

Without so much as a glance at me, Jillian scrambled over the inclined seat and out of the open passenger side door. Joshua touched the inside of my elbow softly, indicating that we should follow her. I looked down at the place where his hand rested—where my skin had already started to tingle and burn. Then I sighed, so low Joshua probably couldn't hear me, and pushed myself up.

After I'd climbed out of the SUV, I walked over to the uneven sidewalk and waited for Joshua to climb out too. While I waited, my eyes strayed upward, to the buildings that surrounded the narrow street on which we'd parked. Each separate structure—whether made of brick or colorful clapboard—flowed seamlessly into the next; each of their wrought-iron balconies almost but not quite connecting, hanging heavy with flowering plants and ferns. Beneath the balconies, most of the windows looked dark and unlit behind tall, wooden shutters. Something about the houses gave off a well-cared-for but unoccupied air.

The town house in front of us, however, had its shutters thrown open, and warm yellow light poured from its windows onto the street. Behind the curtains I could see figures moving. On both sides of the front door, someone had lit the gas, outdoor lanterns. Their flames flickered wildly, casting shadows onto the sidewalk and into the corners where this town house met its neighbors.

Before I had time to survey the rest of the house, the front door flew open and an enormous crowd of people came rushing out to greet us. Leading the charge was a pretty brunette woman who could have been Ruth's middle-aged doppelgänger. Behind her, what seemed like fifty other relatives gathered, all smiling and all talking at once.

"Whoa," I muttered. Joshua came up behind me, bag in hand, and subtly placed a few fingers on the small of my back.

"Meet the Mayhews," he said through the side of his mouth. "All nine hundred and seventy-five of them."

"No kidding. Did your entire family tree decide to visit for Christmas?"

"Basically." He shot me a sheepish, sideways look. "Which, um . . . kind of means we're sleeping in the attic."

"Fine by me." I shrugged, and fought the urge to add, *I can't sleep anyway.* Obviously, that just wasn't true.

As I continued to stare at all the new faces around me, Jillian walked up to my side and hissed, "Hey, Casper—forget your bag, or do you just *like* wearing the same thing every day?"

I raised one eyebrow. "I thought I didn't exist in your world?"

"Obviously I'm not that lucky," she whispered, and then sauntered away toward a group of what had to be more aunts and uncles.

With a tired sigh, I turned to Joshua. "Please tell me no one else in your family can see me. I don't think I could stand any more compliments tonight."

He gave me an apologetic smile. "Not according to Ruth. When she told me about all this Seer business, she also said we were the only ones who've had our triggering events. Oh, and now Jillian. So you're in the clear."

"Thank God for small favors."

A few feet away I saw Jeremiah hug the pretty brunette woman. While returning the hug, the woman leaned around Jeremiah's shoulder and waved directly at us. Well, at Joshua anyway.

"That's my aunt, Patricia Comeaux—Trish," Joshua said from the corner of his mouth, waving back at her. "I don't see Annabel or Celeste anywhere . . . guess they're inside."

Joshua had given me a brief lesson in Mayhew family history during the first hour of our car ride. But I could only keep a few crucial details straight.

Ruth Mayhew—formerly, Ruth Angeline—had grown up in New Orleans. She'd also met and married her late husband here. They had one son and two daughters before moving to Oklahoma, ostensibly for her husband's business (although Joshua and I knew the real reason: so that Ruth could lead her own group of Seers). Once grown, only Jeremiah chose to stay in Oklahoma;

both of his sisters had returned to Louisiana, settling down to raise families in or near the French Quarter, where many of their relatives still lived.

Watching the Angeline and Mayhew descendants flock together on the sidewalk tonight, the only names I could remember were those in Ruth's direct line: Aunt Patricia and her daughters, twenty-year-old Annabel and ten-year-old Celeste; Aunt Penelope and her nineteen-year-old son, Drew. Who I couldn't pick out of this crowd if someone paid me to anyway.

But there was one conspicuous absence on the curb tonight: Ruth. Not that I was complaining.

"Josh," Trish called across the crowd. "Most of the kids are in the drawing room. Why don't you go say hey before you put your stuff up? I think Annabel's got something planned for you all."

"What is it this time?" he asked. "Movie night? Ritual sacrifice?"

Trish chuckled, letting go of Jeremiah to extend another hug to Rebecca. "She's saving that last one for Christmas morning, actually."

When Joshua laughed loudly, she gave him one final smile before turning away to talk to his parents. Joshua waited until everyone's attention was otherwise occupied and then looked fully at me. He tilted his head toward the open front door and mouthed, *Inside?*

I felt a sudden twang of nerves. But I nodded and held out my arm, pointing to the town house.

"Lead the way."

With a last, fiery brush of his fingers against the back of my hand, he walked past me toward the front door. I took a deep breath, told myself that not every Mayhew house held a nasty surprise for me, and then followed him.

Normal, I reminded myself. *These are your last moments to feel normal. So take advantage.*

But as I passed by the gas lamps at the entrance of the town house, their flames sputtered, plunging the nearby sidewalk into darkness. From behind me a chorus of voices cried out in protest. After that I could swear I heard a rush of whispers from somewhere close—maybe from Joshua's family . . . maybe not.

I stopped, one foot on the cobblestones and one foot hovering in the doorstep. Then, unthinkingly, I let that foot drop onto the welcome mat inside the house. The moment I did, I heard two soft pops, and the gas lamps brightened again.

I gritted my teeth and shook my head, hard. *That doesn't mean anything. Those lamps are probably a century old—I'm sure they go out all the time.*

"Amelia?" Joshua whispered from inside the house. "You coming in?"

"Yes," I whispered back, like I was one who needed to worry about my volume. Then I laughed softly.

You know, I told myself, *for a ghost, you get spooked way too easily.* So I straightened my back and stepped fully across the threshold.

There, in the tiny foyer, the light was almost as dim as it had been outside. The only illumination came from an electric-lit pendant hung above a winding staircase down the hall and from the rooms leading off of the foyer. Through the archway to our right, I could see a tiny dining table, still half covered with the remains of tonight's meal. To our left, a set of young voices filtered through the opening between two French doors.

Joshua angled his head toward the doors. "Sounds like Annabel and Drew are in there. Want to 'meet' the rest of my family?"

I blew out one sharp breath and said, "Okay. Sure."

He paused for a second to study my face. Then his expression softened. "You know I'm really glad you're here, don't you?"

The little ache in my heart uncurled itself ever so slightly, and I had to clench one hand to my side to keep from pressing it to my chest. "Thanks," I said, managing a smile. "Me too."

He gave me that boyish grin, all dimples and full lips and inevitable heartbreak, and then pulled open one door. I heard a girl cry out a greeting, so I ducked behind him, feeling oddly shy as we entered the room together.

Once inside, however, Joshua moved aside too quickly for me to hide. At that moment I had a full view of the room. All over the walls, from the tops of the antique furniture to the base of the crown molding, were hundreds of framed photographs. I could just make out Joshua's smile in a few that hung near the fireplace. But aside from some current family photos, most looked ancient, clustered together in groups of black-and-white or sepia-toned portraits. Generations of Angeline Seers, all staring eerily out at us.

On the other side of the room, two teenagers sat together, draped over each other on a red velvet couch. The boy looked up briefly at Joshua and made a gesture with his head that was either a nod of acknowledgment or just an attempt to get his floppy dark hair out of his eyes. Almost immediately he turned back to his companion, a pretty blonde with a chic bob who'd snuggled suffocation-close to his side.

Across from us, another couple huddled together in a pair of overstuffed armchairs near the fireplace. The couple leaned so close to each other, I thought they were kissing. But when their heads turned toward Joshua, I could see they'd just been talking, heads together in intense conversation.

The girl broke away first, leaning back in her chair and flashing Joshua a wide grin. She brushed back her hair—jet-black like his, but cut ultrashort on one side and longish on the other. The long side flopped back, but not before I saw that she shared Joshua's midnight blue eyes.

As Joshua had promised, the girl didn't seem to see me. But when we came close, her friend abruptly sat up like someone had pinched him. He rested both his hands on his knees and then slowly turned his upper body toward us.

For a full minute he stared at Joshua. As he did so, an awkward silence fell over the room. I looked around and realized that everyone else—the black-haired girl, the two lovebirds on the couch—watched him, as if waiting for some kind of signal.

Aside from being creepy, their behavior also didn't make a lot of sense. After all, this boy didn't seem like someone this small crew would follow. First of all, he was significantly older—at least twenty-two. Then, the others wore artfully messy clothes and up-to-the-minute hairstyles. But the boy in the armchair appeared more like a young politician, in his white dress shirt and crisp gray suit. His light-brown hair was so short, I'd be hard-pressed to call it anything but a buzz cut, and I could barely see his eyes through the glint off his wire-rimmed glasses.

When he turned his head slightly to the right, however, the gleam off his lenses disappeared and I had a clearer view. His eyes were a cold gray—steely, almost. And unless I was imagining things, they moved from Joshua . . . to me.

"Well," the boy said, "nice to see the two of you made it safely."

I froze. From the corner of my eye, I saw Joshua arch an eyebrow. "Uh . . . the 'two of you'?" he asked.

"Yes," the boy said. "The two of you."

"Who—," Joshua began, but the boy cut him off midsyllable.

"You, and the ghost next to you," he said matter-of-factly. Then he locked his eyes directly—unmistakably—onto mine.

Chapter
NINE

I stayed frozen near the entrance of the drawing room even when the boy in the suit began to smile. The smile seemed genuine enough, its warmth spreading to his gray eyes until they lost their steely edge. But the moment he pushed himself out of the chair and into a standing position, I jerked backward, taking two quick steps into the foyer.

The boy, however, reacted much faster than I did. Almost as if he anticipated my fear. With two broad strides of his own, he stood right in front of us, hand extended like he wanted me—not Joshua—to shake it.

"Welcome to New Orleans, Amelia."

My jaw dropped.

I wasn't sure what I'd expected when I'd walked into the room, but a formal welcome certainly wasn't it. I peeked at Joshua, who stood motionless beside me. Judging by his expression—eyes wide, mouth slightly gaping like mine—Joshua had no idea who this boy was, either.

The boy in the suit could see me, obviously, which meant he was a Seer—one who'd already had his triggering event. But how did he already know my name? The only person who could have told him about me had to be . . . Ruth? That didn't make any sense, since he greeted me like one might an old friend, not some supernatural enemy.

Suddenly, I felt my defenses rise. I didn't take too well to strangers who knew more about me than I knew about them. Blame it on past experience with a certain blond ghost.

I was just about to tell him to back off when Jillian strolled into the room, flopped unceremoniously into the chair the boy had just vacated, and then glanced up at him with an arch sort of smile.

"See, Alex?" She addressed him directly. "I told you she was annoying."

I blinked back, stunned. *Jillian* had been the one to tell

this boy—Alex—who I was? Not only who I was, but *how* I was?

Even though she'd just entered it, Jillian didn't look the least bit surprised by this strange scene. She sprawled across the wingback chair, legs swung over an armrest and face turned up expectantly to the boy in front of me.

And . . . was I crazy, or did she look rapturous, too? Flirtatious, even? Like she desperately wanted this boy to pay attention to her.

Whatever Jillian may have wanted, the boy's eyes stayed locked onto mine. Waiting for me to react to his greeting. When I didn't, he waited for one more second, hand still hanging in the air, before he swung his body toward Joshua and offered him the introductory hand-shake instead.

"Sorry if I was being rude earlier," he said. "I guess I just feel like I know you already. I'm Alexander Etienne—a friend of Annabel's. We're freshmen at Tulane together, and she invited me to spend Christmas break with your family." He twitched his head sideways, acknowledging the black-haired girl in the other wingback chair. Then he extended his hand a tiny bit closer to Joshua. "Please—call me Alex."

Joshua looked at Alex's outstretched hand for another beat before reluctantly reaching out to shake it.

I thought he would say something defensive to this

Alex person. Make some kind of denial on my behalf. Instead, he eyed the rest of room and then asked, "Okay—how many of you can see her?"

"Joshua!" I cried, taken aback by his sudden frankness.

Across the room, the brown-haired boy laughed. "Oh my God, I can totally hear her!"

"Me too!" the blonde chimed in, clapping her hands together like I'd just performed a circus trick.

I crossed my arms over my chest and glared at them. Neither of the lovebirds looked directly at me, however. They both continued to stare at Joshua, wearing a matching set of self-satisfied smiles.

The only one who didn't seem annoyingly entertained was Annabel. Slowly, calmly, she pushed herself out of her chair and strolled over to us. She flipped back her swoosh of bangs, slipped her hands into the back pockets of her skinny-jeans, and grinned at me.

Well, she didn't grin *at* me, exactly; it was more like she grinned at the place where she *thought* I stood. She narrowed her eyes, peering in my direction like Jillian used to do before she could see me. But unlike Jillian, Annabel looked neither pissed off nor unnerved.

Annabel tilted her head to one side, still peering. "I bet we're freaking you out, aren't we?"

"Yes." Joshua and I answered simultaneously.

Annabel barked out a pleasantly dry, throaty laugh and

then focused on a spot somewhere above my left shoulder. "Sorry. But we've been waiting for this for a while."

"Waiting for what?" Joshua asked in disbelief.

"To meet Amelia."

I balked. Again, another living being saying my name like an old friend. It felt surreal, and I struggled, with only moderate success, to keep my cool.

"So," I said haltingly, "all of you can really . . . hear me?"

"Kind of," said the guy with the floppy hair. "You sort of sound like you're in another room. Or underground." Then his hazel eyes brightened with an idea. "Like . . . maybe you're buried?"

"Shut it, Drew," Annabel snapped. At that moment she reminded me of Ruth—sharply angled face, hawklike eyes, and in obvious command of those around her. And just like Ruth's old followers, Drew promptly shut it.

His girlfriend, however, pushed her mouth into a pretty pout. Under her breath she muttered, "I don't see why we have to do what your cousin says."

Annabel shot her a quick, cold smile. "You don't have to do what I say, Hayley. You have to do what Alex says."

Alex.

While Annabel and the others argued, Alex hadn't moved. Hadn't spoken. From the corner of my eye, I could still see him watching me. When he caught me looking, he ducked his head down so that our eyes were level and gave me a small, reassuring smile.

"I'm the only one who can see you," he said softly, speaking only to me. "Everyone else can just sense where you are. And hear you, thanks to practice."

"'Practice'? Could someone *please* explain all of this to me?"

"Are we making you uncomfortable, Amelia?" he asked in that same just-to-me tone.

"Not really," I lied. I paused, and then amended myself. "It's just . . . well, you're the first Seers I've met who haven't tried to exorcise me within the first ten seconds of meeting me. Except for Joshua, of course."

Annabel let out another raspy laugh. "And we're not going to. Promise."

For so long I'd wanted to hear a Seer speak those words. Now that one did, I felt a little dizzy.

I put my hand to my head. "I'm sorry, I just don't get it."

Annabel slipped her hands out of her pockets, folded her arms across her chest, and leaned back against one of the wings of her chair. Near the fireplace, I caught a glimpse of Jillian's expression; she obviously wanted Alex to mimic Annabel and lean against her chair. When he didn't, Jillian scowled heavily and then returned to chipping at her nail polish.

Either unaware of or unconcerned about her younger cousin's angst, Annabel nodded.

"I guess we owe you both an explanation, huh?"

"That's an understatement," Joshua said. He moved even closer to me and wrapped his arm around my waist.

I looked up at him in surprise. He hadn't touched me so blatantly in front of living people in . . . ever.

I heard a shuffle of movement as Drew and Hayley joined our makeshift circle in front of the fire. Drew draped one arm across Hayley's thin shoulders and then the two of them settled backward, evidently ready for story time.

With her audience now prepared, Annabel nodded once more and launched into her explanation.

"I don't know about you, but I've always been able to . . . sense weird things. I don't think I fully understood it at the time, and maybe I'm just imagining it now, in hindsight. Growing up in the Quarter, it's hard not to think you've heard something strange, or seen something out of place, every now and then. But I guess everything officially started about two months ago, right after Grandma Ruth moved in with us. I remember—it was fall break, so Drew was here eating all our food."

"Uh, you mean partying with you on Bourbon Street," he interjected.

Annabel rolled her eyes. "Like I said, Drew was doing his best impression of a human sponge. But on our last free night, it was raining too hard for us to go out. That's when Grandma Ruth cornered both of us and gave us the Seer talk."

Joshua nodded. "I got the same one when I brought Amelia home."

"Then you don't need me to give you the details. What might have been different from your talk, though, was Ruth's change of heart. She told us about you and your ghost, and about how she failed to do her job with Amelia. I guess that's when Ruth realized that her whole wait-until-their-triggering-event *thing* didn't work. Now, she's decided to tell everyone who's 'of age'—meaning over eighteen, I guess."

"Which is why she left me in the lurch," Jillian complained, not looking up from her nails. "I hate being treated like a little kid."

"You hate everything." Annabel laughed. Then she turned her attention back to us. "Anyway, that night, after we got the supernatural 'birds and bees' from Ruth, she introduced us to someone."

Annabel paused, and, for just a fraction of a second, her eyes darted over to Alex.

I jerked upright. "*Ruth* introduced you to Alex? And I'm not supposed to be freaked out right now?"

Alex sighed and shook his head. "Annabel, may I take over?"

"But, of course," she said, smiling and giving him a mock bow of her head.

"Let me just start by saying that I don't believe in exorcism." Alex shook his head again, looking mildly disgusted. "I think it's unfair, not to mention unnatural. Let the dead take care of the dead—that's my perspective."

Like Eli wanted to take care of me, I thought, but I kept my mouth shut as Alex went on.

"When I moved here three years ago for college, I immediately sought out a group of local Seers so I could keep learning. I knew *them* before I met Ruth Mayhew."

"Wait," I interrupted. "How did you already know what Seers were?"

Maybe I imagined it, but something in Alex's eyes went cold again. He tugged at his collar with one finger, pulling the fabric down to reveal his collarbone. There, carved around his neck and across the bone, was an old, ropy scar.

One that looked like he shouldn't have survived it.

When the fabric slipped back, hiding the scar from view, Alex shrugged. "Triggering event."

"How—"

"Car accident," he said tersely.

There was more to the scar than that, I could tell. But Alex obviously didn't want to discuss the topic. A muscle in his jaw flexed, just once, before his face softened again. Then, with a much warmer expression, he continued.

"I could see ghosts long before I joined the New Orleans coven. And to give the New Orleans Seers credit, they're far more progressive than the group Ruth used to lead. Still, many of their ideas are too . . . ecclesiastical for my taste. When I met Ruth and she told me about her family, I knew I had an opportunity to be a part of something different. So I encouraged her to introduce me to all the young people in her family at the next Seers' meeting."

"What he didn't tell her," Annabel interrupted with a wide smile, "is that he didn't want to teach us to exorcise ghosts. He wanted us to learn how to coexist with them . . . and how to be aware of them without having to have a triggering event."

"Which is awesome," Hayley said, shifting forward in Drew's arms. "My mom's a Seer; and ever since I was a kid, she made me go to their meetings. In the Quarter they have this rule that you have to have a triggering event before you get a say in what the group does. And do you think I want to drop a toaster in my bathtub just so I can vote no against exorcisms? Um, no thank you. So I stopped going as much this year. I mean, I'm eighteen now, so I can do what I want, right? But I'm glad I went to last month's meeting, because that's when I met everyone here."

Drew smiled broadly and pulled her closer to him. "When Hayley found out we were trying to contact ghosts without having to go toe-up for a few minutes, she was in."

With a girlish giggle, Hayley lifted onto tiptoes and gave him a quick peck on the cheek. "I was 'in' when I met you, sweetie."

A retching sound came from the direction of the fireplace. I looked toward it just in time to see Jillian stick her tongue out like she was gagging. A little smile tugged at the edge of my lips before I turned back to Annabel, who'd started talking again.

"Alex has been helping us for the last month," she said. "Teaching us how to listen for ghosts' voices. You wouldn't believe how much concentration it takes."

Drew laughed. "Yeah, except when they're in the room with you."

"Totally," Hayley bubbled. "You're pretty clear . . . , Amelia."

She tried out my name, saying it with a touch of uncertainty. Her eyes focused on something at least two feet above my head, and she pressed her lips together, waiting.

"Um, thanks?" I managed.

Upon hearing my voice, Hayley flashed that spot above my head an enormous smile. At that moment she annoyed me a little less than before. There was something endearing about her enthusiasm. Kind of.

"There's one thing I don't get: where does Jillian fit into all this?"

Joshua's voice startled me.

I'd been too engrossed to realize it, but throughout this entire conversation, he hadn't moved a muscle. Instead, he'd stood next to me silent and unmoving. I took a peek at his face and saw that he'd composed it into that rare, expressionless mask—the one he wore whenever he didn't trust what was going on around him.

"Jillian called Annabel a few weeks ago," Alex explained, not looking directly at Joshua, "to complain about your new girlfriend. One thing led to another and . . . I've been counseling Jillian. Teaching her what it means to be a Seer."

Beside me, Joshua visibly bristled. No one needed him to say aloud what he thought about Alex "counseling" his little sister.

"Oh." Joshua's voice was cold. "So that's why Jillian's been such a sweetheart to Amelia lately?"

"That's all me, bro," Jillian piped up from her chair. "I accept that I can see her now. Doesn't mean I want to have a slumber party and braid her hair."

Despite myself, I chuckled and looked back at Joshua. "You have to admit—at least she's honest."

He barely reacted, his icy stare still locked onto Alex. I reached over and ran my hand, just once, down the sleeve of Joshua's sweater. I couldn't feel the fabric beneath my fingers, and he probably couldn't feel the weight of my touch on his arm; still, he could see the gesture, and his face relaxed slightly in response to it.

"How are you handling this?" he asked me quietly, although everyone could hear us. "Are you okay with all of it?"

I looked around at the new, strangely expectant faces, and then I did a quick self-assessment. What I discovered inside surprised me.

"Yeah," I said, a little stunned at how easily the answer came. "Yeah, I am."

"You're sure?" Joshua pressed.

I nodded, feeling an odd mix of lingering apprehension and relief.

"It's actually sort of . . . nice that other people know I exist. And that they aren't trying to kill me." I shrugged one shoulder in qualification. "Figuratively, of course."

Everyone laughed, albeit a little awkwardly. I guess I couldn't blame them—no matter how enthusiastically they greeted me, most of them hadn't joked about death with a dead girl. Except, perhaps, for Alex.

"Where's Ruth?" I asked Alex quietly. It seemed strange to ask him instead of Annabel, but he obviously had many of tonight's answers.

Alex flicked his eyes up toward the ceiling and then met my gaze again. "Migraine. She hasn't come down all day, and I doubt she will tonight."

I couldn't help my audible sigh of relief. Then, inexplicably, I felt myself giving Alex a tiny smile. After all, he engineered this meeting. And whether he knew it or not, he'd just made my last days with Joshua more pleasant: less speaking in whispers; less skulking in corners, avoiding people who might think Joshua had gone crazy if they saw him talking to himself.

Almost imperceptibly, Alex returned my smile—like we'd just shared a private joke or I'd just thanked him. Which, in a way, I had.

After that Alex's eyes shifted away from mine for the first time since I'd walked into the room. He and Annabel exchanged a quick glance, and then she cleared her throat.

"Well, now that that's settled," she said, "go unpack your crap. We're going out."

"Out?"

Joshua still sounded skeptical, although his voice had lost some of its chill; obviously, the fact that I'd made peace with the situation had calmed him down too.

Annabel's lip curled in amusement at her cousin's tone. "Yeah, 'out.' As in, not 'in.'"

She reached behind her and picked up something she'd left in her chair—a sheet of green paper, which she handed to Joshua. He held it up for me to read with him. Then he raised one eyebrow and looked up at Annabel.

"'*Navidad de los Muertos*'?" Joshua quoted from the sheet, which was printed with what looked like black skulls.

"Christmas of the Dead," Hayley said. "It's a costume party at our new favorite club. It's got a kind of dark theme instead of happiness and presents and Santa. Totally subversive, right?"

Drew gave her a noisy kiss on the cheek. "Good vocab word, babe."

Hayley grinned widely in my direction. "I'm trying to get into Auburn next year," she confided. "That way Drew and I can be together every day."

"Yeah, yeah, yeah," Jillian droned, swinging her legs around and making a little jump out of the chair. "Less talking, more barhopping."

"You're only sixteen—you're not going with us," Alex said firmly.

"What?" Jillian shrieked. "But Joshua's only eighteen."

"She's got a point," Joshua said. "How exactly am I supposed to get in if she can't?"

Annabel let out another dry laugh. "Let's just say that the carding policy here is a little more relaxed than the one in Wilburton."

"It's not that strict in Wilburton," Jillian grumbled.

"That's beside the point," Alex snapped. "Drew and Hayley and Joshua can all pass for twenty-one. You can't. And anyway, you should be perfectly able to entertain yourself here."

Jillian nearly growled as she folded her arms across her chest. But after a moment of glowering, she fell back in the chair to stare sullenly into the fire. She looked, for all purposes, like she would obey Alex's command.

Hearing how this stranger spoke to his sister, Joshua bristled a bit. But he must have decided that Alex was probably right, because he didn't press the issue. Instead, Joshua turned back to Annabel and shook his head.

"What about your mom?" he asked her. "Won't she be pissed that all of us underage kiddos went to a club?"

"Josh, I grew up in the French Quarter. The fact that I didn't have an after-school job at an S&M shop is enough for her." She gave him a wry smile, one that strongly reminded me of Jillian's. When Jillian wasn't scowling anyway.

"Besides," Annabel added, "what are you afraid of? That you'll wake up without a kidney?"

"No, that I'll wake up without *any* internal organs."

Annabel snorted. "This club is totally safe, I promise. And anyway, we thought it was the perfect place for Amelia to have some fun—kind of creepy, really crowded. No one will notice or care if you two are dancing, making out, whatever."

I blinked back. "That's really . . . thoughtful. Thanks."

All around me, everyone except for Jillian beamed. Alex, in particular, looked pleased, which made me wonder whether the club had been his idea originally.

In contrast, Joshua still looked doubtful. He leaned his head toward me and whispered, "You really want to go?"

"Well . . . yeah. I really want to go."

The crazy thing was, I *did*. At this moment I couldn't think of anything I wanted to do more than enjoy myself for a while. I wanted to touch Joshua without fear of discovery, or fear of disappearing. I wanted to spend a few hours not worrying about what lay in store for me. I even wanted to *dance*.

The idea of it was so freeing, I actually giggled. My first genuine, truly free laugh in what had to be months. When Joshua heard that, a slow smile spread across his face.

"Okay then, Club Kid," he said. "Let's go unpack."

Chapter
TEN

"Y ou should stop worrying about your outfit, Amelia. You look perfect."

The compliment startled me, and I jumped a little to the side, away from its speaker. It was something that Joshua would have said. In fact, he *had* said it, many times. But right now Joshua walked at least twenty feet ahead of me. He was so engrossed in his conversation with Annabel, he didn't even notice when I began to lag behind.

If Joshua and I had kept pace, he might have seen me

twist at the fabric of my skirt with one hand, might have noticed me gnaw on my lower lip.

But Alex obviously noticed. And although he'd only known me for a few hours, he obviously felt comfortable leaning close and whispering that compliment into my ear.

Upon seeing me jerk away, he held up both hands in a pose of surrender.

"Sorry," he said. "I didn't mean to scare you."

"You didn't. . . . It's just . . . I'm . . ."

I floundered with my words and then took a quick, shallow breath. "I'm just not used to people talking to me. Besides Joshua."

We passed into the circle of light from a gas lamp, and I saw Alex's gaze shift forward, to Joshua. Just before we crossed back into the shadows, Alex's eyes reconnected with mine.

"It doesn't bother you, does it?" he asked. "That I can see you too?"

Even in the darkness I could see his smile. It was playful, teasing. The smile of someone who considered himself my friend.

I automatically wrapped my arms around my waist, hiding the tightest portion of my dress. I don't know why, but I got the strangest impression that Alex didn't just see me, he saw *through* me. As if he could read every hope and fear on the planes of my face.

I shrugged, trying to keep my expression impassive. "It's a little unexpected. But no, it doesn't bother me."

"I hope not. You have no idea how nice it is to finally meet you."

I felt one corner of my lip tug downward. "Am I the first ghost you've met, Alex?"

He shook his head. "No. But you're definitely the nicest."

"So far."

The sound of Alex's laugh reverberated off the walls of the narrow street. "Okay: you're the nicest so far."

I was about to correct him, to tell him that I'd been cautiously nice—so far—when I heard Joshua's voice calling out to me.

"Amelia? Where are you?"

"I'm back here," I answered loudly. Then I added, "With Alex."

Suddenly Joshua reversed course, pushing between Drew and Hayley and walking toward us.

"Sorry," he said when he got closer to me.

His eyes darted briefly toward Alex. For just a second Joshua let his hand hang in the air near my waist, like he wanted to place a possessive hold on me. He must have thought better of it, though, because he then dropped his arm and tucked both his hands into the pockets of his black slacks.

"I lost track of you for a minute, didn't I?"

I shrugged one shoulder. "No big deal. Besides, it's not like you left me completely alone."

I turned to Alex, to ask that he make room for Joshua on the sidewalk. But without warning, Alex had already disappeared. I squinted into the darkness and saw that he'd taken Joshua's place next to Annabel, far ahead of us. I hadn't even heard him walk away.

"Weird," I murmured.

I turned back to Joshua and saw that he'd stopped in the street. He now stood a few feet behind me, motionless except for the hand he ran through his hair and then left on the back of his neck. Inadvertently adopting that nervous pose I loved so much.

Maybe Joshua worried about abandoning me for a few minutes since things between us had been so strained lately. Or maybe he worried about leaving me alone with Alex for more than a couple of seconds.

At the thought that even Joshua occasionally got jealous, I laughed softly. The corner of my mouth lifted slightly, into a little half smile. I clasped my hands behind my back and took a few deliberately slow steps toward him.

"Whatcha doin' back there, Joshua?" I teased.

"Trying to figure out how to tell you I *am* sorry for

leaving you alone," he said, smiling back at me sheepishly. "Really."

My grin lifted higher as I sidled up beside him. "Don't be. It gave me a chance to check you out from behind."

Joshua's eyes widened, and then he laughed. "Isn't that supposed to be my line?"

"Not tonight," I said, slipping my arm through his. I ran my eyes down his outfit: black pants and shoes; a white dress shirt, its sleeves rolled to his elbows underneath a winter coat. It was the closest thing Joshua had brought to a costume, and it managed to make him look more photo-shoot than costume-party ready.

Not that I was complaining.

I released a small sigh—half contented, half wistful. "You look great, Joshua."

He chuckled low as we began to stroll forward together, obviously not in a hurry to catch up with the rest of the group. He pulled me closer to him; and, for the briefest second, I felt the brush of his coat's wool against the crook of my arm.

From the corner of his eye, Joshua gave me a lingering appraisal. "You always look great, Amelia."

I shook my head. "I always look the same, Joshua."

"Yeah—*great*."

"Huh," I grunted. "Sure."

I absently ran my free hand across the top of my skirt

and then pulled my fingers through the thick waves of my hair. This time it was Joshua who noticed me fidget.

"Stop second guessing yourself," he said gently. "You look beautiful. Perfect."

Perfect.

The same description Alex used. But when Joshua said it, I didn't feel as though I was being scrutinized. Instead, I felt an undeniable warmth spreading out from my core and up to my face. Once it got there, I couldn't stop it from bursting forth into an enormous smile.

All of a sudden that impulse returned. The one that made me want to tell him about *everything*: Eli's warnings, the bizarre dream of my father, my plan to disappear.

Mostly, I wanted to tell him I loved him. I wanted to say it out loud, at least once.

I had just opened my mouth, preparing to let fly my deepest secrets, when Annabel's voice stopped me.

"We're here," she called back to us.

My mouth snapped shut, and I felt the strangest rush of longing *and* relief.

I had no time to deal with either since the group had slowed enough for Joshua and me to finally catch up. All together, we rounded a corner, and suddenly a loud clamor assaulted us. The noise was so great, I don't know how I hadn't previously noticed the wild tumult of shouting and laughter and pulsing bass.

In front of us, spilling patrons and music into the side alley, was the club. I could hardly see the entrance through the thick mass of people pressing to get inside. On the second and third stories, iron balconies looked ready to collapse under the weight of too many bodies and too many strands of red Christmas lights.

Everyone was in costume, as Hayley had promised. I caught glimpses of pitchforks and black capes and elaborately gory makeup. Many of the partygoers also wore identical masks: skeletal faces, sparkling red under a thick coat of glitter.

While Joshua and I stared up at the spectacle, a group of girls pushed past us, all dressed in gauzy sheeting and slathered with white face paint. Ghosts, apparently.

Watching them, Drew leaned around Hayley and yelled over the noise: "Hey, Amelia—do those girls have it about right?"

"Oh, yes," I drawled. "When we die, we all get white sheets. Standard issue."

Our group laughed loudly in approval—particularly Alex, who I'd swear gave me a quick wink. When he turned away, I swept my eyes over the people I'd just met. Drew, Hayley, and Annabel had all dressed in refreshingly unspooky costumes: as a giant chicken, an angel, and a ninja, respectively. Alex, however, stood out most from the crowd in that he *didn't* stand out. Aside from a pair of gloves and an overcoat, he hadn't changed for the party. He still looked every bit the young politician.

Maybe that is *his costume,* I thought.

"Let's go," Annabel commanded us. "Before the wannabe ghosties take our private room."

Everyone turned in unison to follow her toward the club. Although we moved along with them through the crowded alley, Joshua pulled me back slightly and leaned close to my ear. He spoke in a normal tone; but with all the noise, his voice sounded like a whisper.

"What do you think about all this?"

"It's definitely . . . festive."

"Not exactly Bing Crosby and hot cocoa, is it? Do you just want to go back to the house?"

Looking up at the masked figures writhing all over the club, I grimaced. Then I shook my head and reminded myself to stay positive. To *enjoy* tonight.

"Nope," I said, grabbing his hand and tugging him forward. "I want to dance."

I didn't wait to hear his response, nor did I look back for his reaction. Instead, I focused on Hayley's broad white wings bobbing their way through the crowd in front of me. Soon we made it past the sea of bodies and up a few steps to the front door.

Where most entrances in the Quarter had solid wooden doors, a pair of black iron gates guarded this building. Next to them, a hugely muscled man stood with his arms folded across the chest of his tight T-shirt. He looked like a living gargoyle, all scowl and stone. I half expected him to breathe fire when we approached. But to my surprise, Annabel leaped over the final step, used his shoulders to hoist herself up, and gave him an enormous kiss on the cheek.

"Annie," he cried over raucous sounds coming out of the gates. "Where the hell have you been?"

"Finals," she shouted. "Missed you."

"Missed you too, babe." With a brawny arm, he pushed open one of the gates. "Claudette said you'd be here tonight—your room should be ready by now."

Annabel gave his forearm a pat of thanks and made a motion with her head that meant we should go inside. The others followed her; but Joshua and I lingered in the doorway, which was too jam-packed with bodies to permit much of a view into the club.

"Are you *sure* you're sure?" he said, trying to talk over the drumbeat of a new song.

I simply nodded, tightened my grip on his hand until the fire ignited between our palms, and then crossed the threshold.

The club was so dark inside, we could hardly see the path forward. High above, I could just make out a chandelier entwined with Day of the Dead masks and shimmering tinsel. Someone had replaced the chandelier's normal bulbs with red ones. Aside from the little pools of flickering light from the candelabra on the walls, everything glowed bloodred: the mirror behind the bar; the gigantic Christmas tree decorated with plastic skeletons; even the dancers themselves.

Annabel turned a red-hued face to us and mouthed something. Joshua held one hand to his ear, showing her that we couldn't hear ourselves, much less her. So she extended an arm, pointing to the spiral staircase at the back of the room.

We continued to shove our way through the dancers who clogged the path to the stairs. I didn't even try to avoid touching people, so every now and then, I felt a dull press in the numbness where someone came too close to me. Judging by Joshua's pained expression, he could actually feel every misplaced elbow and knee.

As we struggled and shoved, I stared at the rest of club's decorations. Underneath its veneer of eerie Christmas paraphernalia, the place actually looked quite chic. It had a sort of old-world elegance to it, with damask paper and velvet booths running along its walls. The chandelier, the candelabra, the gilded mirrors—creepy in the dark, but I bet they looked lavish in the daylight.

And although the dancers wore nightmarish outfits, I could tell through their glittering skeleton masks and makeup that these people weren't actual ghoul-seekers. Most looked just as chic as their surroundings, probably part of New Orleans's young, painfully attractive set.

Suddenly, it seemed to me as though the club and its attendants were merely playing at the macabre. No real spooks waited in the corners. No demons lived under the stairs. Other than Joshua's relatives and their friends, I doubted anyone in this building could even sense me, much less hear or see me.

Realizing that I had nothing to fear, I felt a heady sense of relief. Excitement, even. It shot up my spine and through my veins like adrenaline. Made me want to react. Made me want to set myself free, if only for a few minutes.

Joshua had just stepped past me on his way to the staircase, so I tugged at his arm. He met my gaze and then tilted his head to one side, questioning. I gave him a sly grin and used my free hand to point to the crowded floor we had just crossed.

Dance? I mouthed.

He raised both eyebrows questioningly. Then he started to grin too. He shrugged off his coat and passed it to Drew to carry up to the private room.

Free of the coat, Joshua looked . . . well, great, as I'd told him earlier. The word "delicious" sprang to mind, and I had to repress a giggle. I took one steadying breath, trying to stay cool. But as I watched him walk toward me, my excitement intensified. He placed both his hands in mine, and the fiery sensation burst across my skin, tingling along my palms and wrists.

At that point I did giggle. Then I said an immediate prayer of thanks that the loud music covered the sound.

Still grinning, Joshua spun us out into the crowd. He guided us past the other dancers and held me tighter, running his hands to my shoulders then down my back. His touch was so electric, I almost didn't notice the effort it took to get to the center of the dance floor, directly beneath the red chandelier.

Once there, Joshua pressed closer—closer than we usually allowed ourselves to be. Suddenly, I felt the brush of his skin, real and warm against my own, and my breath caught in my throat. All around us, the music began to swell. As we swayed together to its rhythm, I felt dizzy, drunk off the heavy drumbeat and the dark, hypnotic melody.

My eyes met Joshua's, and even through all the red, I could still see their striking midnight blue. By now his hands had strayed down my shoulder blades, leaving a trail of fire wherever they crossed. He rested them against the small of my back and then, with the slightest tug, pulled me so close I could almost feel his heart beat through his shirt. When he leaned down to brush his lips against my collarbone, I arched my neck and took one shuddering breath.

And that's when I saw them.

Faces.

Ones that obviously didn't belong here. And by *here* I meant the living world.

They were scattered throughout the crowd—ghastly, stark white and motionless against the undulating red. And all of them stared at one thing.

Me.

My head snapped forward, and I pressed my hands against Joshua's chest. We continued to dance, but I now stared into the crowd, my head whipping to the right and left. Through the thick mass of dancers, I caught only the briefest glimpses of pale white, standing out in the sea of red. The faces were so isolated, so obscured by the movement of the dancers, I couldn't be sure I saw them at all.

For a second I wondered whether I was just seeing the wannabe ghost-girls.

But I didn't think so. Not when everything else in here—the lights, the walls, the people—looked like it had been dipped in blood.

While I kept searching, Joshua started to dance us in a circle. Although he moved slowly, the circular movement soon coupled with too much head swiveling, and my earlier dizziness returned in full force.

Worse, actually. Although Joshua and I continued to move to the rhythm, I felt like we were spinning out of control. My head swam, and a real, disorienting wave of nausea hit me.

I clung to Joshua, leaned over his shoulder, and tried to catch my breath. Tried to quell an overwhelming need to retch.

And there, mere inches away from me, a face stared back. Like it was waiting for me.

It was so close I only saw its most prominent features: pale flesh, black eyes. And row upon row of sharp teeth, glittering in a crazed, wicked smile.

I felt its breath, icy and insidious against my cheek, and I screamed.

Chapter
ELEVEN

After that, I didn't think. I just reacted.

Within seconds I had Joshua at my back, my arms stretched behind me and wrapped around him in my best attempt to protect him from whatever had just come after us. I felt a feral snarl spring to my lips; and, for the briefest moment, I closed my eyes. To calm myself. To prepare.

But when I opened them, the menacing face was gone. No leering grin, no cold breath, no black eyes.

Gone.

Still keeping my arms clasped tightly around what had to be a very confused Joshua, I spun in a circle, searching the crowd again. This time I saw nothing but a swaying sea of red. Besides mine, the only supernatural faces left in this club were made of plastic and glitter.

All the ghastly beings must have disappeared in an instant. Vanished, as if they'd never been there at all.

As if I'd imagined them, just as I'd imagined my father this afternoon.

At that thought my arms dropped from Joshua's sides. My hands immediately flew to my mouth, and I pressed my fingertips to my lips, trying to hold back a gasp. Despite the effort, I started to sound like I was hyperventilating.

The entire time, I kept asking myself the same question: *Is it possible for a ghost to go crazy?*

If those faces weren't real, then I had hallucinated twice in one day. Which didn't bode well for my sanity.

But assuming for a moment that I hadn't totally lost it, then I was probably in even worse trouble. Because I'd seen those kinds of faces before, on the night I'd finally stood against Eli upon High Bridge.

I watched one of them swoop in like a bat, dragging Eli into the darkness. Before fleeing the netherworld for the last time, I had a conversation with another one, which—unfortunately—gave me plenty of time to familiarize myself with how they looked.

Deathly pale and unnaturally still. Beautiful at first, and then hideous.

Those were the faces of demons.

And those were the faces watching me tonight. Maybe not the same demons I'd met on High Bridge, but similar enough.

How had they found me? More importantly, how were they here? If they stayed cloistered away in what I assumed was a place even darker than the netherworld, then what were they doing in living, breathing New Orleans?

Unfortunately, that question seemed to answer itself.

A handful of demons—if that's what they actually were—had appeared tonight because they *didn't* always stay away. They *didn't* always hide in places darker than I could comprehend.

Sometimes they came to the living world to take matters into their own hands.

Maybe tonight had just been a glimpse of things to come. A warning that they *could* find me, whenever they wanted to.

Which meant my presence served as a lightning rod for evil, putting anyone who happened to stand nearby at risk. But only one person in particular stood nearby, almost all the time . . .

"Amelia?"

Immediately, my head snapped up and my eyes refocused. Then I jumped slightly, shocked to find myself standing outside the club with my back pressed against the brick wall. I'd been so intently drawing my conclusions that I must have walked outside, leaned against this wall, and clawed into it as if clinging for dear life.

Judging by the concerned faces around me, I'd had an entourage while doing so.

Joshua stood closest—he'd been the one to call my name in that sharp, frightened tone. A few steps behind him, Annabel waited. She looked worried, casting glances at Joshua and then back at the club —making sure we wouldn't be caught, even though we probably weren't the strangest things in the alley tonight. At least, not on the surface.

"Everything okay?" Annabel asked.

I nodded and then remembered that, to her, I probably looked like a brick wall right now.

"Yeah," I said out loud. "I just . . . I needed some air. That's why I came outside."

In front of me, the darkness of the alley hid part of Joshua's features. When I gave my feeble excuse, the illuminated half of his face twisted.

"Really?" he said, his voice dripping with skepticism. "You screamed, then you freaked out, then you wandered out of the club without hearing me . . . because you needed air?"

I startled a little; I hadn't realized that my behavior had been that frenzied.

"Um . . . yes?" My voice didn't sound very convincing, but I went on, forcing a note of conviction into it. "Didn't you notice how I was . . . getting sick? There were just too many people in there. I couldn't breathe."

"You couldn't breathe," he repeated in a flat, disbelieving voice. He was kind enough not to point out that I technically didn't *need* to breathe.

In response, I simply gave a defensive shrug. Joshua watched me for a moment, waiting for a more plausible— or at least a more honest—explanation. When I didn't produce one, he sighed.

"Okay," he conceded. "You couldn't breathe. Which probably means it's our cue to go home."

"*My* cue," I blurted out. "My cue to go home."

"Huh?"

"I'll go," I insisted. "You need to stay here and . . . and spend some more time with your cousins."

Joshua tossed a quick glance back at Annabel and then shook his head. "It's Christmas in three days—we'll have plenty of time then. But I think *you* need me right now. So I'll just come with you, okay?"

"No!"

I shouted the word. When Joshua flinched in surprise, I suppressed a curse. I took one quiet breath for restraint and then went on in what I hoped was a less desperate voice.

"I just . . . I need some time to think. Tonight's been a lot to take in, you know?" I nodded meaningfully in Annabel's direction. "It would be nice to have some time to myself. Just for a while."

Joshua's brow furrowed. In those dark blue eyes, I could read every one of his emotions: hurt that I obviously wanted to get away from him; fear about me being alone—if relatively invisible—on these dark, unfamiliar streets; and finally, reluctant surrender. He sighed again, and the sound was so full of defeat that the little ache in my chest writhed.

"Okay," he said quietly. "Whatever you want, Amelia. Just wait for me in the courtyard behind the town house, okay? I'll let you in when I get back."

"Thank you," I said, sounding too enthusiastic. Before I could think it through, I sprang forward and gave him a grateful kiss. Then, just as quickly, I jerked away—so fast, I wouldn't blame him for feeling a little rejected.

With the fire of our touch still burning on my lips, I raised my eyes to his. In them I saw his longing, his uncertainty.

Considering the fact that I'd only recently discovered

who I was, Joshua knew me about as well as I knew myself. He knew when I held back, and he knew when I was distracted. He knew when things weren't quite right between us, and he knew when I was lying.

Like right now.

Realizing that my next words would be lies, too, I bit my lip, lifted onto my toes, and leaned in close to him.

"I'll see you back at the town house," I whispered. "I promise."

I leaned back, just long enough to memorize the lines of his face one last time. Then I closed my eyes and willed myself away from there.

Chapter
TWELVE

O f course I hadn't planned to materialize back to the town house. If the demons had really found me, I didn't have the luxury of time to figure out my next move. So, by materializing tonight, I intended to follow through with my plan early: send myself away from New Orleans, the Mayhews, and Joshua. Permanently.

But my ridiculous sense of direction and my poor, weak-willed heart evidently had other ideas.

Wherever I now stood looked much the same as where

I'd just been: old, shuttered buildings; elaborate balconies; crowded streets, even in the dead of night. The only difference was that now those things were out of reach, just beyond the lush, iron-fenced park in which I'd opened my eyes.

All around me, palmetto trees and live oaks defied the winter, their leaves green and full through either their own strength or that of a diligent gardener. Considering the clean paths and neat flower beds that radiated out from where I stood, I guessed the latter.

It was a beautiful place, I couldn't deny that. But I had one little problem with the park: it lay at least ten feet below me. Maybe even twenty.

From what I could tell, I'd materialized on top of some tall, stone platform. I looked up and then stumbled in surprise. A gigantic, metal horse and rider loomed above me. I had to grab one of the horse's extended hooves to steady myself. Once I regained my balance—and composure—I realized that the platform upon which I stood was actually the base of an enormous statue. One that looked like it wanted to attack me.

I stared back up at the statue with a grim smile.

"Any hint where I am?" I asked it.

"About to be trampled by General Jackson." The voice called out from somewhere below in a heavy accent I couldn't quite identify.

Before I could react, someone else drawled, "*President* Jackson, actually."

"As if you remember," the first voice snapped. "You just read it on the base of the statue."

"As if you didn't."

My head jerked downward to the speakers, who, while obviously too busy arguing to pay me further attention, also obviously *heard* me.

When I caught sight of them, my flight instinct surged again. I scrambled, clawing backward until I'd practically soldered myself to the metal statue. A foolish effort, probably, considering how far below me my audience stood. But as I peered closer at them in the dark, I realized that maybe my instincts weren't so foolish.

The five beings circling the hedges at the base of the statute didn't exactly *stand*: their legs faded somewhere around their knees, and through the places where their feet should have been, I could see the outline of the pathway. Although their bodies appeared more substantial, the dark shapes of the trees bled through the contours of their faces.

It was those faces that finally made me realize that the demons had not, in fact, followed me from the club. Because the demons, though pallid and otherwordly, weren't translucent. And because these figures glowed faintly in the dark.

Just like me.

"Who are you?" I demanded, although I'd already guessed the answer.

"Dead," one of the figures said, giving me a languid smile.

He reminded me vaguely of Eli, with his arrogant features and long blond hair tied back from his face. Still smirking, he folded his arms over the breast of his military jacket. "Isn't that obvious?"

"Yes," I said. "But I still don't know what *kind* of dead you are."

"Same as you." A gray-haired woman in a high-collared black dress gave me a brusque nod. "Dead *is* dead."

"No, the girl is right," another figure argued. "At first there are many kinds of dead. But those who stay become like us, in the end."

Recognizing the strange accent of the first speaker— the one who'd told me about the statue—I leaned forward cautiously. The man caught me looking and beamed up a radiant, if slightly flawed, smile. Even through the nasty scars on his mahogany-dark skin, I could tell he'd once been handsome. Before getting into about five hundred knife fights, from the looks of his cheeks.

"Hello there," he said, touching the brim of what looked an awful lot like a pirate hat. "Welcome to the Place d'Armes."

"It's called Jackson Square now," a nasally voice corrected him. "They haven't called it Place d'Armes since they hung people like you here."

I immediately recognized this voice as the one that had corrected the pirate guy about President Jackson. The nasally speaker stood aloof, slightly apart from his fellow ghosts, wearing an old-fashioned tuxedo and a pinched expression. If I had to guess, I'd bet he was once a blue blood and still harbored some leftover disdain for his present company.

Which begged the question: Why was he here, with these other ghosts? Why were *any* of them here?

"None of you really answered me," I said cautiously. "Who are you?"

The last of the ghosts moved forward, stepping in front of her companions. She was the youngest, probably only a few years older than me when she died. Her long black braids fell across the shoulders of a dark cape clasped at the base of her throat.

"We are what is left," she answered in a soft, vaguely French accent.

For some reason I shivered. "What do you mean 'left'? Left of what?"

"Those who have died in the Quarter," she whispered. "We five are the last to walk unclaimed."

I twisted one corner of my mouth. "Are you saying

that you're the last ghosts left in one of the creepiest places in America? Because I find that hard to believe."

She shrugged, her wide, dark eyes never leaving mine. "Your belief or disbelief does not make it any less true."

"O-kay," I said, drawing out my *O* like Joshua always did when he didn't necessarily trust something. "Then who are your masters?"

The sound of the pirate's booming laugh echoed off the statue. "We have none, girl. And those of us who did can't remember now."

I shook my head, still skeptical. "The only other ghost I've met was working for other beings. All the other ghosts had either gone to heaven or . . . someplace else."

"Not you, though," the dark-haired girl pointed out. "You have no masters, and you're still here."

"Well . . . yeah." I frowned. "Not me."

"As you are now, we once were," she said. "Lost in the fog, without guidance. Over the centuries, we have awoken and found one another. Together, we have hidden from the dark ones."

Upon hearing her last words, my stomach clenched. "'Dark ones'? You mean . . . the demons?"

"Those things with the horrible, pale faces?" the pirate asked. When I nodded, he grunted roughly. "If that's what you call them, demon is as good a name as any."

I felt a chill inch up my spine. "So they *are* here, in New Orleans?"

"They're everywhere, girl," he said with a dark laugh. "The demons and their dark caves are everywhere. They hunt all over the world, for the likes of us."

"They *still* come after you?"

The five ghosts exchanged looks, and then, slowly, each of them nodded.

"Them," the pirate said, "and those damned ghost hunters. Exorcising souls left and right. Course, they're easier to avoid than the dark ones."

In the calmest voice I could manage, I asked, "How do you keep the demons from finding you?"

"By vanishing," the soldier said. "Often."

"Materialization," I muttered to myself. Just like I intended to do. I felt a small flush of relief that at least part of my plan might go right. Louder, I asked, "How has it worked so far?"

"It's not without sacrifice." The gray-haired woman gestured down the length of her transparent body. "This is the result of too much vanishing. Soon, you vanish too."

I had to repress a gasp. "Are you telling me that *materializing* does that to you?"

"Among other things. Too much of it and you lose whatever connects you to the living world: your body, your memories."

"Your memories?" I sunk a little against the statue. "You lose your memories?"

"Course you do," the pirate stated matter-of-factly. "If I remembered anything, I've lost it now. My life's gone. Even my name. Hazard of the trade."

"Is it . . . worth it?" I asked. "To escape the demons?"

The black-haired girl gave me a bitter smile. "If you had ever seen one of their dark worlds, then you would know that escape is your only option. Loss of memory, loss of form—they are nothing compared to those places."

Several images instantly ran through my mind: sensations I'd remembered in my flashes; the sight of my mother in the morning sunshine; Joshua's face, smiling at me.

Did these ghosts have such memories to weigh against the value of their afterlives? If so, then I dreaded even more the moment when I had to make their choice. Especially since that moment suddenly seemed all too close.

"Why are you here?" I asked them softly. "With me, I mean?"

"*You* found *us*, girl," the pirate said.

"Maybe. But none of you looked too surprised to see me tonight."

The black-haired girl moved a fraction of an inch closer. "We are never surprised to meet the dead in this city. What is more unusual is when we find a soul that has not yet been claimed. If we see someone like that, then we try to help them. Before the dark ones come."

The corner of my mouth pulled back again into its skeptical little twist. "That's . . . awfully nice of you."

Missing my sarcasm, the girl bowed her head as if to say *You're welcome*.

The blond soldier huffed an irritated sigh, clearly bored with the drawn-out explanation of his bleak afterlife. "We've told the girl enough," he barked. "Let's finish this."

"Finish what?"

"Finish by offering you our company," the pirate said hurriedly, his eyes darting to the soldier and then back to me. "If you're running . . . you can always run with us."

For a moment I kept silent. All five ghosts watched me, their faces turned up expectantly.

I bit my lip and pressed my hand flat against the statue. This wasn't my first offer of help from another ghost, so I suppose you couldn't blame me for suspecting this group's motive. Especially since I'd learned the hard way that ghosts didn't take denial very well.

But . . . did I *want* to deny them?

Whatever their motive, they obviously knew how to do the very thing that I needed, if not wanted, to do: survive, in a sense. Escape the demons and keep myself—and the people I loved—from the darkness.

Even if I had to trade my memories to do so, I knew this option would always be worth it. I just had to decide *how* to carry it out.

And with whom, apparently.

"Thank you for the offer," I said slowly, thoughtfully. "I hope you understand that I need a while to consider it."

"Were I you, I would not take too long," the dark-haired girl warned. "We intentionally make ourselves difficult to find."

I nodded. "That's fair. How about Christmas night, three days from now? I'll try to materialize wherever you are . . . if I decide to show up at all."

"Settled." The soldier finally uncrossed his arms and turned to his fellow ghosts. "Now can we leave? We've been in the open too long already."

The pirate grunted in agreement. As if that was their signal, the ghosts moved in unison, gathering closer together. They continued to watch me with those sheer faces that had probably seen more centuries than I could comprehend. For a moment they hovered silently in their eerie little cluster, and then, without another word or warning, they vanished all at once.

Jackson Square now seemed creepier, even without a cadre of ghosts trying to add me to their ranks. The cackles of laughter from the side streets, the palmetto leaves shifting noisily in the wind—all of it made me wonder whether darker things were on their way, too.

Things that I had possibly imagined?

Listening to the Quarter ghosts tonight, I couldn't believe that the *real* demons would have disappeared so quickly—would have let me go so easily. Maybe I really had hallucinated the confrontation at the club, just as I'd dreamed the prairie where my father spoke to me. That scenario seemed far more likely than a terrifying but otherwise harmless encounter with a huge crowd of demons.

This conclusion—that I was going a little crazy—also gave me a weak excuse to do something I desperately wanted to do before I joined the Quarter ghosts for all eternity.

So for at least one more night, I closed my eyes and wished my way to Joshua's side.

Chapter
THIRTEEN

When I opened my eyes, I found myself standing in front of the only familiar town house in the Quarter. Although its gas lamps still shined brightly, the windows were dark and shuttered for the night. Obviously, the place didn't look empty like the neighboring buildings. But it certainly didn't look as warm and welcoming as it had earlier tonight.

Since I'd only been gone for an hour or two, I doubted that the younger Mayhews had made it back from the club yet. But the materialization had brought me here, which had to mean that at least *Joshua* had returned early.

"Only one way to find out," I said aloud, and then cringed. Call it paranoia, but I suddenly felt like any noise I made might attract unwanted attention.

Tiptoeing gave me some foolish comfort, so I moved quickly and quietly to the left of the town house. There, in between the house and its neighbor, a heavy black gate lay open by several inches. I brushed past it, holding my breath as I crept down the narrow alley running alongside the house. Though the rational part of my mind knew I couldn't rattle them—not without some effort anyway—I dodged a group of metal trash cans before stepping into what looked like the courtyard behind the town house.

As I'd suspected, the space was gorgeous. A twisted live oak tree hung heavy over the flagstone patio, where a marble fountain bubbled next to some expensive-looking teak chairs. The thing I noticed most about the chairs, however, wasn't their quality; it was the fact that they were unoccupied.

Unoccupied, as in no Joshua.

Without thinking, I let out a loud, frustrated sigh and then clasped my hand to my mouth. For a second I waited for something creepy to swoop into the courtyard and demand that I go with it. When it didn't, I released my hand as well as the breath I'd inadvertently held.

You're being ridiculous, I told myself. *No one's tried to get you here.*

Then my brain added a snarky little *Yet.*

I stifled a groan, walked over to one of the patio chairs, and dropped myself into it.

Why had the materialization brought me here when I'd willed myself to wherever Joshua was? For some reason, today's materializations kept going awry, landing me in all the wrong places at the wrong times.

Discouraged, I tucked my hands beneath my chin and propped my elbows on my knees, preparing to wait until someone else arrived. Then I remembered that Jillian had stayed home tonight. It was a long shot, but perhaps I could call out just loudly enough to get her attention so she'd let me inside. I looked up at the house, trying to figure out which window was hers.

That's when I noticed the back door.

In the darkness, I'd almost missed it. But now I could see that it stood ajar by nearly a foot, leading into the pitch-black of the house.

I stood and walked over to the door, again trying to move as quietly as possible. From the looks of it, as long as I could squeeze through the opening I could get inside and wait for Joshua in relative safety. It might be an equally lonely wait; but, if nothing else, I could make noise inside without fear of demonic abduction. Probably.

At this point "probably" was good enough for me. So I lifted one foot to take a step inside the town house.

Except . . . I didn't.

Despite the attempted step, I found myself right where I started: standing in the courtyard, just outside the back entrance.

I tried again, pushing across the threshold with more effort. But like before, I met with the pressure of an invisible barrier. On impulse I looked down at the flagstones. There, just at the edge of my toes, was a familiar line of chalky gray powder sprinkled across the doorstep.

This time I didn't try to hide my sigh of frustration.

Ruth.

She'd pulled this trick on me in Wilburton, barring me from Joshua's house with some kind of magic Seer dust. Looking down at tonight's handiwork, I snorted softly. For such a devoutly religious woman, Ruth sure did like her witchcraft.

Staring down at the dust, I tried to summon the power within me—something that would help me counteract Ruth's spell. After all, if I could rend a bridge in two and make myself shine like a bonfire, couldn't I move a little dirt? But no matter how hard I concentrated, no matter how strongly the breeze rushed through the courtyard at my whim, that stupid dust stayed put.

With a frustrated little growl, I raised my head. Then I shrieked in surprise.

There, smiling out at me from the darkness of the hallway, was another ghostly pale face. My muscles tensed, ready to sprint, but they relaxed when the owner of the face moved forward, bringing himself into better view.

"Long night, huh?"

Alex kept his voice low as he stepped easily over the gray dust and stopped just short of bumping into me. Instinctively, I took one step backward, putting a few more inches between us. Alex's eyes caught the movement before they connected with mine.

"You okay?" he asked. "You left so soon tonight, I was worried."

He sounded genuinely concerned, but I still hesitated in answering him. Finally, after an awkward pause, I gave him a slow nod.

"I'm . . . fine. I just got a little dizzy, that's all."

Alex lifted his hand as if to give me a reassuring touch, then thought better of it and dropped the arm to his side. With an embarrassed little cough, he tucked both hands into the pockets of his slacks. When he noticed me staring at his outfit—still the gray suit, although it had to be well past midnight—he gave me a sheepish grin.

"I wanted to make sure I didn't miss you, so I waited to change."

I frowned. Why on earth didn't he want to miss me? The suggestion of familiarity made me inexplicably defensive, so I crossed my arms and smirked.

"What, are you saying you *don't* have a two a.m. shareholders' meeting?"

Alex laughed loudly and then snapped his mouth shut, looking back at the darkened windows behind him. After he made sure no one inside had heard him, he turned back to me. Still smiling, he whispered, "Hey, can I help it if I like to look stylish all hours of the night?"

My own smile twitched involuntarily. "I guess I really don't have room to judge anyone else's fashion sense, do I?"

We both laughed then; and, despite everything, I actually felt myself relax a little. Not much, but enough to continue the conversation without my arms folded protectively across my ribs.

"So," I said, circling around him until I was the closest to the door. "I don't suppose you know how to undo the mojo from Seer dirt?"

"Voodoo dust," he corrected automatically.

I shook my head, blinking. "Voodoo dust? Honestly?"

Alex gave me that sheepish grin again. "Honestly. You can buy the fake stuff on practically every street in the Quarter. What you have right there, though, is the real deal. Classic banishing dust, good for warding off evil spirits."

"Or just spirits in general," I murmured, kicking ineffectually at the gray line. I turned back to Alex. "Did Ruth really think this was necessary?"

His grin shifted into a smirk. "What can I say? She's a very religious woman."

I snorted. "Yeah, except for the fact she practices magic and Voodoo in her spare time."

"Voodoo *is* a religion, Amelia. A lot of people down here practice it. Besides, it's a religion that doesn't consider itself mutually exclusive with Christianity. The New Orleans Seers have been using it for centuries."

"What about Ruth?" I asked.

"She grew up here, according to Annabel. So I guess she imported some of its tenets to Oklahoma. And then brought them back home with her, obviously."

"Well," I said with a small noise of discontent, "I guess I should feel lucky they don't make Voodoo dolls of ghosts then, huh?"

Alex raised his eyebrows suggestively. "Oh, but they do."

I threw my hands up in the air. "Fantastic. Just what I needed."

"Don't hate the magic," he said, laughing softly. "Hate the magician."

Then, abruptly, his expression grew serious. He walked back toward the door, hands still in his pockets, frowning thoughtfully. This time I didn't edge away from him but held my ground, even when he stopped right next to me.

When Alex leaned close, my breath caught unexpectedly in my throat. Then, suddenly, he dropped into a crouch. He stared down at the dust and, with a quick flick of his wrist, swept half of it into the dirt of a nearby flower bed. He wiped that hand on one knee of his pants and then used it to push himself upright.

"There," he said, smiling at me. "The house is all yours."

"Just like that?" I marveled.

"Just like that."

I stared wistfully at the cleared stones. "Is it weird that I'd give just about anything to touch *dirt*?"

"Dust," he reminded me, chuckling. He stepped back over the threshold, turned around in the hallway so that he faced me, and then held his hand out to me palm up. Like an invitation.

"Coming in?" he asked.

Without thinking, I reached out to take his hand. But right before we touched, I paused. My arm hung in the air until, abruptly, I yanked it back to my side. Afterward, I simply stood there, awkward and stiff.

I couldn't really explain why I'd so nearly taken his hand, just like I couldn't really explain why I *hadn't*. Maybe because I'd only been able to touch one living person since I died, and I didn't want it to happen again with another living boy. Especially one with whom I'd just shared a surprisingly pleasant conversation. It felt wrong, the idea that I might experience something like that with someone other than Joshua.

Feeling strangely confused and guilty, I snuck a peek at Alex's face. In the darkness, I couldn't gauge his reaction clearly. I probably imagined what I saw shifting in his eyes: eagerness, frustration, anger . . . then back to that calm amusement he'd shown earlier.

I definitely heard the humor in his voice when he again asked, "So, Amelia: into the house, or not?"

I nodded, relieved that he hadn't read too much into my hesitation. "Inside. Absolutely inside."

He backed up against a wall, making room for me to enter. This time I didn't hesitate. I stepped right through the doorway, leaving behind the broken line of Voodoo dust.

I walked by Alex, and, in the split second I passed him, I felt a strange itch of anticipation. For what, I don't know. It made me vaguely uncomfortable, so I hurried on, moving farther down the dark hallway toward the foyer.

Other than the tick of a nearby clock and an occasional, muffled snore from upstairs, the house was silent. I crept through the foyer and up the first few steps of the staircase, moving with extreme care. Even if my feet couldn't make the floorboards creak, something about being in a house full of sleeping, dormant Seers made me want to keep quiet.

Once I'd made it to the first landing I turned back to Alex, who still waited at the bottom of the stairs with one hand on the banister. I raised my eyebrows questioningly, and he shook his head. He pointed one finger toward the ground several times.

Waiting, he mouthed. He traced the outline of a rectangle in the air and then pointed up to the ceiling. *Door open. Go on.*

I nodded, pleased that I wouldn't have to go through this routine again when I got to my own room. I'd just turned to continue up the stairs when I paused.

If Alex knew the door to the attic was open, then that meant he'd gone up there. To my room.

Suddenly suspicious, I looked over my shoulder to where Alex had just stood. But he must have slipped back out to the courtyard, because the foyer was now empty of everything but a Persian rug and the ticking grandfather clock. Again, I hadn't heard a thing when he left.

That boy can disappear like a ghost.

Then, inexplicably, I shuddered. For some reason the sight of the empty foyer gave me the creeps. I turned back to the stairs and began to race up them, my fear about making noise momentarily forgotten.

Chapter
FOURTEEN

I only had to spend about twenty minutes in nervous silence, pacing the tiny floor space in our room, before Joshua came walking up the stairs to the attic bedroom.

"You're here," he said in a quiet, relieved voice. The room was so small, one stride brought him next to me. Without another word, he drew me close. I couldn't help but melt into him, wrapping my arms around his waist in a numb but fierce hug.

"I swear," I murmured into his shirt, "I shouldn't miss

you this much after only a couple hours."

He laughed low and began running his fingers through the waves in my hair. "Actually, I wanted to come back here right away. But Annabel told me to quit being a stalker-boyfriend and give you some time alone."

I bent my head back and looked into his dark eyes. "I've had plenty of time alone in the last decade."

In my head, the snarky voice whispered, *And you'll have plenty more of it soon enough.*

I sighed, so quietly I doubted Joshua heard, and lifted onto my toes to give him a small, sweet kiss. When the kiss ended, I lingered there for a moment, waiting for . . . something more. To feel the heat rising off his skin maybe, or smell a whiff of his cologne.

But nothing happened. It never did when I wished for it this much.

I sighed again and rocked back to my heels. "So," I said, trying to hide my disappointment as I ran my hands over the lapels of his jacket without feeling them. "Did you like the club?"

"Hated it," he said instantly, and we both laughed. Then his face grew serious. He tucked one strand of hair behind my ear, too quickly to set my skin tingling. "Are you ready to tell me what really happened back there? Because I don't believe for a minute that you got claustrophobic."

I shrugged, averting my eyes to the tiny bed against the wall. "Believe it, buddy. Just a case of way-too-crowded. Mystery solved."

Joshua made a soft sound of derision. "You're a terrible liar, you know that?"

"But you love that about me," I teased, shying away from him with a playful, departing tug on his sleeve. If I kept it light enough, maybe he'd drop the conversation entirely.

I was so intent on keeping him distracted that he completely took me by surprise with what he said next.

"I love a lot of things about you, Amelia," Joshua said, his voice rough and low.

Oh, God.

I gulped, and then experienced what felt an awful lot like a flush across my cheeks. I hadn't expected his response, or its obvious meaning. I suddenly knew that if I acknowledged it, we'd finally share those confessions I'd so desperately craved.

And avoided.

Once again I wanted to give in. I wanted to spill that four-letter word and have it mean something. Not *I love your eyes* or *I love your laugh.* But I love *you.* Just you.

Instead, I started to babble inanely.

"You know what I love? Christmas. I've loved Christmas ever since I was little. Well, I think I did, anyway, since I haven't gotten those memories back yet. But it's a safe bet that I loved it, right? The tree, the food, the presents—"

Joshua interrupted me by grabbing my arm, encircling my wrist with a ring of fire. The supernatural warmth of his touch, however, couldn't match the very real fire in his eyes. He looked like a man about to say the most important words of his life, and I suddenly found myself silent, hypnotized. If I had a functioning heart, now would be the time it raced uncontrollably.

Joshua's lips parted—either to kiss me or confess something to me, I was certain.

But to my surprise, he did neither. He paused for another long second as if deciding between several options and then gave me a crooked grin.

"Want to know what your Christmas present is, Amelia?" he asked.

"My . . . what?"

"Your Christmas present."

I struggled to make sense of his words and then, finally, the pieces fell into place. I began to sputter in protest.

"That's . . . that's not *fair*, Joshua."

He laughed quietly—obviously pleased with himself. "When did I tell you I'd be fair?" he joked.

I shook my head, undeterred. "Joshua, I can't even make you a reindeer ornament out of pipe cleaners, for pete's sake. How am I supposed to buy you a gift?"

"I didn't buy you one, either," he reassured me. "I didn't even get the idea for this present until tonight. But now . . . well, I think it's pretty awesome."

"Oh, great," I groaned, deflating. "Every time you make up your mind, it's *impossible* to talk sense to you."

His grin widened. "Yup. I become an immovable object."

"Oh yeah?" I grumbled. "And did you ever think that maybe I'm the unstoppable force?"

His smile softened as he placed his fingers at the curve of my waist. "If anything in this life is unstoppable, it's you, Amelia. Just ask Eli."

I tried not to wince at the mention of Eli's name. It provoked thoughts of other things. Things that I almost but not quite forgot each time I stared into Joshua's eyes.

I suffered a near unbearable pinch of guilt when I thought about the Christmas present I'd planned for Joshua: abandonment.

Abandonment for his own protection, but abandonment still. Whether on my own or wandering with a pack of ghosts, I had no intention of staying.

"Amelia? Are you really mad about the Christmas thing? 'Cause if you are . . ."

Joshua's voice called me back to the present, especially when he trailed off. The uncertainty in his tone reminded me to stay anchored in this moment. I had to maximize my time so that both he and I could remember our last minutes as happy ones—probably a disservice to him but a necessity for me, if I wanted to survive the rest of my eternity without him.

I mustered all my courage and flashed him my brightest smile. "I'm not mad at all. Not one bit. But I do have one requirement, okay?"

Joshua nodded. "Name it."

I curved up one corner of my mouth and placed one hand on the front of his shirt.

"Let me give you your present tonight," I said in a low purr.

Delight soon replaced the momentary surprise in Joshua's eyes. "I wouldn't dream of stopping you, Amelia."

"Good," I answered, almost roughly. Then, without further warning, I pressed my hand on Joshua's chest. Hard.

The force of my shove knocked him off balance, and he flew back toward the tiny bed, taking me with him. In the fraction of the second that we fell together through the air, I stopped his surprised laughter with a fiery, blissful kiss.

We landed on the bed in a tangle, pulling each other into another kiss as quickly as we could. His fingers in my hair, my arms around his neck: everything felt warm and fantastic and *right*.

While we kissed, I mostly focused on Joshua. But that quiet, desperate part of my brain continued to pray for three things: that Joshua and I would never have to stop doing this; that when we inevitably did, I would find a way to leave him kindly and safely—at least, safely for him; and finally, that just for tonight I wouldn't have to disappear from his side.

The next morning came too quickly. Though we hadn't done much more than kiss, I wanted to spend the rest of the day luxuriating in our time together. But Joshua was all jittery excitement as he jumped out of bed and hurriedly threw on new jeans and a sweater. Too soon, he dragged me down the staircase and into the tiny dining room where most of the Mayhew clan had gathered for breakfast. Even then—surrounded by family, friends, and a mouthwatering feast of fruit, bacon, and breakfast gumbo—he bolted down his meal without taking the time to chat, much less breathe.

While he threw down his napkin and gave his aunt Trish a mumbled thank you, I cast a final glance around the room. Ruth had once again failed to join her family. After last night's little trick with the dust, I more than suspected that had something to do with my presence.

All the more reason to follow Joshua on his mission today and get out of the house from which she'd tried to ban me last night.

Before we left, however, I noticed that another face was strangely missing from the breakfast table: Alex's.

With the exception of their leader, the entire crew of young Seers had made it to breakfast. Annabel, Drew, and Hayley (who evidently had permission to stay over) all huddled together over steaming cups of chicory coffee, each looking the worse for wear after last night's partying. Jillian also looked inexplicably tired as she glowered at her plate of fruit. She'd probably paced in her room all night, silently bemoaning her tragic social life.

But Alex must have chosen to stay in bed.

Odd, I thought. He didn't strike me as the late-to-rise type. Then I reminded myself that I hardly knew most of these people.

And in two days I would no longer know them at all. . . .

The warm grasp of Joshua's hand in mine stirred me from that thought. After giving Annabel a knowing look (which I assumed meant she knew what my present was), Joshua pulled me gently from the dining room. I followed him through the foyer—a far less menacing place in the daylight—and out onto the sidewalk.

The French Quarter looked quite different in the sun, as well. No longer mysterious and shadowed, the streets were welcoming, their colorful shutters flung open to the day. Despite the bright winter air, green ferns cascaded over the balconies above us, some of their tendrils reaching up toward the sky. And although the Mayhews' town house was in a somewhat residential area of the Quarter, the sidewalk bustled with camera-wielding tourists and harried residents carrying bags full of last-minute gifts.

Joshua gave my hand a quick squeeze before releasing it so that we could move less conspicuously down the street. From the corner of his mouth, he said, "Your present is a couple blocks away. That okay?"

I just nodded, too absorbed in the sights and sounds of the Quarter to answer. We rounded a corner and crossed onto what looked like a more commercial street. As we walked, I couldn't help but gape into all the shop windows, which displayed everything from ornate, antique furniture to mannequins in outrageous clothing and wildly colored wigs.

When we crossed another street, I could see a motley group of street musicians about half a block away, setting up some makeshift seats next to an open guitar case on the ground. Only after Joshua and I walked out of view did I hear their music: lush, classical jazz . . . amazing, when I realized it came from their battered instruments. Listening to the music fade into the distance, I sighed wistfully.

To my surprise, my next breath brought with it a brief whiff of scent. Some sharp, delicious spice overlaying the briny smell of seafood. The sensation faded quickly, as my sensations always did, and I groaned softly. Once again I felt that all-too-familiar rush of satisfaction and frustration.

Hearing my groan, Joshua turned back to me with a concerned expression. I shook my head, indicating that I was fine.

Still, his steps slowed and he looked around the street . . . to make sure it wasn't too crowded, apparently, because he reached back to take my hand. As he guided me into another alley, I held tight, letting the fire of our touch spread up the veins of my wrist.

I enjoyed the electric tingle so much, I almost didn't notice that Joshua and I had left the busiest sector of the Quarter. When I started to pay better attention, I saw that our surroundings had shifted from flashy and eclectic to dusty and worn. Here, the shops looked grayer, shabbier. Nor did they boast crowds of onlookers and shoppers. In fact, only two other people were walking on this street. And judging by how they hurried along, they weren't here on a leisurely stroll.

So I was more than a little surprised when Joshua stopped suddenly in front of a diner with a dirty, cracked front window. Inside, I could just make out the sputter of a neon light, sending off its death glow above several rows of empty tables. The place made me think of a few choice words, "sketchy" and "shady" being the fore-runners.

Joshua pulled a slip of paper from his pocket, unfolded it, and frowned down at a bunch of scribbles. He looked up at the diner—the Conjure Café, according to the chipped red paint on the window—then back at the paper.

"Um, Joshua?" I prompted. "What are we doing here?"

"I don't want to tell you, but maybe I need to warn you in advance . . . ?" he mused, more to himself than to me.

"Warn me about what?" I demanded warily.

He flashed me an anxious, close-lipped smile. Then he flicked his head in the direction of the diner.

"Well . . . your present—it's kind of inside."

I blanched. "In *there*? What are you trying to give me, the Plague?"

He shook his head, snickering nervously. "We're not hanging out in the diner, Amelia. We're going to the back. In the kitchen, I think."

"Joshua, honey, I appreciate the effort, but I don't

really think I need to see the Conjure Café's culinary masterpieces in the making."

"I promise this isn't about the food," he insisted. "We're supposed to meet someone in there is all."

"Who?" I gasped, trying not to imagine someone holding my present in one hand and a meat cleaver in the other.

Joshua hesitated, about to say something. Then he shook his head again, obviously reversing course. "Please, Amelia. Just trust me."

I pulled my eyes from his and peered into the dim interior of the diner. When I turned back to Joshua, I practically had to rip my bottom lip from my teeth to answer him.

"Against my better judgment, I trust you. But if I see Sweeney Todd back there, so help me God I'm running in the opposite direction, and you can fend for yourself."

"Deal," Joshua said, letting out a strangled laugh that made me wonder what made him more nervous: my possible reaction to his gift, or the fact that he'd have to go inside this place to get it.

Before I had the chance to ask him, he crossed in front of me and walked up the two crumbling steps to the front door of the Conjure Café. He pushed on the door, holding it wide-open for me since we didn't have much of an audience. I took a little gulp for courage, sent up a silent request that I wouldn't regain my sense of smell when we were inside, and followed Joshua into the diner.

The bell above the entrance gave a weak chime as the door shut behind us. I glanced up quickly, worried that a patron might notice Joshua holding the door open for thin air. But no one occupied the tables scattered haphazardly near the windows.

As Joshua and I moved cautiously toward the back of the dining area, I studied the place further. Besides the fact that this had to be the least-populated restaurant in New Orleans, something about the café felt . . . off.

The few tables held none of the "extras" you saw in normal diners: no napkin holders, no bin of sugar packets, no salt and pepper shakers. In fact, there didn't seem to be enough chairs to serve a small dinner crowd. I couldn't see a cash register anywhere, either. Not even on the long counter in the back, where a bored attendant stood flipping through a tattered magazine.

Something told me that, if people patronized this café at all, it certainly wasn't for food. My suspicion only grew stronger when Joshua and I approached the back counter.

The attendant, an acne-scarred man who looked well past fifty, hardly stirred when Joshua leaned against the counter directly in front of him. Finally, after being ignored for longer than reasonable, Joshua cleared his throat.

"Um, excuse me?" he said, checking the slip of paper one more time. "I'm looking for . . . Marie?"

Still silent, the attendant raised one arm and pointed to a curtained doorway at the very back of the restaurant.

"Can we . . . I mean, can I just go on in?" Joshua asked.

The attendant merely nodded without looking up from his magazine. Joshua caught my gaze and shrugged. I could see my own discomfort reflected in his eyes, but I could also see his determination to follow through with this project. Gnawing wildly on my lip, I nodded reluctantly.

We walked toward the curtain together, and my misgivings intensified with each step.

"Will you just give me a little hint about what we're doing here?" I murmured, grateful that the attendant completely ignored us.

My question must have made Joshua uncomfortable, because he paused with his hand only inches from drawing aside the curtain. In the softest whisper he could manage, he said, "I'll tell you if you promise not to be mad."

"I could never be mad at you," I whispered back. "But you have this uncanny ability to seriously freak me out."

Joshua bit his bottom lip—a bad habit he'd obviously

picked up from me—and his gaze shifted to the closed curtain. He was silent for so long, I became impatient.

"Could you at least tell me where we are? I mean, where we *really* are?"

His hand lingered beside the curtain a moment longer, and then as if to answer me, he tugged back the fabric.

For nearly a full minute I had no idea what I was seeing. Instead of a sterile, brightly lit kitchen, this café had some kind of cavelike storage room in the back. At least that's what it looked like at first.

The room had low ceilings and narrow walls painted dark brown and lined with endless rows of shelves, which were stocked with jars and books and little statues. Roughly hewn candelabra flickered through the dark haze of smoke pouring out of several incense burners.

I peered closer at the strange powders and liquids swimming in the jars, and at the skeletal-faced statues surrounding them. Then I recoiled.

"Oh my God," I whispered through clenched teeth. "You brought me to a Voodoo shop."

Chapter
FIFTEEN

My brain was in the process of sending a "run away" signal to my muscles when Joshua began to spill forth a rush of words, half of which made no sense.

"I know you're mad," he sputtered, "but I just had to tell Annabel about all the problems you've been having with materializing, and about all your bad dreams and worries and stuff, and then she told me about this place and how they might be able to help you feel better, or more 'at peace,' or something. And maybe it was a bad idea, but I've wanted to help you so badly that I sort of—"

While Joshua rambled through his explanation, I felt my vision blur with anger and fear. But before I had the chance to chew him out, someone else beat me to the chase.

"And just who might you be?"

Joshua and I turned simultaneously toward the paper-thin voice that came from the far, unlit corner of the room. There, hidden underneath a canopy of dried herbs, I could just make out the rounded shape of a person.

When the shape moved, I took an involuntary step backward. But I straightened my spine, steeling myself for what might come out of the shadows. Once the shape revealed itself fully, I took a tiny breath of relief.

As far as I could tell, the stately looking black woman who emerged from the shadows was neither a demon nor a ghost. Just a very, very old human. Thousands of wrinkles creased her face, around which only the slightest wisps of white hair—free from her severe bun—curled. She held her hands in a formal clasp in front of her dress and appraised Joshua suspiciously.

"Are you Marie?" Joshua asked.

In the shifting candlelight, I thought I saw the woman smile.

"That depends on who's asking," she said.

"Um . . . me?" he offered.

"Me, who?"

This time I definitely heard a laugh dancing its way through her words. For whatever reason, she was having a little fun at the expense of the young man who had so foolishly entered her shop.

Joshua, clearly intimidated by this woman, took a tentative step forward and extended his hand to her. "Joshua Mayhew, ma'am. My cousin, Annabel Comeaux—she sent me to you?"

The woman ignored Joshua's hand. "I've never heard of the girl."

Now her tone was cold and unyielding—all her amusement gone like a wisp of incense. She remained motionless in the corner, hands still clasped imperiously in front of her like some statue of an unfriendly god.

I watched Joshua flounder beside me for a few uncertain seconds. But quickly his resolve returned. He didn't intend to leave here empty-handed, no matter how much wiser that course might be . . . no matter how much I might want him to.

"Ma'am," Joshua said with more force. He dropped his hand but inched closer to her. "A person I care about needs help with her . . . afterlife, actually. My cousin told me you were someone who could do stuff like that."

A beam of candlelight fell across the old woman's face, revealing an arched eyebrow. "And what do you think

I could do for this person's afterlife, young man?" she asked.

Joshua gave me a quick glance. "You could help her learn more about why she is . . . the *way* she is maybe? Help her learn how the dead can control things. How *she* could control things."

Before he'd even finished his request, the old woman shook her head forcefully.

"I don't provide those kinds of services, boy. I might help protect you from a ghost that means you harm, or make an offering to a spirit. But I don't presume to guide the spirits myself. Besides, my spells are for the living— for their luck, power, or money. You want something like that, I can help you."

"No," Joshua insisted. "This isn't for me. This is for someone who's already dead. I want to help *her*."

"I already told you, boy, I won't do that." She unclasped her hands and folded her arms across her thin chest. "Since you clearly can't listen—and I suspect you're cursed by this spirit—I'll ask you to leave now."

She can't see me, I realized. She hadn't once looked in my direction, and now she only *suspected* that Joshua was haunted. For all her potions and powders, she had none of the sight that Joshua and his family possessed.

I turned to tell Joshua as much, but he was too focused on the task at hand to hear me.

"I'm not cursed," he replied angrily. "I just need your

help. Are you refusing to give it to me because you won't do anything, or because you can't?"

Now Joshua had gone too far. I didn't realize the woman had more inches to gain; but when she drew herself up to her full height, she seemed to tower over us. Her frail appearance was gone, as was her shaky, paper-thin voice.

"You *will* leave," she commanded in a deep, resonant voice that seemed to reverberate much louder than it should in that tiny room.

"But—"

Suddenly, from another corner of the room, a jangling crash interrupted Joshua's objection, and all three of us whipped around toward the noise.

Almost immediately, the woman uttered a foreign oath and pulled a bristly knot of what looked like hair from the pocket of her dress. She rubbed it furiously as she crossed the room and then bent down to examine the remains of the glass jar that had dropped to the floor.

Joshua and I, however, were more focused on the person who'd done the dropping. She stood in front of the doorway leading farther into the recesses of the café, and she now stared back at us in what could only be described as shock.

Even in this dark room I could tell she was one of the most beautiful people I'd ever seen up close. She looked about my age—if not a little younger—but she was much taller and curvier than me. Beneath a gorgeously wild Afro, her smooth coffee-and-cream skin perfectly offset her radiant blue eyes.

Eyes that were looking right into mine.

The girl let loose an incredibly vulgar string of words. Then her gaze darted to the old woman, who'd started to remove shards from the puddle of whatever the jar had held. The girl pressed her lips together, obviously debating something, before releasing them to blow out a low whistle.

"Sorry, Marie," the girl mumbled. "I'll clean that up after my break."

The old woman ignored the apology and continued sifting through the soggy mess, muttering to herself in some foreign language. Apparently, this girl was her employee, and, apparently, this girl was clumsy.

"Sorry," the girl repeated halfheartedly. Then, after giving her unresponsive boss a flippant shrug, she brushed past Joshua and me without acknowledgment.

Once the girl had drawn the curtain back by a few inches, however, she paused. In a soft hiss—so quiet I almost couldn't hear it—she whispered, "Both of you: outside. Now."

The words "both of you" echoed in my head even after she stormed out and let the curtain fall back into place behind her.

Afterward, the room was completely silent except for

the wet sounds of Marie's cleanup efforts. Joshua and I stayed rooted in place until—finally—we exchanged matching looks of confusion and misgiving.

He twitched his head toward the curtain. *Follow?* he mouthed.

Catching my bottom lip with my teeth, I peeked at Marie. She hadn't stopped her frustrated muttering, nor had she looked up from the broken jar and its contents. Clearly, the mess meant we'd been forgotten. Which also meant she probably wouldn't put a hex on us for bothering her.

I turned back to Joshua, placed my index finger to my lips, and flicked my eyes in Marie's direction. Understanding my meaning, he nodded and pulled the curtain aside for me. As quietly as possible, we slipped out of the room and then hurried through the diner before anyone could stop us. Joshua opened the door with a minimal amount of chiming, and we practically flew out of it. We bolted down the crumbling steps, only jerking to a stop when we realized that the shop girl had actually waited for us outside as she'd promised.

She leaned against the gray brick of the building just out of sight of the café window. Because she had rushed outside without her coat, she now furiously rubbed her hands against her bare upper arms in an attempt to protect herself from the wind. Really, her entire outfit—a billowy, gunmetal dress over bare legs and thigh-high gray boots—looked less than winter friendly. I wasn't surprised to hear her teeth chattering as we approached.

Despite her clear discomfort, the girl was all business. Joshua had barely introduced himself when she cut him off with a wave of her hand.

"Don't bother, Lover Boy," she said. "I got all that info back at the Conjure. The walls aren't that thick in there, you know."

Joshua nodded, looking relieved that he wouldn't have to repeat the same story. "Then you already know why I need help?" he asked. "And who I need it for?"

The girl jerked her head in my direction. "For Princess Paleness over there, right?"

"Excuse me?" I said, folding my arms defensively. "I don't know if you've picked up on *what* I am, but I haven't exactly had the opportunity to get a tan lately."

"Yeah, yeah, yeah," she said with another dismissive wave. "And I'm sure there's some fascinating story about how you got stuck in that dress, too. But I'm more interested in what brought you here today."

Joshua began to speak, but she cut him off again with an impatient sigh.

"No offense, Lover Boy, but I'd rather hear it from the horse's mouth."

I pulled back one corner of my lips. "The 'horse' being me?"

"Yeah, the horse being you. So tell me, Princess, what's so wrong with you that you need Voodoo to fix it?"

"Nothing," I said bluntly. "And incidentally, my name's not Princess. It's Amelia."

A tiny smile skirted across her lips. "Hi, Amelia. I'm Gabrielle—I'll be your Voodoo priestess for the evening."

"You expect us to believe that *you're* a Voodoo priestess?" I scoffed.

Gabrielle shrugged one shoulder. "You tell me, Amelia. Between me and Marie back there, which one of us can actually see you?"

I snorted softly. "That just makes you a Seer."

"Yeah, it does. And I'll bet you fifty bucks that you've met some powerful Seers, haven't you?"

I pinched my lips shut; she had me there. In my experience, a knowledgeable Seer had the ability to affect the dead in some pretty intense ways.

I met Gabrielle's eyes and saw a glimmer of victory in them. She nodded at me, almost imperceptibly, and then reset her mouth in that straight, businesslike line.

"Speaking of fifty bucks," she said, turning back to Joshua, "that's my fee for helping you tonight."

"But we haven't even told you what kind of help we're

asking for," he pointed out.

Gabrielle shook her head, sending her delicate silver earrings jingling. "No need to. I bet it's the standard fare: can't touch stuff, can't control your disappearances."

Joshua and I shared a meaningful look. I hated to admit it, but this girl knew her ghosts.

"It's . . . kind of more like that last one," Joshua hedged, and I silently blessed him for not confessing other things that were just too personal, too private.

"Huh." Gabrielle looked slightly surprised. "Well, whatever the problem, I think I can take care of it."

"Really?"

However much discretion he'd just shown, Joshua's exclamation definitely revealed too much now—I could see it in Gabrielle's sharp blue eyes. Again, victory sparkled there like a flame.

"Really, Lover Boy." She rubbed her hands together—in triumph or to warm them, I couldn't tell. "So here's how it's going to go down: you guys meet me tonight, ten minutes before midnight, in the St. Louis Number One Cemetery. It's the aboveground cemetery off Basin Street, near Iberville. It's usually locked by three p.m., but I'll find a way to get the front gate open. Once you're inside, go toward the center until you find a tall concrete vault that's been painted brickred. You can't miss it—it's right by the tombstone that looks like a dinner table.

When you get there, we'll start the ceremony."

I placed a restraining hand on Joshua's arm before he could agree for us again. Remembering something that Rebecca mentioned during the car ride yesterday, I frowned.

"Aren't the cemeteries here supposed to be dangerous without a tour guide?" I asked. "Especially at night?"

Gabrielle barked out a laugh. "Well, you're dead, so no worries there. And you," she said, turning to Joshua and giving him a contemplative once-over. "Maybe you should carry a baseball bat or something."

I balked, but Joshua just nodded decisively.

"Done," he declared, and extended his hand for her to shake.

For the first time this morning, Gabrielle's confidence seemed to falter. After all that bravado, I had no idea why something as harmless as a handshake should have bothered her. But she stared warily at Joshua's outstretched hand as if any physical contact with him would result in something terrible. Her firing maybe? I couldn't read the reason in her face. . . .

"No can do, Lover Boy," she said in a weirdly choked voice. "Shaking hands is, uh . . . it's a big no-no in Voodoo."

Joshua dropped his arm to his side with an embarrassed grin. "Sorry. I don't really know the rules yet."

Once again Gabrielle shrugged—a gesture of studied indifference that I was beginning to recognize. "No biggie," she said offhandedly. "But you've got to get out of here before Marie decides I've taken too much time for my smoke break."

She didn't have to tell me twice. I grasped Joshua's hand—a move that Gabrielle watched closely, I noticed—and tugged at it.

"You heard the girl," I murmured. "Let's get out of here."

But Joshua held firmly in place. As if he just couldn't help but be doggedly polite, he flashed Gabrielle a grateful smile.

"I appreciate you helping us. Really."

"Yeah, yeah, yeah." Gabrielle ducked her head and made a little "shoo" motion with her hand. "I'll see ya'll tonight at the St. Louis. Now seriously, hit the road."

This time I didn't let Joshua express any more gratitude. I yanked his hand as hard as I could, feeling the pins and needles heat of our touch spread all the way up to my shoulder. Finally, Joshua got the hint. He gave me an apologetic grin and—without another word to Gabrielle—turned with me to hurry away from this café, this street, this *neighborhood*, as quickly as we could without running.

Chapter
SIXTEEN

Almost as soon as we rounded the corner of Ursulines, I dropped Joshua's hand. When he made a soft, questioning noise, I trained my gaze severely to the right—away from his—and put at least a foot's distance between us. We hadn't said one word or looked at each other the entire walk home, and I didn't intend to change that now.

Still not speaking, I followed him into the town house and waited while his mother told him that Annabel and company had left on a day trip to Lafayette (also leaving me without the option of chewing out Annabel). Upon hearing this news, Joshua looked hesitantly in my direction. I refused to meet his eyes, choosing instead to keep silent while he said hello to the rest of his family and then led me outside.

There, only a few sounds filled the courtyard: the scratch of live oak branches above us and the twin scrape of the two chairs he pulled out from one of the tables so that we could sit.

All the while, Joshua kept his mouth firmly shut. Once we'd both sat down, however, he trapped me with those arresting blue eyes . . . probably anticipating the effect they'd have on me. He clearly wanted to know what I thought about everything that had just happened—I could tell by how frantically his fingers worked the edge of his sleeve.

But I wasn't ready to give him my reaction yet. Not until I had better control of my thoughts, which were currently screaming at me that, if Joshua was pursuing such a drastic measure, then he knew as well as I did that our relationship was set up for failure. Of course, another set of thoughts screamed back that I didn't want it to be true. Not now, not ever.

As the minutes passed, the branches continued to clatter noisily above us, from either the errant gale that had found its way through the alleys or the poltergeist force of my emotions—I couldn't be sure. Finally, after what probably felt like an eternity to Joshua, I met his gaze.

"So," I said, keeping my voice tightly controlled. "That was my Christmas present?"

"That was *going to be* your Christmas present," he explained cautiously. Then he leaned forward, scrutinizing me. "But you have a problem with it, don't you? Even after finding out what I meant it for."

Despite his effort to hold my gaze, I broke eye contact and stared down at my hands, which I'd absently begun to wring in my lap.

"Yes," I said, and then shook my head. "No. I don't know."

With my eyes still cast downward, I sighed heavily and sank back into my chair. True to form, Joshua seized upon the opportunity that my ambivalence gave him. He leaned even closer and tucked his forefinger beneath my chin, lifting my head until I faced him again.

"I'm not going to push you into anything," he said softly. "I've done that before, with some mixed results."

I gave him a tense, close-lipped smile. "I can't say I haven't done it to you, too. O'Reilly's barn burner comes to mind."

Joshua chuckled quietly. Keeping his finger beneath my chin, he began to brush his thumb across my cheek.

Where he touched, heat erupted in an arc. Like a blush, only better.

This time I didn't pull my eyes from his. I stared at him until all I could see was midnight blue. Until all my warring thoughts quieted and left me with something that at least resembled peace.

Now calmer and more resolved, I gave him a stronger, broader smile—one that I didn't necessarily feel, but certainly meant.

Joshua grinned back. "Does that smile mean you don't hate me?"

I placed my hand over his, stopping his thumb but doubling the heat on my cheek. I didn't speak. But an irresponsible part of me wished he'd read a reply in my eyes, one that revealed I could never hate him when I loved him this much.

After a prolonged silence I squeezed his hand and then released it. In a soft, almost unfamiliar voice, I said, "You won't have your cousins to blame for staying out late tonight. So I guess you'd better start thinking of some excuse for why you need to go somewhere at midnight. Otherwise, you're just going to have to sneak out."

Joshua arched one eyebrow. "Oh, really?"

"Really."

"What made you change your mind?"

"I hadn't made my mind up *against* the idea," I said. "It just kind of threw me for a loop, that's all."

"And . . . now?"

"Now I kind of want to see what happens. See if she can help me control the materializations and freaky dreams."

Or even help me protect my loved ones without having to flee or join a troop of rogue ghosts, I thought. *No harm in asking once we're there.*

The strained half smile tugged at my lips again, helping me to keep those thoughts from playing themselves out on my face.

"Just promise me one thing, okay?"

"Anything," he said earnestly.

"If she's lying, and she's actually on the Ruth side of things . . . if she ends up trying to exorcise me—"

"We get the hell out of there," he finished, and then gave me a surprisingly wolfish grin. "And stiff her the fifty bucks, of course."

I laughed. "Of course."

My one, weak laugh was all Joshua needed. Suddenly excited, he clutched both of my hands and gently pulled me forward until I balanced precariously on the edge of my chair. With my lips precariously close to his too.

"I really want her to help you tonight," he whispered, serious again.

I sucked in a sharp breath, which brought with it the briefest scent of his cologne. When the scent evaporated, I nodded slightly, dizzily. I let Joshua hold me there—on the edge of my seat, and on the edge of something potentially momentous.

But I didn't—and wouldn't—tell him the truth: that I was knee-quaking, bone-shaking scared.

Not that I might see last night's ghosts or demons spending the witching hour in what had to be one of the more haunted places in New Orleans. Not that Gabrielle—who struck me as someone with more than a few ulterior motives—might hurt me.

I *was* somewhat afraid of those very real threats, obviously. But they weren't what filled my heart with an icy sort of dread; they weren't what I struggled to hide from Joshua's perceptive gaze.

Because, in the end, I was most afraid of what would happen if Gabrielle couldn't do a damn thing for me.

The sun set too quickly that night, disappearing over the slate roofs of the Quarter and pulling the streets back into the shadows. I sat alone upon the front steps of the town house, with my arms wrapped around my legs, watching the darkness descend.

Inside, I could hear the raucous sounds of the Mayhew clan crowded around the dinner table. Tomorrow, the entire group would travel to one of the many gourmet restaurants in the Quarter to celebrate Christmas Eve in style. But tonight they were supposed to dine together in their family home, filling every available inch of the first floor.

The only exceptions to this tradition were the young Seers, who still hadn't returned from their trip to Lafayette. (I couldn't remember my own parents' curfew rules, but I imagined they were far less lax than those of the Mayhews.) Sitting outside, I absently wondered whether Joshua missed their company.

If I listened carefully to the clamor, I could distinguish his voice as he laughed and joked with his younger cousins. If I stood up, I'm sure I could peer through the front window and see him sitting closest to the glass so that he could keep a watchful eye on me.

Considering what we might face in a few hours, I probably should've taken a covert place beside him in that cramped dining room. Especially since he'd warned me that this first family dinner might run long into the night, giving us no time alone together before we had to leave for the cemetery.

But like some scared little rabbit, I'd fled the house only minutes after I'd caught my first glimpse of someone I'd half expected never to see again.

I'd seen Ruth Mayhew before anyone else in the family

had, standing at the top of the main staircase. In the shadows, she looked like some aging heroine in an ante-bellum movie, tall and grand and patrician, with one hand on the banister and the other clutched to her shawl.

Very briefly, I'd thought about confronting her—asserting my presence in this house for whatever limited period of time I intended to occupy it.

When she'd taken a few, unsteady steps down the main staircase, however, I took my own steps toward the front door, practically flinging Joshua against it and begging for him to let me outside. Somehow, being outdoors felt safer than staying inside with her.

But before Joshua had moved to shut the door behind me, a beam of light from the dining room fell across her face. At that moment I'd gasped. Even when the door closed, my mouth stayed open in shock.

I had no idea how someone could age so much in only three months, but tonight Ruth Mayhew didn't even look like the same person. Her glossy white hair had dulled, and her skin had sagged even further. Instead of carrying herself ramrod straight, she now hunched like an old woman. Worst of all, her normally hawk-sharp eyes looked bloodshot and vague.

Granted, she was emerging from the stupor of a two-day migraine; anyone would look terrible after something like that. And she'd obviously had the energy, at some point between the time we'd arrived in New Orleans and the time I returned from Jackson Square, to decorate the back stoop with Voodoo dust.

But as I watched her through the dining-room window, I couldn't help but notice that her relatives treated her like a helpless invalid. They very nearly carried her to the dining-room table and, once they had her there, flocked around her as if she couldn't even lift a spoon. Which, judging by her shaking hands, she couldn't.

Despite all the horrible things she'd said and done to me, I felt the strangest twinge of sympathy for her. People aged, people died—I knew that better than anyone. That didn't mean I wished it upon Ruth, though. Nor did I want Joshua to have to watch it firsthand. Of course, there was nothing I could do to stop it from happening. And even if I could, I'm pretty sure Ruth would still use her last ounce of strength to banish me to the Antarctic or somewhere equally unpleasant.

So, however weak and hollow she might look, however much sympathy her appearance might elicit, that woman was *still* Ruth Mayhew. And because I had no intention of angering her, I stayed put, alone outside with my own dark thoughts.

Anyway, I told myself, *tonight's going to be hard enough without adding her to the mix.*

As if responding to my mood, the gas lamps above me

sputtered violently, sending an army of shadows dancing across the street. The movement startled me, and I pulled my legs more tightly to my chest. Call me crazy, but aging enemies, flickering shadows, and midnight rituals in cemeteries all made me jumpier than usual.

The image of another, more familiar graveyard in rural Oklahoma popped into my head, and I couldn't seem to get rid of it. As the evening dragged on, I mulled over the shape of the lettering on my own headstone, the way its concrete looked at sunset, the curve of the ground over my grave. . . .

Finally, after nearly a full hour of this torture, I groaned loudly. I ran my hands through my hair, covered my face with them for a moment, and then leaned my head against the brick wall behind me. I had to think about something else while I waited for Joshua to sneak out for the night. Otherwise, I really *would* go crazy.

So instead, I pictured the prairie I'd dreamed about during the car ride to New Orleans. I envisioned the lush grass and the endless blue sky. Then I imagined my mother and father, sitting with me on a blanket spread over the carpet of wildflowers. I pretended that I could taste the food from our picnic, smell the flowers as the breeze hit them, feel the sun on my skin.

And since I was fulfilling all my wishes in this little fantasy, I added Joshua to the scene. In my imagination, he was sitting next to my father, laughing with him about something my mother had just said. The dream-Joshua, still talking to my dad, absentmindedly reached across the blanket and took my hand—a real touch, without sparks or electricity, but somehow better. So much better.

I sighed happily and reached my hands out in a big, satisfied stretch. But the second my fingers touched something icy and wet, I jerked them back, fast. I opened my eyes, and then let out a small, choked sound.

It wasn't possible. What I had just touched shouldn't be there. Yet here it was, as real as the gas lamps that had suddenly disappeared. A garishly colored metal girder, with my fingerprints still visible on its shimmering, frosty coating. The kind of girder you'd find on a bridge.

The kind I'd seen before.

I took an automatic step backward, away from the icy girders. Then I looked wildly around me. Instead of old buildings and narrow streets, I was now surrounded by twisted metal bars, all colored in bizarre, wounded shades of black and red and purple. Like some insane, life-size version of a birdcage.

This was definitely not the French Quarter; this was a bruised and ugly place, encrusted in ice and plunged into darkness. I hated it, almost as quickly as I recognized it.

High Bridge.

The words whispered in my mind, like a curse. This place looked exactly like the netherworld version of High Bridge.

But a second look told me I wasn't on High Bridge—just a different structure that closely resembled it.

I had to be in the netherworld. But *where* in it, I couldn't say.

As far as I could tell, I was standing in some sort of metal pavilion. Its girders extended up, over my head, to support a steeply pitched roof. In the back, behind me, the pavilion opened onto what looked like a metal boardwalk. Beyond that I couldn't see very much since this part of the netherworld was as shadowy as the part I knew. In the front, where I'd just been, a few rows of twisted girders were the only things between me and a sudden plunge.

Whatever that plunge led to, it did *not* look welcoming. Even in the impenetrable darkness I could tell I wouldn't want to lean over the edge of the pavilion. And yet I felt an irresistible tug toward it—an urge to creep just a bit closer and find out what waited below. The longer I resisted it, the stronger the impulse became, until I could hardly keep still. It gnawed at me, making me squirm and wriggle in an effort to stay in place.

Finally, I couldn't stand it anymore. I took one lurching step toward the edge.

But before I could take another, a faraway shrieking sound made me freeze. When I looked up, in the direction of the noise, my mouth dropped open.

Above me, the ceiling of the pavilion seemed to have disappeared, replaced by a sky of purples and grays that teemed and seethed around each other like storm clouds. Their movements were too rapid, though. Too unpredictable and chaotic to be part of any earthly storm.

And there in the cloud forms, so high I nearly missed them, were swooping black shapes. Hundreds of them.

If I squinted, they looked like enormous, high-flying crows or ravens. But I knew those shapes weren't birds.

They were demons. Real ones. And suddenly, they were moving in a flock formation to take a downward dive.

Toward me.

Chapter
SEVENTEEN

A scream began to build in my throat. I tried to choke it back. Tried to keep silent. Despite that feeble effort, it ripped its way out when someone gave my shoulder a rough shake.

Then, all at once, a fiery glow burst across my skin.

I hadn't seen the fire, hadn't been able to re-create it since that night on High Bridge. Now, without any warning or effort on my part, I burned like a torch—hot, vivid reds and oranges, shining against the darkness.

Immediately, I felt stronger. Bolder. Finally armed

with my glow again, I spun around to face my attacker.

For a split second the reflection of the fiery glow glinted back at me from his eyes. But as soon as I realized who he was, the glow vanished. Extinguished by some invisible force.

"How did you get here?" I whispered, snatching Joshua's hand from the air and using it to pull him against me. I wanted him closer to my flame, in case the glow reappeared. Maybe it could protect us both from the things that were about to swoop down upon us.

Judging by his expression, Joshua was also afraid. But he wasn't looking up at the sky, where an army of demons prepared to descend. He was looking at *me*.

"Amelia?" he said tentatively. His eyes were wide with alarm, and he'd actually pulled a few inches away from me. "What's going on?"

"Joshua, you've got to get out of here," I warned, frantic. "We're about to be—"

Yet something made me stop short. Maybe it was Joshua's pained expression, or maybe it was the fact that the scenery had finally registered in my peripheral vision.

Still holding Joshua's hand, I slowly turned my head to take in my surroundings: centuries-old buildings, cramped together; long, iron-railed balconies; sputtering gas lamps.

Somehow, between the moment I saw the demons and the moment I looked into Joshua's eyes, the netherworld pavilion had disappeared. And now I stood shivering in the French Quarter, clinging for dear life to a very confused boy.

Finger by finger, I unclenched my hand from his. I forced myself to stop shivering, but I couldn't get my lips to relax out of their terrified grimace.

There were two explanations for what had just happened to me, neither of them good.

"Joshua," I whispered, "if I asked you to be really honest with me, would you?"

His mouth lifted into a faint, worried smile. "Come on, Amelia. You know you don't have to ask me that."

"I know," I said, nodding stiffly. I took a deep breath and then released it, along with the most essential question of the evening.

"Tell me the truth, Joshua: did I disappear just now, or have I been standing on this sidewalk the whole time?"

He frowned, tilting his head to one side to scrutinize me.

"Well," he said, "there were a few seconds when I didn't see you, when I left the dining room to sneak out the front door. But as far as I know, you've been sitting here the whole time. I guess you stood up at some point, though. . . ."

Joshua trailed off as I sagged against him. I turned my face into his sweater, not even looking up when, after a moment's hesitation, he wrapped his arms around me.

We stayed like that for a while: him holding me, me desperately wanting to hold him, too. But I was more afraid than ever to do that now. Especially when I heard his answer to my next question.

"Just one last thing," I murmured into his shirt. "Can you tell me if you saw the fire again?"

Joshua stirred a little, but didn't loosen his grip on me. "What fire?" he answered, as casually as if I'd asked him what time it was.

I bit my lip, holding back a sob. Those two little words—"what fire"—told me so much about my mental state. About my future, and Joshua's place in it. Even if I could keep the demons away from me, and therefore away from Joshua, there was still an obvious problem brewing.

Me.

It seemed as though I was becoming like those ghosts I'd met last night: terrified; half crazy; running scared at the slightest sound. And if I was bouncing between real threats and hallucinated ones, how could I justify being anywhere near Joshua for any longer than tonight? Unless someone, somehow, could end the dreams and hallucinations. Maybe even empower me against the demons for good measure.

It seemed as if I really did have one last hope: a girl I barely knew, and trusted even less.

With a deep sigh, I leaned away from Joshua's sweater and then looked up into his beautiful, worried eyes. I gave him a light smile—one that I knew he could see through but hoped he appreciated all the same.

"Okay, Mr. Voodoo Conjurer," I said, forcing a positive note into my voice. "Is it time to go yet?"

"Yeah, it's already eleven thirty. The party's still going strong inside; I don't think anyone realized I even left the table."

"Well, that's good. At least we won't have . . . anyone . . . you know, *following* us."

He grimaced and ran a hand through his hair. "You mean Ruth? I don't think she's going to be doing any following any time soon."

"Don't say that." I placed a few fingertips on his chest. "She's just getting over a really bad headache."

Joshua shook his head uncomfortably, looking away from me. We both knew that when I was the one expressing optimism, things might not be so great. I'd lifted my hand, ready to guide Joshua's face back to mine, ready to say something reassuring, when his expression changed.

"Taxi's here," he murmured.

I turned in the direction he was staring. Two headlights

bounced unevenly toward us as a battered white vehicle pulled forward and stopped in front of the house. The driver's window lowered.

"You call for a cab?" a rough voice barked out to Joshua.

"Yeah," Joshua said, stepping closer to the car.

At that moment it hit me that we were *really* about to go perform a Voodoo ceremony, and my stomach did a sudden flip. But I followed Joshua anyway, coming close enough to see the cabdriver: a grizzled old man with one arm slung carelessly out the window. He jerked his head toward the back, indicating that Joshua could let himself inside. Clearly, this driver wasn't interested in getting up to open the door for a teenage fare.

The only effort he expended was to raise one eyebrow when Joshua held the door open for me—or for thin air, from the driver's perspective. Before I ducked into the cab, however, I saw him shrug dismissively. He'd seen weirder things in his career; he'd probably seen weirder things tonight.

When Joshua finally climbed in and closed the car door, the driver cleared his throat. "Where to?"

Joshua leaned toward the opening in the clear plastic that separated the front and back seats. "St. Louis Number One Cemetery, please."

The cabdriver chuckled, but he abruptly stopped when

he realized Joshua wasn't joking.

"You're serious," he stated flatly. In the rearview mirror, I could see his bushy white eyebrows rise again.

Joshua nodded. "Yes, sir. St. Louis Number One."

The driver turned slightly so that we could see his profile through the plastic divider. He no longer looked bored or unconcerned.

"Listen, kid. I know people say the Cities of the Dead are safer than they used to be, but that doesn't mean you should be traipsing around them at night. Including this one."

"I appreciate the advice," Joshua said with an air of finality.

"But it's locked after dark," the driver pressed. "So there's no point in wandering outside in that part of town this late."

When Joshua didn't answer, the driver hesitated, still eyeballing his young—and possibly crazy—fare. Then he shrugged again and spun back around in his seat. He pressed a few buttons on the console with one hand and turned the wheel with the other.

"It's your funeral, kid," the driver muttered, guiding the cab back into the flow of traffic on Ursulines Avenue.

"If you think about it," Joshua pointed out, "that's kind of ironic."

The driver snorted and then fell back into silence as he navigated the cab northwest. No one spoke while he drove, carefully moving the car through the thick press of milling partyers at the intersection of Ursulines and Bourbon. Only when the driver turned onto the long, less-crowded stretch of Dauphine Street did Joshua break the silence, leaning forward again.

"It's off of Basin, right?" he asked. "Near Iberville?"

The driver merely grunted in reply. Joshua settled back against the seat and folded my hand into his. He gave it a quick, reassuring squeeze.

I looked up at him in the darkness, watching the streetlights illuminate and then hide his profile in turns. He caught me staring and gave me a broad grin. I could see his optimism shining out at me from that confident smile—he was sure that tonight would go well. That I would get the help I needed.

And God, did I want him to be right. If Gabrielle could stop the disorienting visions, if she could help me regain my glow and my poltergeist strength, then maybe—just maybe—I didn't have to leave. I could fight off the demons, avoid the transparent ghosts, and stay by Joshua's side, for at least a little while longer.

These bewitching ideas were still chasing one another around in my head when the cab pulled to a stop along the curb next to a long, white stone wall. Up ahead I could see a break in the wall where a gate of bars guarded the entrance.

The cabdriver placed the car in park, fiddled with his meter, and then flopped back into his seat with a resigned sigh.

"The St. Louis Number One," he announced.

"Thanks," Joshua said, tossing a wad of bills through the opening in the divider. He pushed open the door and climbed out, then stood aside so that I could climb out too. After slamming the cab door shut, he gave the driver a casual salute, as if to say *Thanks, and don't worry about me, pal.*

Instead of driving off—his money earned and his obligatory warning delivered—the cabdriver leaned out the front window one more time.

"Look, kid," the driver said, "I have a grandson who's reckless and stupid, too. So I'm going to say it again: don't try and go in there. It's a bad, bad idea. How about I take you home? Free. No fare."

Joshua shook his head, hard. "Like I said: thanks, but I'm good."

To emphasize his point, Joshua patted the roof of the cab. The driver understood the "move-along" signal well enough. He took a last look at Joshua, lifted one shoulder in another dismissive shrug, and then pulled the car back onto the road.

Staring at the cab's fading taillights, I didn't share Joshua's cavalier attitude. In fact, a small part of me just wanted to heed the driver's advice and get out of here.

But instead, I folded my hand back into Joshua's and followed him toward the entrance of the St. Louis Number One.

In just a few shorts steps, we'd made it to the half-way point of the white wall surrounding the graveyard. There, the entrance was decorated with some historical plaques and a large iron cross atop the gates. Which happened to be locked.

Although I'd expected to find them open as per Gabrielle's instructions, both sides of the gate were held together by a chain threading through their bars—shut tight against any nighttime visitors and their intended Voodoo ceremonies.

I peeked over my shoulder: not another cab in sight, and the bright lights of the Quarter seemed awfully far-off. I wasn't worried for myself necessarily; my ghouls appeared to me even in crowded places. But I certainly didn't want *Joshua* loitering around outside a New Orleans cemetery all but begging to be mugged.

My fears were short-lived, however, when he gave one of the gates a light shake. The chain holding the gates closed slithered off, falling to the concrete path with a *thunk*.

"Huh," Joshua said, staring down at the chain and then at the small opening between the gates. "Looks like the Voodoo girl made good on her word."

"Oh. Yay."

Those two unenthusiastic syllables just slipped right out of my mouth.

Honestly, I didn't know which was worse: being locked outside, scared that Joshua might get stabbed, or going in and finding out exactly what Gabrielle could—or couldn't—do.

Hearing my lukewarm response, Joshua grinned back at me.

"Come on, Amelia Ashley," he teased. "Where's your sense of adventure?"

I've had more "adventures" in the last three days than I care to ever have again.

That's what I should have said out loud. Instead, I conceded.

"Okay, okay. Lead the way, Captain Adventure."

Joshua laughed quietly and then opened the gates farther. After we both stepped through the opening, he bent down to pick up the chain. As he threaded it back through the bars, he explained, "This will keep anyone from getting suspicious that people are in here."

I snorted softly. "Captain Adventure also happens to be the captain of covert operations?"

"Yup," he whispered back. "I'm an expert in both fields."

Then he took my hand again and began leading me down the concrete path, deeper into the cemetery.

As we walked, I couldn't help but gawk at the scenery. Here, all the graves appeared to be housed in above-ground mausoleums. Many were tall—a good three or four feet above my head—but a lot of them rose only to my knees. These crypts, which crowded together around the pathway, stood in various states of repair. Some had walls of gleaming white stone, firm and strong against the elements, topped with weeping sculptures and carved urns. Others were nothing but piles of crumbling brick held together by a network of scraggly weeds. Various bits of these crypts lay fallen on the pathway, and I had to skirt them as I walked.

Joshua, who led our way through the weaving, labyrinthine paths, whispered back to me.

"They look like creepy little houses, don't they?"

"Cities of the Dead," I murmured, repeating the cab-driver's phrase. When you put it in those terms, this really was a fitting place for a Voodoo ceremony.

I peered closer at the tombs, trying to read their weathered epitaphs. But all I could really make out were a few of the clearer surnames: Deforges, Morphy, Charbonnet. Beneath those I could barely discern long lists of more names, and dates. Illegible, weathered reminders of the people who lay buried inside . . . and who had perhaps walked these paths after their deaths just as I'd done in my own cemetery.

Maybe I'd even met a few of them last night in Jackson Square. Maybe they would soon become my only companions.

The thought chilled me. I followed Joshua more closely, keeping silent until, suddenly, he stopped short and I nearly bumped into him.

He whispered back to me, in a voice so low and reverent I could hardly hear him:

"We're here."

Chapter
EIGHTEEN

The instant Joshua announced our arrival, a thousand goose bumps—real ones—erupted across my skin. I clung tightly to his back, not sure I wanted to move forward. Ever.

But eventually, Joshua's stillness and my curiosity got the best of me. I leaned to one side to peek around him. Then I reeled backward.

As promised, a tall, bloodred crypt loomed to our left. The pathway it faced intersected another row, which bore the dining-table headstone that Gabrielle had mentioned, along with more standard, shoulder-level tombs.

And there, waiting in the intersection of these pathways—looking every bit the Voodoo priestess—stood Gabrielle.

A small fire burned in a metal pot at her feet and illuminated her from below, casting mysterious shadows across the planes of her face. This lighting somehow made her look older. More powerful. Her loose, floor-length dress shifted in the wind, as did her wild hair. She caught my eye and raised an arm in welcome; her other arm was occupied, holding a large, vine-wrapped black book.

A family Bible, the same kind of item I'd seen Ruth use in her exorcism rituals. Not necessarily a sign of good things to come.

Gabrielle beckoned again with one hand, signaling us to join her.

"It's almost midnight," she called. "Let's get started. Amelia, I'm going to need you at the center of this ring."

I looked down to where she had gestured. There on the ground, drawn in a broad circle that encompassed both Gabrielle and her small fire, was a ring of dust.

Voodoo dust.

I shook my head vigorously. "You *do* realize there's no way I'm stepping into that thing, don't you? I mean, even if I could."

Gabrielle laughed low.

"This isn't banishing powder. This is the protective stuff. It keeps out whatever means us harm." As if to demonstrate, she lifted her arms and spun around, letting the gauzy hem of her dress twirl with her. "We're safe in here, to do whatever we like."

Still unconvinced, I frowned. "What about Joshua?"

Gabrielle shook her head. "He needs to stay out of the circle since he isn't a part of the ceremony."

Joshua wrapped his arm around my waist and gave me a slight hug. "It's okay," he whispered. "I'm right here, watching. If anything goes wrong . . . I'll be here."

I hugged him back, not wanting to tell him that I wasn't worried that I would need his help; I was worried that he would need *mine*. But he looked so intent, so certain, that I nodded.

"All right. I'll give it a try."

"Good," Gabrielle said, sounding relieved. "Now hurry. We don't have a lot of time left."

I stepped forward reluctantly while Gabrielle knelt to arrange a collection of items at her feet. She placed the first—a small, portable stereo—just outside the circle. When she noticed me watching her, she gave a one-shouldered shrug.

"Drums," she explained. "Since it's just me, we've got to make do with recorded drumming."

"Oh," I said, feeling incredibly out of my element. "Drums. Of course."

As Gabrielle arranged the other items—a small bowl, a plastic bag full of dried herbs, some kind of gourd, one bottle containing clear liquid and one containing dark— I took another tentative step toward the circle. I inched one foot and then the other closer to the outer line of chalky white powder. With a deep breath for courage, I muttered, "Here goes," and took my first step inside the circle.

This time my foot landed where I wanted it to; this time I didn't feel the solid, impenetrable barrier of Ruth's magic. Instead, I felt . . . nothing. Nothing at all.

I sighed in relief, and stepped fully into the ring. Gabrielle glanced up from her work with a wry half grin.

"Congrats. They say the first step's always the hardest."

I rolled my eyes and folded my arms protectively across my chest. Just because I'd made it inside her circle didn't mean I trusted her yet.

Gabrielle, however, didn't seem to care much about my disdain. She was too busy placing the empty bowl near the fire and then crumbling the dried herbs into it. She grabbed the bottle of clear liquid, removed its cork, and began pouring it in careful increments into the bowl.

"Rum," she said distractedly. "A gift for the Loas, so that they'll help us."

Again I couldn't manage much more than a bewildered "Oh."

Gabrielle dipped her fingertips into the bowl and withdrew them to make little splashes upon the ground at my feet. She splashed a few more drops on herself and then ran her wet hand down her face, murmuring something incomprehensible under her breath.

Finally, she grabbed the gourd and the bottle of dark liquid, and stood.

"Sit," she commanded me, gesturing to the ground with the bottle. So I crossed my legs and dropped to the concrete. Then I folded my hands in my lap and turned my most skeptical expression up to her.

"Look," I said. "I'm not sure what you have planned for tonight. But mostly I just want the bad dreams to stop. Do you think you could do that?"

I couldn't tell whether she'd decided to ignore me or just silently process my request. Either way, she didn't respond as she bent down to press the PLAY button on the stereo. Immediately, the pounding sound of drums filtered out, as well as other, jangling noises.

Finally meeting my gaze, Gabrielle hissed, "Stay quiet until I say."

Then she raised her arms. In a strange, melodic

language I didn't recognize, she called out to the midnight sky. I tried to catch some of the words—*Legba, souple, lavi*—but wasn't really sure what I'd heard.

Still chanting, Gabrielle closed her eyes and slowly began to spin in a circle. With one hand she shook the gourd, which made a dry, rattling sound. With the other she held the bottle upright, letting its dark liquid slosh with her movements.

Soon, the sloshing and rattling synced with the drums. Combined, the noises started to take on their own rhythm—a kind of music to which, I now realized, she was dancing. The chiming of her chandelier earrings and clanging of her bracelets only added to the effect.

Despite everything I'd been through, I remained a skeptic about things like this. Yet as I listened to the music swell, as I watched Gabrielle's dancing grow more hypnotic and frenzied, I felt myself falling into a sort of trance. I had no idea where Joshua was, but I couldn't turn my head to look for him. I just couldn't pull my eyes away from the clamor occurring in front of me.

"Loa," Gabrielle chanted over and over. "Loa."

She repeated other words, too, like that *lavi* I'd heard earlier. Then she added a mantra I actually recognized: "Please." She whispered it frantically, like a prayer.

After God knows how long of this chanting, she dropped the gourd to the earth and continued to dance as she uncorked the bottle of dark liquid. She poured its contents carefully onto her hand, which she lifted to the sky and then flung to the earth, splattering the ground with dark drops.

I leaned forward, just an inch, to examine the splatters closely in the firelight. Then I recoiled.

The dark droplets, which I'd first taken as black, were actually red. Deep, arterial red.

Bloodred.

I gasped, but Gabrielle ignored me. She'd stopped dancing and was now swaying, occasionally pouring more of the bloodred liquid into her cupped palm before flinging it onto specific places around the circle.

Suddenly, I was desperate to find Joshua. I craned my neck, searching for him in the darkness outside of the Voodoo ring. I found him quickly enough, leaning against the side of the brickred tomb. Unfortunately, he looked as transfixed as I'd just been.

I spun back around to Gabrielle, whose arms were now covered in trails of red streaks from where the liquid had escaped her palms.

"I want this to stop now," I demanded. "You stop this right now, Gabrielle."

The sound of drums and jangling metal, however, drowned out my demand. Gabrielle either didn't hear me or didn't care, since she kept swaying and chanting and pouring.

I thought that the ceremony would never end—that I would forever sit in this circle, watching a ghastly display of fire and blood—when Gabrielle froze midsway.

For a long second she remained completely motionless, completely silent. Then, without warning, her eyes flew open and she turned them on me.

What I saw in them made me choke.

Where her irises had once been a stunning, vibrant blue, they were now the color of tar. As black as her pupils, as deep and dark as the abyss I'd seen under the netherworld High Bridge.

I was choking, struggling to warn Joshua that he should run, when Gabrielle dropped into a crouch and lunged for me.

I shrieked and tried to scramble backward, out of the circle. But I suddenly found my back pressed to some barrier—one that I instinctively knew wasn't visible.

Despite her promise, Gabrielle's protective circle had turned on me. Trapped me.

Gabrielle reached a hand for me. This time, however, I lunged forward. She was alive and probably couldn't touch me, but *I* was the poltergeist. I could at least try to fight her off. To keep her from Joshua, if I could.

But instead of clawing at me as I'd expected, she leaned in and softly pressed her blood-tinged fingertips to my collarbone. With an eerie smile, she whispered one Creole word:

Rete.

Then, with that simple oath delivered, her eyes rolled back in her head and she collapsed, unconscious, upon the ground.

For a moment I didn't move. Didn't breathe.

I stared down, mesmerized by Gabrielle's slumped form, which had fallen across the hem of my dress. While I stared at her, I didn't feel anything. Just numbness. Emptiness.

But the longer I sat there, the more a hot, uncomfortable stirring began to grow within me.

At first it felt like fear. Like adrenaline and nausea and fire mixing together in my core. Soon I could tell that it wasn't just in my mind, wasn't some mental side effect of what I'd just seen. This sensation was real, spreading out from my abdomen and tendriling its way to my limbs.

I thoughtlessly let it burn me for a few seconds more, until suddenly, my legs twitched beneath me. I jerked them out from under Gabrielle and sprung to my feet. I spun around toward Joshua, who was still looking gape mouthed at the Voodoo circle.

With a sharp intake of breath, I threw myself at him and very nearly shouted a prayer of thanks when I landed in his bewildered arms. Apparently, Gabrielle's barriers had faded with her consciousness, releasing me from the hellish circle.

"Amelia?" Joshua murmured, still fighting his way out of the trance.

"We have to leave," I said, grabbing his hand. "Now."

He didn't protest when I dragged him down the pathway, moving as fast as his stumbling, muddled pace would let me. I would've sprinted if I could, but there was no way I intended to leave Joshua stranded in this place.

A few times I took a wrong turn and ended up in a dead end of crumbling tombs and weeping statuary. Each time that happened I would groan in frustration and then spin around, tugging Joshua along with me on an alternate path.

Finally, blissfully, we made it into the broad, open area where the cemetery gates waited. I pulled Joshua toward them.

"The gates, Joshua. You have to open them."

He shook his head, obviously still disoriented, but began to fumble with the chain. When his hands kept slipping, I moaned softly. "Please, Joshua, hurry."

As if he were a zombie under my command, Joshua deftly removed the chain and let it slither to the ground beside him. He'd only had time to pull one gate open before I was shoving him out of it and onto the sidewalk. I followed him out, folded one of his hands back in mine, and pulled him onto the street.

There I started to run, picking up my pace once Joshua gained better control of his feet. The sound of his shoes pounded on the pavement as we dodged the traffic on Rampart Street and crossed back into the French Quarter.

Even though we'd made it back into the Quarter, we both continued to run mindlessly in the direction of the town house—holding each other's hand and sprinting past pedestrians and restaurants and shuttered town homes.

While we ran, my brain buzzed with thoughts. Unpleasant ones. Each beat of my feet against pavement brought me closer to a horrible, inevitable conclusion.

This is it, isn't it? I asked myself. *This is the end.*

And I knew, without a doubt, that the answer was yes.

I couldn't keep letting things like this happen. I couldn't keep placing Joshua in danger with these constant, hopeless attempts to stay with him. Fleeing Oklahoma, only to wind up in potentially demon-infested clubs; participating in failed Voodoo rituals? These were crazy, desperate acts that hurt him far more than they helped me.

He could have been possessed tonight, by whatever dark force had taken over Gabrielle. Worse, he could have been killed. Besides, the longer I lingered by his side, the more opportunity I gave the evil netherworld spirits to find me, and thereby him.

Every second he spent with me, every instant he touched me was like a slow-working poison. Which meant that everything I'd done in the past few days was unforgivably selfish. Done to prolong my time with him instead of to protect him.

So I didn't have two nights left with him. I didn't even have one night.

I had to end this, now.

When I saw that we'd made it to the relative safety of Ursulines and Royal, just north of the Mayhew house, I yanked him to a stop. He instantly flopped back against a brick wall, panting, looking grateful for the chance to rest.

I, however, didn't rest. I paced madly in front of him, trying not to cry. Trying to think of exactly what to say. It didn't help that the weird, burning sensation was still snaking its way through my body. It made me feel heavy and jittery at the same time, simultaneously light-headed and weighted down.

Joshua looked worse for wear too. He clenched and unclenched his hands a few times and then ran one hand through his hair, letting it rest on the back of his neck.

God, why did he have to do that? I thought. *This would be so much easier if he wouldn't do things like that.*

"You okay?" he asked me, sounding winded. "What

the hell happened back there?"

"It doesn't matter." I shook my head bitterly. "It's not going to happen again."

Joshua made a small noise somewhere between a grunt and a laugh. Then he grinned widely, like someone under the influence of a danger-induced rush.

"Oh, I agree—we won't be going back to the St. Louis Number One any time soon."

I shook my head again, more strongly. "No, Joshua. You don't get it: it's not going to happen again, because nothing's going to happen again. Not between us. Not anymore."

Joshua's smile held, but faltered at the corners. "Amelia? What's going on?"

I steeled my back, and my voice. "I've been lying to you, Joshua. You called me out for acting weird lately, and I lied to you about it. So now I'm going to tell you the truth: I've been thinking a lot about us, and our future."

"And?" he said softly.

"And we don't have one. A future, I mean. Tonight just proved it."

His smile disappeared. "But . . . but tonight was just about me helping you. I thought you were okay with that?"

"I . . . I lied."

Panic edged into his eyes. "Look, I won't try that again. I promise."

"N-no," I whispered, my voice finally cracking. "You probably won't. But will it matter? When five, ten, twenty years pass, will it really matter that we just sat back and enjoyed each other? Are you really going to be a forty-year-old man with a dead, eighteen-year-old girlfriend?"

Now Joshua's eyes burned. He lunged forward, clasping his hands to my upper arms. He didn't intend to hurt me, but he grabbed me forcefully enough that the movement lifted me onto my toes.

"I will, Amelia," he said roughly. "I *will*."

"It doesn't matter," I moaned, trying to pull away from him. I cursed myself when the tears began to flow, filling my eyes despite my resolution to be cold and immovable. "I'm leaving you, Joshua. Right now."

He leaned in, trying to hold my gaze. But I closed my eyes so tightly, I forced the tears out onto my cheeks. I had to get out of here, had to materialize before my willpower completely crumbled.

So I ignored him. Ignored the heat I suddenly felt rising off his skin. Instead of his smile, his hands, his eyes, I pictured the ghosts I'd met in Jackson Square. Though they didn't expect me for another day, I pictured myself finding them, joining them. Fading with them.

The effort worked. I could feel the soft pull of the

materialization tugging me out of Joshua's arms. Helping me vanish from his life forever.

Just before I slipped away, I heard him call out to me.

"Amelia, don't do this! Stay with me."

"Why?" I sobbed, though I could no longer see him. But his fading whisper still followed me into the darkness.

"Because I love you, Amelia."

Chapter
NINETEEN

I love you.

The words whispered in my mind long after they'd been spoken. They echoed, haunting me, distracting me in the darkness.

Maybe *they* were the reason my materialization didn't work. Not entirely anyway.

When I opened my eyes, I didn't see the other ghosts. Instead, I saw a throng of drunken, living people, laughing and shouting and surging around me. Beads were flying, drinks were sloshing, and loud music was pouring out from every window and door.

Bourbon Street.

For all I knew, I'd landed right in the middle of a parade, or what might have been just an average night in the French Quarter. Either way, it was nothing but utter chaos, and it mirrored perfectly how I felt inside.

I began to stumble through the crowd like a zombie— mindless, uncaring, blind. I wanted to be numb, too, but my body wasn't complying with that wish. As I walked, I grew dizzier and sicker, burning and reeling inside. It felt like my veins were filling up with kerosene and my brain was just seconds away from striking a match.

At this point, I probably wouldn't stop it. While I stumbled and burned, one word repeated itself on an endless loop in my mind.

Mistake. Mistake. Mistake.

I pushed my way through the mass of bodies, moving without direction or coherent thought. With nothing on my mind but that one repeating word and the impulse to get *away*. Every now and then I would catch the stench of rot, alcohol, and centuries of decadence. Even though they vanished quickly, these momentary sensations just made my head spin faster.

The farther I walked, the dizzier I got and the more the crowd pressed smothering-close. Their drunken laughter disoriented me so much, I started to superimpose the scene on other memories.

Memories of another party, on a bridge, many years ago.

A lifetime ago, technically.

That night—the night of my death—I'd seen shapeless black forms writhing their way through the crowd, inciting my friends and classmates to attack me. But tonight I couldn't distinguish the living beings from the supernatural.

Until I smacked right into one.

The force of the contact knocked me off balance, and I stumbled backward. My legs tangled in my skirt; and, despite a clumsy attempt to right myself, I began to fall. I threw my hands behind me in time to land palms-first upon the dirty curb.

The moment my hands slapped pavement, a nasty, stinging sensation slashed across my palms—surprising me not only with its force, but with the fact that I felt it at all. Even stranger, the jolt of the fall actually knocked the wind out of me. I sat there stinging and gulping for almost a full minute before I had the sense to look up and figure out who I'd just run into.

When I saw the face leering down at me, I shivered—a reaction that had nothing to do with the cold wind suddenly biting into my exposed skin.

He tipped his flamboyant hat in acknowledgment

and then bent his knees so that he crouched at my level. Of course, from my vantage point, he didn't really *exist* below the knees.

"That felt good, running into you," the pirate said, giving me a crooked grin. "Our group doesn't ever touch. But I wouldn't mind doing it again with someone who looks like you do."

Before I could react to his innuendo, another voice hissed in my ear.

"Trying to seduce one of my own? Or are you just out for an evening stroll, dear?"

I jumped slightly and then shuffled backward on my stinging hands, away from the hiss. I moved even faster once I saw the speaker: the gray-haired woman from Jackson Square. Once I'd backed a safer distance away from her, I straightened my spine and gave her my coldest glare (despite the fact that my veins were now *scorching*).

"I don't like your tone," I told her icily.

A harsh, ugly smile cut across her face. "It doesn't matter what you like, girl. You came to us—you're ours now."

As if they'd been planning this confrontation, the other three ghosts appeared out of thin air, materializing to form a circle around me. The soldier, with his arms folded menacingly across his chest; the sneering aristocrat; and the black-haired Creole girl whose dark eyes—now that I could see them more closely—looked a little manic. Those three must have agreed with, or at least overheard, the gray-haired woman, because they all flashed me triumphant, possessive smiles.

This wasn't exactly how I pictured this scene going down: burning on the inside, freezing on the outside, and outnumbered by five spirits who I'd started to suspect weren't my allies. Glowering back at them, I pushed myself off the pavement, dusted off my skirt in mock indifference, and then drew myself up to my full height.

"Other ghosts have tried to control me before," I warned. "Trust me when I say it didn't turn out too well for them."

The soldier eyed his companions and then smirked. "I like our odds."

The other ghosts shifted in response to his threat, moving as one to tighten their circle.

"What do you want from me?" I demanded.

"A trade," the aristocrat said.

"For what? I don't have anything to give you."

He laughed. "We don't want to trade with you; we want to trade *you*. We plan to exchange you for something else."

My mouth dropped open, and I took an involuntary step backward. The dark-haired girl moved with me, pressing in closer to block my escape. I turned toward her, hoping to appeal to someone nearer to my own age. Even if she did look totally crazy.

"I just wanted your help," I whispered to her. "Like you promised. You and I probably have a lot more in common than you think."

To my surprise, she grinned. Then she held up her forearms for me to see the vertical scars on them. "I don't think so. Not unless you slit your own wrists, too."

When I recoiled, her grin only broadened.

She's nuts. They all are.

I repressed my horror and tried to keep my expression smooth, confident. Although I suspected that the girl was past the point of reasoning, I asked, "Is what you'd get in this trade really worth trying to hurt me?"

"Oh, yes," she whispered, her eyes widening. "Yes, it certainly is."

I spun back around to the rest of them. Louder, I asked, "What price are you getting for me?"

"Our freedom," the soldier said. "From the demons. We have it on good authority that they want you. Badly."

My rigid posture faltered, right alongside my bravado. I knew that *I* would do just about anything—aside from murder and betrayal, obviously—to avoid the demons. And I'd only been running from them for less than a week. So how could I expect these ghosts, half rabid from centuries of hiding, to feel any differently? How could I reason with all that fear and desperation?

"So they offered you your freedom," I asked softly, "in exchange for . . . me?"

"Not exactly," the pirate said. "An intermediary has agreed to negotiate on our behalf, as long as she—"

"Silence!" The gray-haired woman cut him off with another hiss. She held him in her cold stare as she addressed the rest of their companions. "We're done explaining things to her. Let's get on with it."

Upon hearing her command, they each nodded. Then they began to take slow, stalking steps toward me. Almost in unison, they extended their hands like claws, reaching for me.

They looked like predators. Dead, crazy predators.

Panic and terror boiled inside me, along with that damned, searing heat. But I still clenched my fists and let loose a feral snarl.

"I won't go without a fight," I growled.

Still moving in, the soldier chuckled darkly. "Good."

Once again, something about him reminded me of Eli—of his cruelty and sadism; his pleasure in my pain.

And just like that, I was infuriated beyond rational thought. Suddenly, mindlessly, I began to stalk forward, too. Ready to meet them headlong.

But just as abruptly, they scrambled away from me,

skittering back across the uneven surface of Bourbon Street like leaves. Only two ghosts remained close enough so that I could still see their eyes, which shined with fear.

When I peered closely, I realized they shined with the reflection of something else, too . . .

Something almost neon, and blue.

I didn't even have time to register what I'd seen in their eyes before the burning inside me doubled. So much so that I felt like my brain had finally dropped that lit match into the kerosene.

The blaze was so hot, so blistering that I arched my back and then hunched forward, flailing in some sub-conscious effort to put out the fire. A particularly strong wave forced my head downward so that I faced my hands. When I saw them—still clenched in defense—a soft shriek escaped my lips.

My protective glow was back.

Sort of.

Instead of fire, traces of blue light raced each other up and down my hands, my wrists, my arms. I *glowed* again.

But not with the ghostly flame I knew. That flame had never harmed me. This glow *hurt*. Wherever the light moved it seared, leaving lines of pain in its wake. Roasting me from the inside out.

After a few seconds of mindlessly staring at my hands,

I realized that the light followed the tracks of my veins. In fact, it looked as though the veins themselves were shining through my skin. Like blistering hot, illuminated pathways that followed the course of my dead circulatory system. Blue lights, crisscrossing the places where my blood once flowed.

This isn't possible, I thought. *It can't be.*

Then it struck me: *this* is what I'd been feeling since Joshua and I left the cemetery. This is what had been boiling inside me. The slow, hot buildup of an internal lightning storm.

What did Gabrielle do to me?

With my mouth hanging open, I raised my head and faced the other ghosts.

None of them had vanished yet. They still hovered cautiously, at least a few feet away. But although the ghosts still watched me, none of them actually looked me in the eye. Instead, they seemed hypnotized—entranced by the light that snaked its way across my skin.

Slowly, one by one, they stirred. While I still writhed in pain, they leaned in to get a better view of my light show. And as they did so, their frightened expressions began to disappear.

They started to *smile*.

"Now this," the pirate hissed, "is interesting."

"What do you think?" the aristocrat whispered. "That

she'll be worth more to them like this?"

The soldier moved one scuffed boot closer to me. "What do you say, troops? Should we find out?"

The other ghosts nodded again and took slow, careful steps toward me.

Obviously, my light had only provided a momentary distraction. In a few more seconds, the ghosts would completely regain their confidence. Once that happened, they wouldn't hesitate to capture me and serve me up to the darkness like a meal.

I had to get away from the ghosts; I knew I had to. But I just hurt so badly. I tried to move forward so that I could run, but the pain intensified. Instinctively, I curled into a ball and crossed my burning, glowing arms against my chest.

That move, however, was a mistake.

It was as if my arms had marked an X. All at once the fire contracted, rushed through my limbs and veins toward one target.

My heart.

The fire blossomed in my chest, unfurling petal after petal of pain. I thought my heart might explode, ending my existence right there on the grimiest street in New Orleans. But it kept scorching me—so fiercely, I actually screamed aloud.

Thank God I didn't scream too loudly to hear someone

calling out to me, shrill and urgent.

"Amelia! Holy hell, Amelia, get out of there!"

I didn't recognize the voice, and I had the fleeting impression that I'd simply imagined it. But while I sucked in rapid, shallow breaths, I heard it again.

"Amelia! *Run!*"

And suddenly, I did just that.

Despite the incapacitating pain in my chest, despite the bloodlust shining in the Quarter ghosts' eyes, despite my suspicion about who had shouted that last-minute warning—I ran.

I broke through the ghosts' ranks easily, shoving in between the aristocrat and the gray-haired woman. As I passed, I felt their hands clawing at my dress, but I shrugged them off without a backward glance.

Free of the ghosts, I ran fast and hard down Bourbon Street. Sidestepping underage girls and bleary-eyed boys, dodging late-night hot dog vendors and people peddling booze in grenade-shaped cups. I flew past them all, pushing my legs to their limit until, finally, I couldn't take another step.

I shouldn't have felt the acidic burn of adrenaline in my legs. Nonetheless, it flooded my muscles with crippling force. I had just made it to the relative safety of a side alley when my thighs gave out and my legs buckled beneath me. There in the darkness I collapsed in a heap on the dirty ground.

All my energy spent, I gasped desperately for air and pressed my hands to my chest, where my heart still punished me with fire. I couldn't breathe, couldn't think, couldn't feel anything but scorching.

I couldn't even open my eyes when a familiar voice spoke from somewhere above me.

"It worked," a girl whispered. "Holy hell, it worked."

"Jesus," a male voice hissed. "What have you done?"

"What she asked me to do," the girl snapped.

"She didn't ask for this. Just look at her chest; look at her heart. Don't you remember how that felt?"

"Yes," the girl answered, surly. But her voice softened as she went on. "She can touch the living, Felix."

"She can *what*?" he gasped.

"I know, I know. Try to touch her."

The voices fell silent for a moment and then the boy whispered, "I can't."

The girl swore and then said, "That doesn't make any sense."

"Well, can't we just figure it out later?"

"Fine." She sighed. "If you stand watch while I grab her—"

The boy cut her off. "Don't I always help you clean up your messes?"

She made a petulant sound. "Don't think you can

lecture me just because you're alive and I'm—"

"Gaby," he warned, "now is not the time for that discussion."

The voices once again fell into a tense silence. Then, so softly I knew I must have dreamed it, a set of arms slipped under mine. As someone lifted my body, I felt an impossible heaviness settle in my chest; and I wondered, deliriously, how anyone had the strength to carry such a weight.

"It's happening," the girl breathed. "Look."

At that point I finally managed to flutter my eyelids open. In the few seconds I stayed conscious, I saw a pair of astonished, radiant blue eyes staring back into mine.

"Joshua," I whispered. "I need to go back. . . ."

I trailed off when my vision doubled. At least, that's what I think it did; that was the only explanation for why I suddenly saw two indistinguishable pairs of blue eyes studying me.

I blinked, trying to clear my vision, but the moment I closed my eyelids, unconsciousness slipped over me.

Chapter
TWENTY

The world had gone dark again, like it had in my dreams. All around me, everything was still and quiet, except for the hushed lapping of water.

This time, however, I didn't panic. I felt peaceful. At rest. And I had no idea why.

I kept my eyes shut, breathing shallowly for who knows how long. When I sensed daylight breaking, I opened my eyes and watched as a uniform layer of dark clouds became visible high above me. A weak sunrise began to filter through them, and I realized that I was somewhere outside, lying on my back and facing the sky.

But instead of leaping up and trying to figure out where I was, I shut my eyes again and did an unrushed self-appraisal. After what had just happened to me, I had the feeling I wouldn't get another quiet moment to assess the damage I'd suffered; I had to take advantage now.

To my surprise, I found . . . nothing. Absolute nothing.

My thighs didn't sting with adrenaline anymore, nor were my lungs straining from the effort of my run. Best of all, the fire in my chest was gone. My heart felt free, unburdened—as if the flame had never burned there.

Because I was suddenly free of pain, I assumed that *all* my physical sensations had disappeared. With my eyes still closed, I wriggled my fingers, expecting the numbness of death. When they touched something grainy and wet, I pulled them back into my palms.

For some strange reason, the sensation didn't scare me. I opened my eyes, splayed my hands against the wet earth, and pressed myself up into a seated position.

First, I checked my body, now free of the blue-glowing veins. Evidently, they'd gone the way of the burning in my chest.

Next, I took in the wide expanse of slate-colored beach stretching out in front me. I sat in its sand, bare feet pressed to the ground, staring into what looked like an endless black sea. Only, I couldn't really tell where the water stopped and the clouds began.

I felt everything now: the cold, gritty sand between my toes; the spray of mist off the water; the brisk chill of the wind.

Again, none of it scared me. If anything, it made me more peaceful than ever. Perhaps that mood allowed a memory to seep into my mind instead of flash suddenly as it usually did.

In the memory, I was a child, so young that the image seemed faded and patchy like an old photograph. I wore a bathing suit dotted with small, blue daisies—my favorite suit, I remembered. But I shivered, too, as I played doggedly on the muddy beach. Every few seconds I would toss a petulant glare back at my parents, who waited impatiently in the car. Seeing the image now, I didn't blame them—it was an unseasonably cold day, and I was the only member of the family who hadn't given up on our day trip to the lake.

The memory faded, until I was once again watching black waves lap at the beach of an unfamiliar sea. I had the sudden urge to touch the mud one more time. To mold it into something important. Something memorable.

Still feeling inexplicably calm, I squished my fingers into the silt. Before I could raise my hand, though, a hushed voice spoke next to me.

"I know what you're thinking," she said softly. "That this is an ocean. But it's definitely not."

I turned toward the voice, strangely unsurprised to see the pretty redhead from my prairie dream. She sat cross-legged next to me, arms propped behind her so that the sleeves of her green tunic skimmed the sand.

Looking at her, my brain did a few automatic leaps: if this girl—an obvious figment of my imagination— sat here, then that meant "here" was just another dream space. Which meant this place wasn't real.

This also meant that my pain might not actually be gone.

"If it's not the ocean," I said in an oddly detached voice, "then what is it?"

Still watching the waves, the girl shuddered. "It's the river."

"What river?"

"*The* river." She nodded toward the shoreline. "Maybe not the biggest in existence, but the biggest one I've ever seen. So wide that when you're sitting beside it, you think it's the ocean."

I looked back at the supposed river, searching for another side. Another bank, matching this one, some-where far across the water. No matter how hard I searched, I found none. Only black waves undulating into the horizon.

Glancing back at her, I shrugged. "Well, it sure looks like the ocean."

"It looks like anything they want it to. Same as our place. They can shift and change it all they want."

"They . . . ?" I said, but she cut me off with a soft *shh*. Wordlessly, she pointed to the shoreline directly in front of us.

At first I didn't see anything. Then, while we watched, a small, dark shape appeared, hanging in the air without support. It was moving too, swirling and spinning around itself like a mote of dust in the wind. As it moved it expanded, stretching and widening until it eventually took the shape of a small house.

For a few seconds it hovered several feet above the ground, and I wondered whether the strange building process had stopped. But then stilts began to form beneath it, anchoring the house to the sand. Next, a steep roof appeared, supported by evenly spaced columns instead of walls so that we could see through to the ocean. Finally, in this state, it settled.

And I gasped.

The structure wasn't a house—it was the dark pavilion. The one I'd hallucinated last night before Joshua and I left for the cemetery. The only difference was, now I sat outside of it. But I would have recognized it anywhere.

We were in the *netherworld*.

"We have to get out of here," I breathed, scrambling backward in the sand. "Any second, High Bridge will show up, and then the demons, and then—"

"High Bridge isn't going to show up," she said. "This is a different part of their world, one that they've intentionally designed to match the living world—or, at least, parts of it. They traditionally stick to moving bodies of water. Transitional places. You know, 'crossing the River Styx' and that whole bit. But don't be fooled; their world is completely interconnected. They can get from Oklahoma to here in a matter of seconds. Besides, every portal—whether in Oklahoma or New Orleans—leads to the same dark place."

Before I could tell her *Thanks for the info, but we should probably still be running,* she spun around to face me. Her bright green eyes were suddenly fervent, wild.

Without warning, she grabbed my wrists and jerked me toward her so hard that the wet sand slopped over my skirt.

"Amelia, you have to stop doing this," she pleaded.

I shook my head and tried to pull away from her. "Let me go. Now!"

My command only made her hold on tighter. "I can't, Amelia. Not until you understand that you have to stop."

"Stop what?" I growled, tugging harder. The longer she held on to me, the more my wrists began to ache. "I don't know what I'm doing wrong!"

Finally, she let go. The moment her hands released mine I clutched at my wrists and tried to massage feeling back into one, then the other. The girl, however, seemed totally unconcerned about my discomfort. Wearing that same fanatical expression, she gestured with one hand down the length of my body.

"This," she said flatly. "This is what you need to stop."

I followed her gesture and then blinked in confusion.

"My . . . dress? Look, I get that it's outdated, but that's no reason to—"

She cut me off with a violent shake of her head. "Not your dress. *You*, Amelia. *You're* the problem. What you're doing is unnatural, and we won't put up with it for very long."

"I don't . . . I haven't *done* anything," I sputtered, now totally lost.

"But you have. You're doing it right now. . . . You just don't know it yet."

"I . . . I'm sorry?"

The girl sighed and tugged at her copper curls. "I know. Trust me, I know. I've seen this coming for a while, and I've been trying to warn you, with all the visions. I've been trying to keep you *away* from this place. But you are so . . . *damn* . . . *stubborn*."

She pronounced each of her last words individually,

as if to emphasize her frustration. For some reason that rankled me. By now my zenlike feeling had completely vanished. So I sat up straight, stopped massaging my wrists, and looked her directly in the eyes.

"Maybe—now, this may sound totally nutso—but maybe you should have tried to make the dreams easier to understand. How about that?"

She groaned. "I have to work within the parameters they set for me, okay? This guardian thing has rules, and I can't just—"

"They?" I quoted. "You keep saying that like I'm supposed to know who you mean. And what's a guardian? Are you my guardian angel or something? Because, if so, you're a really *bad* one."

She waved both hands in front of her, looking distraught.

"No!" she cried. "God, no. I'm just . . . I'm a . . . crap, I can't *tell* you what I am. Just trust me when I say you have to figure out a way to undo this." She gestured down the length of my body again. "Then go home."

I arched one eyebrow. "Home? To Oklahoma?"

"Yes, Oklahoma. Perfect."

"But the demons are waiting for me there."

"They're waiting for you *everywhere*, Amelia."

When I blanched, she rushed on: "Don't worry, though—we'll take care of it. Just go home, stop talking to the living, stop hanging out around that bridge . . . just go back to your old existence."

"You mean . . . the wandering? The fog?"

She nodded vigorously. "Yes, exactly. The fog. You think you could do that again?"

I puffed out a long, frustrated breath before answering her. "Okay, let's just say for argument's sake that I thought going back home was a good idea *and* that I wanted to reenter the fog. Do you know any ghosts who've done it before? And if so, could you give me some tips? Because I have no idea how to unremember everything at this point."

The girl groaned again and flung her arms up in the air. "Truthfully? I have no clue. Almost every soul gets claimed right after death. . . . There are only a few ghosts who wander, and even less of you who wake up."

She surprised me by flopping back onto the wet sand as if she didn't fear the netherworld at all. Lying flat, she released a heavy sigh. "You were doing just *fine* on your own, staying off their radar and ours. But then I just *had* to give in. And things got too complicated, with the living guy and that fire glow, and Eli not doing what I thought he'd do—"

I cut her off. "Wait. You know about the glow? You know *Eli*?"

She darted a guilty look at me and pinched her lips

shut, like a little girl who had just divulged someone else's secret.

"No," she said weakly. "Of course not."

"Are you going to give me any useful answers? Like, what my glow is, and how I can use it again?"

Her subsequent silence didn't surprise me, not at all.

I abruptly shifted my legs under me and pressed myself up so that I towered over her. "Look, I don't need any more supernatural beings mucking around with my afterlife. So thanks for your . . . help, I guess. I have the feeling that you're part of whatever the *opposite* of the netherworld is, and I appreciate the fact that you guys have finally noticed that I exist."

She looked a little stricken by my bitter tone, but when she didn't respond, I went on.

"That being said: I don't want your help anymore. Not unless you can keep the demons from going after me and—"

"We can!" she interjected, right as I finished with "And the living people I love."

Her face fell.

"We *can't* do that," she said. "Rules are rules; they get to make their choices, just like we get to make ours."

"Then I'm making mine, right now. Your help isn't worth anything if it doesn't extend to the living people I care about. I'm not like those ghosts back in the French

Quarter—I wouldn't trade someone else to save myself."

She frowned up at me from the beach without commenting; apparently, she didn't like how I'd summarized her offer. And that was just too bad.

"Okay," I said firmly. "Since that's settled, stay out of my business. And stop giving me creepy dreams and hallucinations—my afterlife is weird enough. I mean, making me imagine my dad's voice in the prairie? That was below the belt."

The girl opened her mouth to object but then popped it shut. When I felt certain she didn't have anything more to add, I turned away from her and examined the endless stretch of water and sand around us. Other than the eerie pavilion—still unoccupied, thank goodness—I didn't see any other structures or objects. No doors or windows or cars or boats . . . nothing to take me back to reality.

I looked down at the girl. "I don't suppose you'll tell me how to get out of here?"

She shrugged—a gesture that looked strange, considering she still lay flat on her back. "Close your eyes tight and say 'There's no place like home' a couple times."

I snorted derisively. "Are you going to tell me I need to click my heels next?"

Even through her scowl, the girl laughed. "Okay, okay. But you've still got to close your eyes."

"Why?" I asked, justifiably suspicious.

"Because I'm going to end this dream, and I can't do it while your eyes are open."

I quirked one corner of my lip in disbelief, and she sighed. "Please, Amelia. Just close your eyes."

I studied her for a moment longer—lying back in the sand like she didn't have a care in the world except for me: a stubborn, anomalous dead girl. Then, against my better judgment, I lowered my eyelids.

Of course, I didn't close them *fully* until she chided, "Stop peeking."

After I obeyed, I heard the soft whoosh of air. When I reopened them, I no longer saw the beach. But my new surroundings weren't exactly comforting, either.

Mostly because, almost immediately, I recognized the small, dark room in which I'd woken. The slatted windows, the slipcovered furniture, the rainbow of pills on the coffee table in front of me—all elements of one of my darkest dreams.

The one in which I saw myself alive.

And dying.

Chapter
TWENTY-ONE

I tried to sit up, but almost every inch of my body shrieked in protest at even the slightest movement. So instead, I lay perfectly still, gazing around with bleary eyes.

Dawn was breaking here, too—I could tell from the light creeping in between the heavily slatted shutters across from me. As the room lightened and my eyes began to clear, I could see more than just the elements I recognized.

Now free of the dream haze, I realized that this room

was actually far nicer than I'd first thought. The walls were painted a rich purple and hung with what looked suspiciously like original canvases of priceless art. The furniture (at least those pieces not covered in white sheets) had an expensive sort of feel to it, all highly polished wood and lush fabrics and gilt accents. Even the coffee table with its collection of spilled narcotics was inlaid with gorgeous mosaic tiles and decorated with clusters of lit, luxe-smelling candles.

Despite the candles, however, the place still smelled . . . odd. Almost palpable, even. Like rich food and humidity overlaying the sweet scent of decay. The longer I lay there, the stronger the smells grew.

But that . . . didn't make sense. I dragged in a deeper breath through my nose, and the scent followed, strong and continuous. It didn't fade like it was supposed to. I just kept right on smelling it.

Even weirder, I felt other things, too: a bitter taste in my mouth, dryness in my throat, and an itch just begging to be scratched on my arm. Sensations I'd never felt long enough to fully experience.

Until now.

I did another self-assessment, noting the raw ache in my legs, the pounding at my temples, the strange heaviness in my chest.

Not a single part of my body was numb. Not anymore.

I was trying to make sense of all this, trying to reason through it, when I heard a soft snore from somewhere near my feet. I gritted my teeth and hazarded some movement, using one elbow to prop myself up on the couch. Although everything—and I mean *everything*—hurt, I craned my neck so I could see over the rolled arm of the sofa.

There, sitting in a dark corner a few feet away from the couch, was a boy. He'd slumped forward in his chair, with his arms dangling over its sides and his head flopped down to his chest.

I listened to one more snore and then I did the only thing I could think to do.

"Hey!" I shouted. "Who are you?"

Except I didn't actually shout. I tried to, but the sound came out scratchy and dry, like I was recovering from a nasty cold.

Still, the boy must have heard me. He stirred, shifting backward in the chair and releasing a final, rough snore. Half yawning, half groaning, he shook himself awake and then wiped one hand from his forehead to his chin.

For that brief moment I couldn't see his face. But when he removed his hand and opened his eyes, I sucked in a sharp breath.

The boy looked *exactly* like Gabrielle, the Voodoo girl. The same coffee-and-cream skin, the same flawless bone structure. Their only difference, aside from gender, might have been age. His stubble and the frown lines around his mouth made him seem older . . . but not by many years.

His luminous blue eyes caught mine, and I suddenly felt dizzy. I swayed for a second; and though I tried to stay upright, my elbow gave out, and I dropped back to the couch.

The boy, however, didn't move. If I angled just right, I could still see him, sitting awkward and stiff in the chair. It didn't look like a comfortable place to wake up, and his handsome face showed the burden of sleeping there all night. Like he'd been keeping watch.

Or watching over me.

I hadn't made up my mind which option seemed more likely when he called out in a voice almost as rough as mine.

"Gaby, she's awake."

I heard a muted curse from somewhere deep in the apartment, followed by the sound of footsteps. Within seconds, Gabrielle emerged from the archway next to the boy's chair. She wore a long, embroidered kimono, and although she didn't look half as tired as he did, she still yawned as she plodded into the room.

Even tired, she was still prettier than the last time I'd seen her: covered in blood and possibly possessed. In fact, compared to last night, she looked positively cheery.

She flopped into a nearby chair, used her fingernails to muss her Afro into shape, and then turned to me with an affected sigh.

"Don't you think you could have let us all sleep for a few more hours?"

I grabbed an arm of the couch and fought through the pain to pull myself upward. While I moved, the weight in my chest grew heavier, stronger. I tried to ignore it until, finally, I managed to get myself into a seated position. From there I shot Gabrielle an angry glare.

"Who are you people, really?" I demanded, panting from my efforts. "Where am I? And what the hell did you do to me?"

"That's a lot of questions for seven a.m., Princess."

"Amelia," I corrected automatically.

"Fine. That's a lot of questions for seven a.m., *Amelia*."

"Gaby," the boy scolded, still not rising from his chair. "Stop taunting her—she's been through enough."

Gabrielle rolled her eyes. "Like I don't know."

"Yeah, but you got to *choose*. From what you told me last night, you weren't exactly forthcoming with this girl, were you?"

"Choose what?" I croaked. "Would someone please start explaining things? I'm grateful you guys saved me from the other ghosts, but—"

"The Faders," Gabrielle interjected.

"The what?"

"Faders," she repeated in a blasé tone. "That's what I call the ghosts who tried to trap you."

"So . . . you've had experience with them before," I said slowly. My brain began to pluck memories and phrases from last night's attack. One word in particular came to mind: "intermediary." When I spoke again, I did so carefully. Guardedly.

"*How* do you know the Faders, exactly?"

Gabrielle and the boy shared a look. When she turned back to me, her eyes seemed decidedly less flippant.

"We'll . . . get to that," she said haltingly. "But maybe we *should* start with the basics. You already know I'm Gabrielle." She placed her fingertips on her chest. Then she pointed to the boy. "That's my brother, Felix. We're the Callioux twins."

I raised one eyebrow. "Twins?"

"Fraternal," she said.

"Yeah, I got that part. It's just . . . you two look like you're different . . ."

"Ages?" Felix offered, grimacing. "Well, we look like that because we are. *Now*, anyway."

"Now?"

Felix didn't respond but instead shot his sister another pointed look. She sighed heavily and met my eyes.

"Felix is twenty," she said. "But I'm seventeen and, like, ten months. I have been, for a little over two years."

I waited for her to tell me she was joking. When she didn't, I balked.

I knew the implication of what she'd said better than anyone. Still, I had to ask the important question out loud. Just in case.

"You're . . . dead?"

"Yup," she said, popping the *p*. "A little ghostie ghost, just like you."

I remained silent for a moment. Then, in a hushed voice, I asked, "How?"

"You mean, how did she die?" Felix said. "In a car accident. The same one that killed our parents."

He spoke plainly enough, with no emotion registering on his face. And yet—even from across the room, even though I hardly knew him—I could see a glint of pain in his eyes. It made my stomach clench, that glint. How on earth did someone lose his entire family in one fell swoop? Even if part of it had obviously returned to him?

"Yes, yes, it's all very tragic," Gabrielle said, drawing my attention back to her. "My boyfriend accidentally jerked the wheel out of my dad's hands, and our car went over the Crescent City Connection Bridge. We haven't seen him or our parents since."

I shook my head in disbelief. "You died falling off a bridge?"

She scrutinized me for a second. Then her eyes widened in genuine surprise. "You too? Seriously?"

When I gave her a dry, close-lipped smile, she barked out a mirthless laugh. "Wow. Of all the dumb luck."

"Tell me about it," I said dismissively, wanting to get back to the subject at hand. "So, you died, Felix survived, and you came back to haunt him?"

Felix shifted forward in his chair, nodding. "Pretty much, yeah. I must have been thrown from the car or something, because the emergency crews found me on the shore a couple hours later. Everyone else in that car died, though, including her jackass boyfriend." Gabrielle made a noise of complaint, but Felix cut her off: "That's too good a word for Kade LaLaurie, and you know it. I don't care if he was some frat boy honors student; that guy was a total freak. I'm still not convinced he didn't intentionally cause that crash. Sorry, Sis, but you had the *worst* taste in guys."

After she shot her brother a withering glare, Gabrielle continued the story. *"Moving on,"* she emphasized. "It only took a couple days for Felix and me to find each other again. Actually, he found me, looking all lost and confused outside our family crypt the day of the funeral."

"At first I thought she'd survived, too," he said, shaking

his head sadly. "I mean, I'd never seen a ghost before, so I didn't really know what I was looking at."

"You are a Seer but didn't know it until you almost died," I concluded.

Felix nodded. "Guess so, although I didn't learn what that word meant until we started researching why she didn't have any senses, and no one could see her, and she couldn't touch anything."

"Nothing?" I asked, trying to keep my tone as bland as possible. I didn't want to reveal the reason for my curiosity to the twins. But since the first moment I touched Joshua, I'd wondered whether the electricity we experienced was specific to all ghosts or just specific to . . . us.

I frowned heavily. Right now I didn't want to think about the fact that "us" didn't exist anymore.

Felix noticed my expression and gave me a curious glance. Fortunately, he didn't press me about it but instead answered, "Nothing. That's what finally made us realize she was dead."

Gabrielle snorted. "Yeah, that and the fact I could send myself to Michigan and back in two seconds." She shifted forward in her chair, rearranging the kimono around her long legs. "Too bad that was around the same time we also realized that our folks were in major debt when they died. The bank sold off our house in Metairie to pay the bills. By the time all the legal stuff was done, Felix was of age and no one was too worried about where he'd live. So after that . . . we were homeless."

I frowned, letting my eyes circle the interior of the apartment. "Looks like you're doing pretty well now."

Felix's gaze followed mine, and he began to squirm. But despite her brother's obvious discomfort, Gabrielle grinned wickedly, clasped her hands, and leaned forward.

"Did you know," she said conspiratorially, "that a lot of Hollywood stars have bought town houses and apartments in the Quarter? Would you believe that some of them don't put in alarm systems? Would you also believe that most of these people hardly ever visit, especially when they're about to go bankrupt *and* a court orders them to six months of rehab?"

She cocked her head toward a framed photograph sitting on one of the side tables. There, flashing a high-wattage smile at the camera, was one of the most famous actresses in the world. Even *I* knew who she was, and I'd been dead for more than a decade.

"Oh, my God," I gasped. "This is *her* apartment? You're *squatters*? Aren't you afraid of getting arrested?"

Gabrielle cackled. "Me? No. But Felix obviously is."

"Hell yes, I am," he chimed in gruffly. "Especially since I'm the one who busted the lock on the downstairs door so you could carry out this epically stupid plan."

His sister, however, just rolled her eyes. "Live a little,

Felix. Besides, if you believe the tabloids, the bank's probably going to foreclose on this place before she gets out of rehab. Other than some clothes and the bedding, we haven't touched anything. The sheets on the furniture, the pills on the coffee table—it looked like that when we got here, it'll look like that when we leave."

I shook my head, incredulous at her daring show of courage and stupidity.

But really, the saga of the Callioux twins wasn't the most important thing in my afterlife right now. Ultimately, I wanted to know why my fingertips could touch the rough slipcover beneath me; why I could still smell the strange scents of the French Quarter; why my body felt beaten and tired long after those sensations should have faded.

"Okay, so now I've got your backstory, breaking and entering and all. But what about me? Why do I feel so weird? Why do I *feel* at all?"

Once again Gabrielle and Felix exchanged wary glances.

"Tell her, Gaby," he urged.

She held his gaze for a moment longer, clearly drawing upon his strength for what she had to say next. After a disconcerting silence, she turned back to me.

"Put your fingers on your neck, Amelia," she commanded softly.

"Put . . . what?"

She demonstrated by taking the fore- and middle fingers on her left hand and pressing them to her neck, just below the jawline. I frowned in confusion but then followed her lead.

After all, what could it hurt?

Only a few seconds after I'd done so, however, I jerked my hand back and shot up to sit rigid-straight on the couch. My eyes widened uncomfortably as I stared at Gabrielle. When she nodded in confirmation, I let out one hissing breath.

Because, although I hadn't experienced it in a very long time, I recognized what I felt in the tender skin of my neck.

A pulse.

Chapter
TWENTY-TWO

Hope surged within me, so strong it made me dizzy again. My pulse sped with excitement. Now that I felt it again, I don't know how I could have mistaken that pounding at my temples for anything else.

"Am I . . . am I alive?"

Gabrielle frowned guiltily and shook her head. "No. Sorry. You're not actually alive—your body just thinks you are. It's sort of like . . . an illusion."

Everything inside me wilted. My right hand wavered at

my neck, just over the place where I'd felt blood and heat coursing through my skin.

"What do you mean, 'an illusion'?"

She wrung her hands in her lap as she struggled to come up with the best explanation. "You're kind of . . . how do I put this? You're kind of undead. Or the living dead. Pick your supernatural euphemism."

My stomach twisted violently. I didn't want to believe her. Yet I knew, beyond doubt, that I'd been dead yesterday. And now I was . . . something different.

"What are you saying?" I whispered. "That I'm a . . . a *zombie*?"

Unbelievably, Gabrielle smiled. "I don't think so. You aren't craving brains, are you?"

I sputtered for a moment, my mind leaping between confusion and anger. Then, weakly, I answered, "No. Not yet."

My stomach let out a sudden, audible growl, and Gabrielle laughed. I clutched my hands to my abdomen and looked down at it in wonder. Then my eyes shot back up to hers.

"Where's my dress?"

Gabrielle gave me a sheepish, one-shouldered shrug. She reached down to the floor and brought up a shapeless bundle of filthy, decaying fabric. If not for the familiar bodice, I almost wouldn't have recognized the tattered silk, which looked like it had been stored some-where damp and dank for . . . well, for a decade. Now the fabric literally disintegrated in Gabrielle's hands. As I stared, gray flakes of it fluttered to the floor like ash.

"The transition affected you, not the clothes. So your dress . . . kind of didn't make it," she said. "I had to put you in one of the actress's bathrobes when this thing started to get a little PG-thirteen."

My eyes flickered to Felix, whose cheeks flushed. I said a silent prayer of thanks that Gabrielle had been the one to dress me . . . even if I couldn't understand *how*.

I rubbed at my temple, where a headache inexplicably pounded. "This all happened because of that ceremony last night, didn't it? Because of Voodoo?"

"Yes—because of a Lazarus spell."

A shiver ran down my spine. "A what? You'd better start explaining. Like, *now*."

Gabrielle shifted, still looking a little guilty. "I will, but I have to go back a bit, okay?"

I gave her one cold nod, and she went on.

"Even before I died, I was into Voodoo. Mostly just for fun, although my grandpa actually practiced it. Once, before he died, he told me about the Conjure Café. He said it was run by an old friend—one of the most pow-erful Voodoo priestesses in New Orleans. So when I realized that I was dead, I started haunting the place.

Watching Marie, learning whatever I could. Mostly about the dead, and how to make my own spells."

About two months ago I hit pay dirt—Marie finally left one of her conjure books open to a page with something called the Lazarus spell on it. It was perfect, exactly what I'd been looking for, except for a few minor details. So I memorized it and added my own little twists. Then I made Felix swipe some items from the Conjure and go with me to the St. Louis cemetery. There, with his help, I performed the first Lazarus ceremony—the one that changed me."

"Like the ritual performed last night?" I asked

"The *exact* ritual. It's similar to all those Haitian Voodoo rituals you see in documentaries but different in one important way. In Voodoo, resurrection magic typically reanimates the body without the soul. But I figured out a way to revive the soul . . . without the living body."

"How?" I demanded, my voice frosty with skepticism.

"The Lazarus spell is based on an offering," Gabrielle said. "An exchange has to be made in order for it to work. When it does, the resurrection gives ghosts a quasi-physical form, and some amazing abilities. Like, we can make ourselves visible to the living whenever we want. And because we aren't really alive, we can't get hurt. Plus, we get to wear different clothes and hairstyles again, which is—in my opinion—an absolute necessity.

The resurrection gives us sensations, too. We get to smell things . . . we even get to *eat* again."

Felix cleared his throat and gave his sister a pointed look. "Except for . . . ?" he prompted.

Gabrielle's mouth twisted in frustration and reluctant defeat.

"Okay, okay." she conceded. "There are a few drawbacks. You see, magic only works on the basis of a trade. To gain a few things, you have to give up some others."

So far she'd given me nothing but sunny reviews about my new, in-between state of being. But I could hear the evasion in her voice.

Fighting my growing nausea, I kept my tone low and dangerous.

"What exactly did I give up for this, *Gaby*?"

She pinched her lips into a thin line, grabbed a loose curl of her Afro, and twisted it wildly around her index finger. Finally, at the moment my patience had almost run out, she spoke. Hesitantly, like she already feared my reaction.

"In order to live this half-life," she said, "you have to deal with a few negatives. First, you had to experience that pain last night, where the force of the change lights you up and makes your heart act like it has restarted. So . . . that was one sacrifice. Next, you can't vanish at will anymore, I think because you're more substantial now. And last, you had to . . . to give up . . . something else."

I gave her a withering look and leaned closer. "What 'else,' Gabrielle?"

She fiddled silently with her hair for a few more seconds and then, in a rush, said, "Touch. We think you've lost the ability to touch."

"But I can touch stuff right now," I argued. I demonstrated by slapping my hand against the slipcover beneath me and tugging on the terry cloth lapel of my robe.

Gabrielle smiled apologetically.

"Yeah, you get *that* kind of sensation back. But . . . well, there's something that made you special. It's the reason why I agreed to help your boyfriend in the first place. I thought you'd keep it after the transformation, but there must have been a complication. We didn't figure out until last night, when Felix tried to touch you." She cringed before finishing: "We're pretty sure you've lost the ability to touch the *living*."

I stared at her blankly. "What?"

Gabrielle tilted her head toward Felix in some sort of unspoken signal. He nodded and pushed himself out of the chair. Then he strode over to the couch and knelt beside me. Frowning, he laid one gentle hand upon mine.

Or, at least, he tried to. Where our skin touched, I felt nothing. No electricity or sparks. Just the standard numbness I'd felt before this transformation.

I yanked my hand from under his. "That doesn't mean anything. That could just be specific to you and me."

"Maybe," Gabrielle said doubtfully. Her expression told me she knew exactly who I was thinking about when it came to touching. "Maybe the only living person you could touch was Lover Boy. We can always get him and find out . . ."

I shook my head weakly. "No, we can't."

She had the decency to look regretful for a moment. Not for a very long moment, however, as she cheerfully offered, "You can still touch me, if that makes you feel better."

I simply scowled at her. After that I sat motionless, trying desperately to process all this information. While I did so, a few sneering comments and denials ran through my head—rebuttals to everything Gabrielle had just said. But instead of voicing my thoughts aloud, I fell back against the couch.

"I don't feel so well," I whispered, and my stomach snarled again as if to back me up. Felix gave me a sympathetic glance before grabbing a designer trash can from under a side table and placing it next to my feet.

"Thank you," I murmured absently, unable to look

him in the eye. For a while I just slumped into the sofa cushions, thoughtlessly monitoring the heavy thud in my chest. My mind had gone empty. Blank.

Until one word whispered in my head.

Joshua.

It felt wrong to say his name, even if I didn't do it out loud.

My head started to spin with questions. Had I really lost my ability to touch him? And did it even matter?

Of course it mattered. It mattered terribly. Although I'd sworn to protect him—even if that meant never seeing him again—I couldn't stand the idea that I would live at least some kind of life without him in it. Every time my heart beat, every time I experienced some previously lost sensation, he wouldn't be there to share it with me.

I couldn't be like this without him; I *couldn't.*

Suddenly, what felt like a sea of venom bubbled up in my stomach. I flew forward, gripping the trash can in time to empty the contents of my stomach into the bin—mostly disgusting, acidic bile since I hadn't actually consumed anything in more than ten years. When that was finished and I felt reasonably certain another wave wouldn't cripple me, I reared back and began to yell at the Callioux twins, who stared wide-eyed and openmouthed.

"What were you *thinking*? And who the *hell* gave you permission to do this to me?" I knew I was wild and out of control, but I didn't want to stop. "If you'd have just listened to me in the graveyard—I told you, I just wanted the dreams to end. And maybe learn how to do something about the demons. But . . . *this*? I didn't ask for this!"

"I know," Felix murmured, but Gabrielle's words overlapped his.

"The demons?" she asked in a tight, strained voice.

"Yes, the demons. They've been after me ever since I met two of them in the netherworld. All I wanted to do was find a way to defeat them, or at least to escape them. And now I can't even do half the things that protected me in the first place. . . ."

Gabrielle lurched forward, diving between Felix and the coffee table until she knelt beside me. Her eyes were abruptly bright, desperate; and she clenched my hands in a painful grip.

"You've gone to the other side?" she hissed. "Into the darkness?"

Her intensity surprised me, and, momentarily, I forgot how mad I was.

In fact, there were only two reasonable explanations for what happened next. Maybe I questioned whether Gabrielle was the Quarter ghosts' intermediary to the demons if she really didn't know anything about my past. Or maybe I'd been so starved for someone who'd not only been through what I had, but also didn't want to destroy me, that I started to spill some of my own history.

"Yeah, I *have* been to the darkness, actually. This ghost, Eli, used to take me there. You wouldn't believe what it looks like, all gray and cold and twisted. I've been trying to get back in there so I can get my dad out of it, but I can't. . . . I haven't been able to. . . ."

When I trailed off, Gabrielle's expression lost its ferocious edge. Suddenly—shockingly—she smiled. Her grin, however, wasn't full of its usual bravado, or even wry, offhanded amusement.

Instead, I saw vindication written all over her face; she practically *glowed* with it.

"I knew I chose you for a reason," she breathed.

"You . . . 'chose' me?" I asked, frowning heavily. "You don't even know me."

"But I know what you can—could—do. I've met other ghosts," she confided, "and none of them could touch the living like I saw you do yesterday morning. Even if that ability is gone, you're *different*. Which means we might be able to help each other."

"Help each other do what?"

She squeezed my hands tightly. "Get our parents out

of there. Your dad, our folks. I've been trying to contact my parents with Voodoo spells, Ouija boards, the works. But if you can actually get *in* there—"

I cut her off with a shake of my head. "I told you: I haven't been able to. Not without help from someone inside it."

"Doesn't matter," she insisted, still smiling confidently. "We'll work together to get in. Once we find our parents, I'll even help you with that demon problem."

Before I could ask her *how* we were supposed to accomplish either of those goals, she let go of me and leaped up from her crouch. After taking one enormous step over the coffee table, she began darting around the room excitedly.

"First things first: clothes. Not that the robe doesn't suit you, but it isn't much better than the melting prom dress. Next, one of the best things about being Risen—beignets for breakfast. You're going to *love* them, almost as much as you'll love eating again."

I quirked one eyebrow. "What was that word you just used?"

"'Beignet'? It's a little French doughnut totally covered in—"

"No, the other word. 'Risen'?"

"Yeah," she said, flashing me a wide smile. "That's my name for what I am. Or what *we* are, I guess. The Risen."

"Huh," I muttered. I looked away from her and leaned back into the cushions, ready to sit here for a few minutes, hours, days to process everything I'd learned this morning. But Gabrielle wasn't having that. She dove forward, grabbed my hands from my lap again, and yanked me to my feet.

"Let's go raid the actress's closet; trust me, it's like Christmas Eve squared."

In a small voice I asked, "Is it Christmas Eve today?"

Felix nodded. Although I stayed on my feet, I sank a little.

Before Joshua's and my abrupt breakup last night— before I'd been transformed into the living dead—I honestly thought that I would spend Christmas Eve with Joshua. One last night with him before I fled. Now I felt sick again thinking that I might have ruined his Christmas.

Or saved it. Nothing destroys the holiday spirit like getting attacked by your girlfriend's demonic stalkers.

I noticed that the twins were watching me with identical quizzical expressions so I shook my head to clear it of those thoughts. As I told myself earlier, I'd made my choice. For my loved ones, for myself.

Which meant I'd be spending Christmas in the company of relative strangers, learning how to control my new form. Deciding how much I did or didn't trust the twins, especially with regard to the netherworld and its demons.

I sighed softly and then shrugged. "Okay, Gabrielle. Let's go play dress up while you tell me more about this Risen stuff."

"Awesome!" she squealed, her blue eyes sparkling. Then she leaned in close and whispered, "Gaby."

"Huh?"

This time her smile actually managed to look a little shy. "Call me Gaby. Everyone who's anyone does."

I couldn't help but laugh. "And by 'anyone,' you mean Felix?"

"Well, I *am* her only friend," he said. Gabrielle angled her entire body around me and stuck her tongue out at him.

He gave her a dismissive wave. "Don't act offended; you know it's true."

A little noise chirped, and Felix fumbled in his pocket. He pulled out a cell phone, flipped it open to check something, and then glanced back up at us. "Work is texting—looks like they want everyone there bright and early to prep for the Christmas Eve banquet tonight. I've got to go."

"Felix is a waiter at Antoine's," Gabrielle explained. "They totally use and abuse him."

"Someone's got to pay for those beignets," he

grumbled. "And it's not like Marie's been handing you a paycheck every Friday."

Gabrielle grinned. "If she could see me, I'm sure she would."

"She can't?" I asked, surprised.

"Not unless I want her to. Which I don't. I'll show you how that works at breakfast, I promise."

And just like that, Gabrielle was dragging me across the room, chattering happily about the actress's well-stocked closet. I peeked over my shoulder at Felix, who still watched us with a concerned frown. Right before Gabrielle pulled me through the archway, he mouthed:

You okay?

Like someone who cared about me. Like a friend.

So I shook my head lightly—a gesture that said *I don't honestly know*—and then ducked under the archway after Gabrielle.

Chapter
TWENTY·THREE

abrielle tugged me through an open doorway into what must have been the master bedroom. Once inside, I couldn't help but breathe a soft "Wow."

I'd expected this room to be as dark and narrow as the hallway we'd just crossed. But here the space was bright and airy, with floor-to-ceiling windows lining two of the pearl-colored walls. Although the windows were shut tight against the winter cold, all their shutters lay open, flooding the room with sunshine. It lit up the rich wooden floor, the antique vanity, the oversize bed and its gauzy white canopy.

While Gabrielle threw open the double doors leading into the master closet, I walked over to a row of windows and peered outside. On one side of the apartment I could see the gray waters of the Mississippi River moving alongside a long wharf of shops and restaurants. On the other side I saw something familiar. Past the hanging ferns and the iron balcony rail, through a thick wall of surrounding trees, I could just make out the tilt of Andrew Jackson's bronze head.

"Jackson Square?"

"Yup," Gabrielle called back from somewhere deep inside the closet. "This is the corner apartment of the Lower Pontalba Building. One of the oldest apartment buildings in the country. Prime view, right?"

"Sure," I muttered. But looking out at the square, I still shivered.

However "prime" the view, I turned away from it and walked cautiously over to the closet, from which several loud clunks and more than several foul words were emanating. I grasped one of the doors—trying not to freak out about the smooth feel of painted wood against my hand—and peeked inside.

At first I couldn't see Gabrielle for all the clothes: furs and silks and sequins and lace, hanging and draped and folded on a labyrinth of shelves and racks. The vast majority of the wardrobe, however, appeared to have landed in a knee-high pile on the floor. In the middle of the pile, almost buried in fabric, Gabrielle knelt, muttering profanity and pawing through the jumbled mess around her.

"You know your whole, 'we've hardly touched the place' philosophy?" I asked her. "Well, this closet sort of makes you a liar."

Gabrielle simply ignored me. Then, to my horror, she pulled out two completely see-through tops and held them up for comparison. When she saw my stricken expression, she sighed heavily and threw those back into the sea of fabric, only to yank out a pair of boots and a bundle of more acceptable garments. She tossed them at me without explanation and then ducked into the adjoining bathroom with her own handful of clothing.

I waited for some further instruction; but when I realized that this bundle of fabric was the only hint I'd get, I looked for someplace more private to change. Finding none, I used the bed's canopy as a cover while I slipped out of my robe.

Everything about this situation felt strange, invasive, so I hurriedly pulled on my new set of clothes without studying them; honestly, I couldn't pay attention to much more than the chilly air and my ongoing feelings of nausea.

By the time I finished dressing, Gabrielle had come breezing out of the bathroom. I don't know how she'd managed it in such a short time, but she looked even prettier than before, in skintight gray leggings, a cream-colored tunic, and purple ankle boots.

"Check it out," she said, twirling in a circle. "It's from a couple seasons ago, but still—it's a Rachel Zoe. Did I break into the right house or what?"

"It's still stealing," I murmured.

Gabrielle scoffed, dumping the contents of a small black bag onto the bed. "We'll put it all back before the bank auctions everything off, I promise."

I glanced down at the items on the bed and grimaced. "Makeup? Is that really going to stay on my face, considering . . . you know . . . ?"

"The clothes are staying on, aren't they?" She shrugged and grabbed a glinting eyelash curler. "Now hold still so I can make you look less like . . . well, what you are."

Ten cringe-worthy minutes later, Gabrielle backed away and gave me an appraising look. Her blue eyes flashed with approval, and she nodded.

"Better. Much." She nodded in the direction of a full-length mirror standing in the other corner of the room. "Go look at yourself. I bet you're just *dying* to. Pun intended."

So slowly I thought Gabrielle might just give up and push me to it, I stood and walked over to the mirror.

Other than a few glimpses of my senior yearbook photo, I hadn't seen myself in a very long time. I knew I wouldn't look like a corpse; besides that, I had no idea what to expect.

I certainly didn't expect to catch a glimpse of the pretty girl staring back at me in the mirror.

Her long brown hair fell in thick waves down her back—almost to the waistband of her skinny-jeans, which were tucked into caramel-colored, over-the-knee boots. As I watched her, she fidgeted nervously with one thin strap of her flowing beaded white tank.

Despite her obvious unease, the girl in the mirror looked stylish. Sexy, even. Her cheeks flushed, and her green eyes sparkled with fire. With life.

At that moment I had a fleeting thought:

What would Joshua think of me now?

Even when I'd repressed the question—and the unbidden, accompanying image of his eyes—I couldn't speak. Couldn't tell Gabrielle what I thought of this transformation.

Until, finally, I asked, "White? Again?"

Gabrielle's laughter filled the room. "That is Dolce&Gabbana—you should be hugging me right now. Besides, after much deliberation I decided you really can rock the white."

Still chuckling, she turned away from me and wandered

back into the closet. While I listened to her rummage around in there, I studied the reflection some more.

I really *did* look alive. Uncannily so.

Yet there were a few telltale signs that I wasn't quite the picture of health. For starters, I was way too thin. Gaunt, actually, which meant breakfast was probably a good idea after all. Then there was the color of my skin: a uniform, chalky white, improved only by Gabrielle's blush and the sprinkling of freckles across my nose.

In the mirror, my reflection bit her bottom lip and tugged at the ends of her long waves. She looked confused, worried, and *very* out of her element.

My reflection kept that wary look even when Gabrielle walked over with another armload of goodies from the closet.

"Here," she said, handing me a cropped leather jacket and a pair of celebrity-sized sunglasses. "I can't let you out of this house without accessorizing you. It just goes against my nature."

With an indulgent sigh, I slipped my arms into the jacket sleeves, shivering a bit when my bare skin hit the cool silk of the lining. Then I put on the glasses and turned back to the mirror to assess Gabrielle's final touches.

Thus disguised, I really *did* look like a different person: not an anguished, heartbroken ghost, but just some pretty, living girl in designer jeans.

Gabrielle nodded at my reflection, obviously pleased with her work. Then she slung on a black, three-quarter-length cape and her own pair of sunglasses. With a wide grin—and absolutely no warning—she grabbed my arm and dragged me out of the bedroom.

"We're going to start easy," she said, pulling me down the hallway, out another door, and toward a dark flight of stairs. "Since we're not supposed to be in this building, it's useful to be invisible when we leave it. Once we get to the café, though, the real work begins."

By the time we reached the bottom of the curving stairwell, everything had gone pitch-black. So when Gabrielle opened the door to one of the interior courtyards of the Pontalba, the high-priced sunglasses couldn't keep me from squinting painfully against the sudden flood of daylight. Nor did my stylish coat protect me from the continuous rush of cold air; the sensation sort of made me grateful that the chills Eli always incited were so short-lived.

Shivering, I followed Gabrielle blindly across the uneven ground. I slowed down only when my eyes adjusted and I saw just how crowded the tiny courtyard was. People milled everywhere: sipping coffee at small iron tables, smoking under canvas overhangs, scurrying to pick fresh fruit out of crates and take it inside to the first-floor restaurants.

Not a single person glanced up at Gabrielle or me.

Granted, everyone looked incredibly busy. But considering the fact that most of them appeared to work—not live—in these buildings, you'd think they'd at least *notice* a pair of young, glamorously dressed girls wandering in their midst. As far as I could tell, though, it was as if we weren't even there.

"Can they see us?" I hissed, following Gabrielle through an alley that led out of the courtyard.

"Not unless they're Seers, or we want them to. Basically, we don't have to *work* to stay invisible. To make ourselves apparent . . . now, that's a different story. That takes intent."

Her last few words came out muffled, buried beneath the cacophony of the street onto which we stepped.

"Welcome to Decatur," she yelled over the noise.

A sea of honking cars separated us from the other sidewalk, where people ducked into shops and cafés along their way. To our right, on the corner where Decatur Street met Jackson Square, a troop of artists and street performers were already setting up shop for the day. There, a lone trumpeter warmed up, adding his own notes to the noise of the street.

Although I could have stayed to gawk for a while, Gabrielle pulled me onward, dragging me to a crosswalk and practically throwing me into oncoming traffic.

"If these drivers can't see us," I shouted at her as we dashed across the street, "doesn't that make them more likely to hit us?"

Gabrielle simply flashed me a mischievous grin, leaping with me onto the curb in time to avoid a speeding taxi. Once she'd steadied herself, she brushed the road dust from her leggings and then twitched her head toward a huge outdoor café, where patrons crowded under a green-and-white striped awning.

"Time for you to experience the deliciousness that is Café du Monde."

"It's awfully . . . full," I noted uneasily.

Gabrielle nodded. "Spot-on. It's the perfect place for you to learn to go visible: if you want breakfast, you'll have to *earn* it."

Maybe because I'd seen her covered in blood, maybe because she'd totally altered my afterlife, but nearly everything Gabrielle said still made me suspicious. I followed her to the café warily, staying a few paces behind her in case of . . . who knows what.

Gabrielle didn't seem to notice or care. She weaved deftly through the busy sidewalk, bypassing the long line to get inside the café and signaling to me from underneath the awning.

"Look—immediate seating," she called out, pointing

to the little table that a waitress had just cleared. As far as I could tell, it was the only open table in the entire café.

"Um, aren't we supposed to wait in line?" I asked, still hovering outside the waist-high gate that separated the café from the rest of Decatur. Gabrielle laughed and plopped into one of the metal chairs.

"We're still *invisible*, Amelia. Now get in here before we lose out to those tourists." She pointed meaningfully to a nearby middle-aged couple who fumbled bags and bumped other patrons in their eager beeline toward the table. Feeling apprehensive and more than a little guilty, I slipped through the opening in the gate and edged my way through the restaurant.

When the tourists beat me to the table, I thought we'd surely lost our spot. But before they could even pull out their chairs, I saw Gabrielle do . . . something.

For a split second her appearance wavered like an image on a staticky old television set. When the effect ended, she leaned casually back in the chair, smiling broadly up at the couple.

"May I help you?" she asked them with arch politeness.

Both tourists blinked back in surprise at what must have been the sudden appearance of this gorgeous young girl.

"You weren't . . . where did you . . . ?" the man

sputtered, obviously confused. But his wife recovered more quickly. She placed a restraining hand on his arm and then smiled apologetically at Gabrielle.

"So sorry, ma'am," she said. "We didn't realize this was your table. We'll just wait for another one. Right, honey?"

When her husband started to object, she spun him around forcefully and dragged him back to the line. As they passed, I heard her mutter, "Don't embarrass me, Charlie. She's *famous*. Don't you remember her from that one movie we saw last summer? You know, the one with all the car chases?"

As the couple rejoined the line outside Café du Monde, I heard Charlie's faint, befuddled "No." I watched them fade into the crowd and then turned a disapproving frown on Gabrielle.

"Well," I said, sinking into the chair next to her and taking off my sunglasses. "You'll be happy to know they think you're some superfamous actress with carte blanche to steal any table she wants."

"Excellent," she crowed, clearly unrepentant. "If I'm playing the part, then I'm glad I can actually pull it off."

Realizing that we had much more important matters to discuss than Gabrielle's audacity, I leaned forward.

"So . . . how did you do that? Make them see you, I mean?"

"Glad you asked," she said, waving to a pretty Asian

waitress who was taking orders a few tables over. "Here's your chance to try it yourself."

"But . . . *what*?" I floundered as the waitress began crossing over to our table. "I have no idea what to do!"

Gabrielle shrugged one shoulder. "It's instinctive, I promise. And it's a lot like how you used to vanish. You just have to concentrate on being seen instead of disappearing. Stay visible while you eat, though. Otherwise it'll look like the floating-breakfast show."

"I don't even know what that means," I hissed. But I fell silent the instant our waitress walked up to the table.

"Order?" she demanded in a brusque, no-nonsense tone.

"*I'll* have a small café au lait and an order of beignets," Gabrielle drawled. She smirked in my direction. "Amelia? What would *you* like?"

Although the waitress looked like she thought Gabrielle had gone crazy, I still felt a dizzying wave of anxiety and pressure.

After all, I'd just lost the first living person who could see me (a fact that stung on so many levels and that I tried desperately to repress again). Now I had the opportunity to appear to an entire city full of living people.

If only I could figure out how.

Do I even want to? I asked myself. Maybe I just wanted to skulk into the shadows, running from the demons and avoiding the living like I'd originally intended . . .

But at that moment, my stomach growled so loudly it hurt. Suddenly, I couldn't think of anything I wanted to do more than to talk to the woman who stood between me and my first bite of food in more than ten years.

I felt a strange current pass over my skin just as I said, "Um, the same?"

Upon hearing my voice, the waitress actually jumped. She turned, openmouthed, to stare at me.

She *saw* me now. A normal, living woman—not a Seer—actually saw me.

I'd done it. I wanted to appear badly enough, and I'd done it.

I gave the server my widest smile. "I'll just have what she's having. Is that okay?"

With her mouth still hanging open, the waitress nodded mechanically. Then she slowly backed away from our table, keeping her eyes on me the entire time. She only looked away when she reached the relative safety of the indoor portion of the restaurant.

"Ha!" Gabrielle clapped her hands together loudly. "Man, you learned way faster than I thought you would."

I shrugged sheepishly. "What can I say? I'm *really* hungry."

Gabrielle was still laughing when our waitress returned a few minutes later carrying two steaming mugs and two heaping plates of fried doughnuts. She dumped them unceremoniously on our table, maintaining as wide a berth as possible. While Gabrielle paid in cash, the waitress kept a suspicious eye on me, hurrying away from the table as soon as she could.

"Obviously, *she* didn't think we were famous," I muttered once she'd disappeared from view.

"You," Gabrielle corrected. "She didn't think *you* were famous. I, however, pull it off fabulously."

When I turned back to see why Gabrielle's voice sounded garbled, I found her tucking sloppily into the beignets. She couldn't have been eating for more than a few seconds, but she already had powdered sugar smeared on her cheeks and dusted all over her designer clothes.

Despite everything—my heartache over Joshua, my distrust of the Callioux twins, my fears about what I'd become—I started laughing so hard I actually snorted.

"Oh, yes. You are the picture of couture perfection."

Gabrielle took another huge bite of beignet and then grinned at me, showing her food in her teeth.

"I'm a vision," she mumbled around the pastry. "And you know it."

I couldn't help but keep laughing, and the sight of all those white sprinkles on her priceless cape just made it worse. I only gained better control of myself when my stomach growled, louder and more insistent than ever.

So I took a few gulped breaths, wiped my tears away so that the carefully applied makeup wouldn't streak, and then gingerly picked up a beignet.

It was hot to the touch and slick with the pastelike mixture of sugar and grease. I could smell it too: sweet and doughy. I reveled in its scent until my head spun and then drew it to my mouth for a tentative bite.

The sugar burst across my tongue, followed by the rich, yeasty taste of fried dough. I took a few more greedy bites before I'd even had time to swallow the first, finishing the entire doughnut in seconds. The moment the beignet hit my poor, neglected stomach, I thought my eyes might roll back in my head.

"Oh my God," I moaned, grabbing my second beignet. "I'd die twice if I could eat this every day."

"I know, right?" Gabrielle spoke through another mouthful. "And you haven't even tried the café au lait yet."

With my pastry-free hand, I picked up the mug and took a sip of the coffee. Again I tasted heaven: smooth chicory and creamy milk, warm and strong beneath a sweet layer of foam. I dropped the second beignet so I could concentrate more fully on the café au lait, practically chugging it in three big gulps. Once finished, I reluctantly set down the mug and licked the last drops from my lips. Even with the caffeine jitters buzzing through me, I felt satisfied. Content.

I slid lazily back in my chair. "This," I concluded, "is awesome."

"Glad you approve." Gabrielle chuckled low, popping the last bite of dough into her mouth. "The best part is that you totally earned it. Now you just have to learn to go invisible again, and we'll be set."

"And how do I do that, exactly?" I asked, picking up the beignet I'd discarded earlier. Then I froze, thoughtlessly dropping the pastry to the ground.

"You just need the proper motivation," Gabrielle said, dabbing at her cape with a wad of napkins. But she froze, too, when she caught the look on my face.

"Amelia," she said. "What's wrong?"

"I think I just found my motivation," I whispered.

Gabrielle followed my gaze and then swore. At that moment she knew exactly why I *needed* to disappear. After all, the one person I wanted to appear in front of was the one person in the world I shouldn't.

And he and his Seer family were now standing about ten feet away from us.

Chapter TWENTY-FOUR

E verything twisted inside me.

It mangled and mashed together until I felt certain that the only thing I could do right now—the only thing I could *ever* do—was fly across the café, throw myself into Joshua's arms, and apologize for the next thousand years.

Then when I finished apologizing, I would finally tell him I loved him. More than anything.

But instead, I closed my eyes and willed myself invisible.

The strange current rippled over my skin again, and I opened my eyes to see Gabrielle's image blink out of, then back into, existence almost too rapidly to catch.

"Just to be clear," she whispered once she finished going invisible. "We're hiding from them, right?"

I nodded and kept my mouth shut. I felt pretty sure I would just start bawling if I tried to speak. It would have been better for my sanity, and my willpower, if I just looked away. Still, I couldn't take my eyes off Joshua.

So many members of his family clustered together that I wouldn't have seen him had he not stood aloof, slightly apart from his relatives. The rest of the clan seemed blissfully unaware of our presence as they debated whether to wait for a group of tables to open up outside or just go into the interior restaurant. Only Jillian threw worried glances over her shoulder at her brother.

I didn't blame her: he looked *awful*. Worse than I'd ever seen him.

He hadn't slept last night, I could tell. Dark purple circles ringed his eyes, which looked bloodshot, even from this distance. My breath caught in my throat when he rubbed a palm over his stubbled cheek and then dragged his hand roughly through his hair—a gesture I loved so much, now a part of his obvious misery.

Almost as if he could sense someone staring at him, he pulled a pair of sunglasses from his back pocket and slipped them on. Then he folded himself deeper into his winter coat, like he just wanted to disappear. Suddenly, it seemed horribly unfair that I could and he couldn't.

Realizing that I'd inadvertently clutched my hand to my heart, I cleared my throat and turned to Gabrielle.

"Let's get out of here, okay?" I croaked.

Gabrielle nodded, looking uncharacteristically serious. "Yeah, I think that's probably a good idea."

She slipped out of her chair without moving it, tilting her head to indicate that I should do the same—no point in going invisible just to alert the Seers to our presence with the scrape of a chair. I followed her lead, wriggling out and then skirting the neighboring tables to better avoid the Mayhews.

I'd almost reached Gabrielle, who waited for me by the café entrance, when I hesitated. Then, like a fool, I reversed course until I stood only a few inches from Joshua.

Stupidly, recklessly, I leaned in close enough to feel the warmth of his presence, to breathe in the sweet, musky scent of his cologne. These were things I'd wanted to experience in full since we first met. And now I had to act like a thief, stealing this moment from him.

I'd just reached out to grab his hand—to see if our connection had in fact disappeared—when I heard Gabrielle choking behind me. Apparently, *I'd* shocked *her* this time. I dropped my hand, but that didn't deter me from lingering beside Joshua . . . waiting.

Waiting for him to notice me. To sense me, even though he could no longer see me.

I wanted some kind of recognition from him, some proof that our connection withstood what happened last night. I wanted to know that, whether I ran from or fought against the demons, there would always be something of us that survived.

I didn't get that reassurance.

Without so much as a glance in my direction, Joshua sighed once and then followed his enormous family to the back of the café, where a large crowd of people ate standing up outside at tall, chairless tables.

Watching him walk away, I sighed, too. Then I turned around and slunk back toward Gabrielle, who ogled me from the gate.

"What the hell was that?" she said through clenched teeth. "I thought we were avoiding Lover Boy?"

I hung my head, feeling embarrassed. "We were. We are. Let's just go."

Thankfully, she simply nodded, slipping on her sunglasses and moving quickly with me out of the café. She didn't speak until we'd made it halfway down the sidewalk. Then she smacked me on the arm.

"Where are your sunglasses?" she demanded.

I reached absently for my face and found nothing. No glasses.

"Crap, I left them in the café." I turned to go back, but Gabrielle grabbed my arm and tugged me to a stop.

"Don't go back there," she said. "It will only upset you more."

I shook my head. "The Mayhews were moving to the back of the café. I probably won't even be able to see Joshua. Besides, we need to get those glasses back in the actress's closet—one less thing that could get Felix arrested."

"Bah," Gabrielle grumbled. "Who cares about the stupid glasses? I'm sorry I even brought them up."

"You can't tell me you don't know the exact designer and cost of those things."

She grinned sheepishly. "Fendi. Three hundred and forty-five dollars. Before tax."

"Now tell me you want to leave them for a stranger to own." When she didn't respond, I shook her hand off my arm and began trudging back down the sidewalk. "See you in less than two minutes, promise."

By the time I'd pressed my way through the line outside Café du Monde, I'd already admitted my ulterior motives to myself. Of *course* I wanted to catch another glimpse of Joshua; I wasn't made of stone.

But when I ducked back into the seating area and

angled over to our table—where a waitress now cleared our mess—I couldn't see the Mayhews anywhere.

Maybe they went inside, I thought as I covertly swiped the sunglasses off the tabletop. *Couldn't hurt to check* . . .

I spun around, more than ready to slink my way into the interior restaurant, and then stopped short.

Alex stood less than a foot from me—eyes wide, expression alert. I hadn't seen him earlier, when the Mayhews entered the café; he must have been buried deep in the crowd. Now he searched, hunted the area where Gabrielle and I had sat only minutes ago.

It's nothing, I reasoned. *This doesn't mean anything.*

But I went cold when he whispered, "Amelia?"

I pressed my lips together, held my breath, and kept so still I thought I could hear my phantom pulse pounding in my ears. Still, Alex inched closer. After another beat, he tried again.

"Amelia, are you there?"

I stayed silent, now biting the inside of my lips to keep them shut. This technique was especially effective when Alex leaned forward until only inches separated us.

"I know you're here," he whispered. "I can smell your perfume. Like peaches, right?"

Despite my resolve to stay silent, a tiny squeak escaped my lips.

I prayed that Alex couldn't hear it above all the

laughing and talking and plate rattling. But he immediately jerked backward, looking triumphant. Then his expression shifted to one of pleading.

"If you *are* here," he said, louder now, "please stay and listen to me, just for a second. I think I know what's going on with you. I think you're afraid of something."

I stayed motionless, silent, as he continued.

"I know I don't know you that well, but I could see it written all over your face the other night. Something has you scared, and I think you're trying to run from it."

He took a step closer, and I jagged to one side. "I'm sure I look like a crazy person right now, talking to thin air; but I have to tell you: we can keep you safe. Me, Annabel, and Drew. Hayley and Jillian. Maybe even Josh. My group of Seers may be young, but we have the power to protect you."

I started to move backward one step at a time, away from him. Perhaps Alex sensed my retreat, because he turned blindly in several directions, his arms flailing. I nearly shrieked when one of them hit me.

Or at least it *should have* hit me.

Like Felix's this morning, Alex's hand slid across me as if we hadn't touched at all. I didn't feel the pressure of the impact; and, judging by his expression, Alex didn't, either.

"Think about it, Amelia," he said, unaware of what

had just happened. "Come back to us, and we'll protect you. *I'll* protect you."

No, I whispered in my head. *You won't.*

Then I spun around, running out of the café before I accidentally answered him out loud.

Chapter
TWENTY-FIVE

I didn't speak to Gabrielle again for at least another twenty minutes.

When I approached her on the sidewalk, I complied with her request to go visible so that we could talk without sounding like disembodied voices. But otherwise I waved off her questions. Then I made some vague gesture, indicating that she could follow me on my blind quest to go anywhere that wasn't Café du Monde. And if she didn't . . . well, I didn't particularly care at that moment.

Eventually, my quest landed us in a small park with a double alley of oak trees, where I found myself pacing frantically. Gabrielle silently watched me for a few minutes and then plopped onto one of the park benches that line the alley.

"Told you not to go back in there," she stated bluntly. "I knew it wouldn't turn out well."

"What, so now you're a Voodoo priestess *and* clairvoyant?" I snapped.

When she held up both her hands in a gesture of surrender, I stopped pacing and rubbed my temples. Cringing, I slouched over and plopped next to her on the bench.

"Sorry," I mumbled, staring off in the distance at a small bandstand where a group of jazz musicians played Christmas music. "I just . . . I have no idea what I'm doing."

To my surprise, Gabrielle wrapped one arm around my waist and gave me a brief half hug. After she released me, she laughed.

"Like I do? I totally destroyed your afterlife in some last-ditch effort to find my parents. And so I wouldn't be . . . alone."

"Alone? You've got Felix."

She lifted one shoulder and then dropped it. "Felix is my brother, and I love him. Of course I'm glad we're together through all of this. But at some point Felix has got to get on with his life. Without me haunting it."

"Yeah," I said softly. "I know *exactly* what you mean."

"Like I told you earlier, I met those Faders once," she said. "After I became Risen, I still haunted my parents' graves at the St. Louis Number One, trying to figure out what to do with myself. One night last summer I ran into them, sort of aimlessly standing around what was probably one of their own graves. At first I was excited to meet them. I thought maybe they'd be—I don't know—good companions or something. But when that pirate guy tried to cop a feel, I decided that they weirded me out too."

I barked out an involuntary laugh, and she smiled slyly.

"Besides," she added, "old Nathan Hale was more my type anyway. I just love a man in uniform."

"The soldier?" I made a sour face. "You really *do* have bad taste in guys."

"Okay, okay," she said, laughing. "Let's just agree that the whole crew is pretty unsavory. Anyway, the real point of this story is that I'd basically given up on finding someone like me. Then you and Lover Boy walked into Marie's, and I thought, 'Holy hell, this is someone I might be able to hang out with.' And when you touched him? Forget about it—I was totally convinced that another relatively normal-acting ghost with special powers was *exactly* what I needed. But I really wasn't trying to ruin your afterlife, or break the two of you up."

"How did you know I left him?" I asked, frowning. "I mean, before Café du Monde?"

"You talked in your sleep last night. Believe it or not, Felix wasn't the only one keeping watch over you."

"Huh," I murmured, leaning back against the park bench thoughtfully. For a while I just sat in silence, absentmindedly listening to the jazz band. Then I turned slowly toward Gabrielle.

"Look, Gaby," I said, trying out her nickname, "I have no idea if I can trust you or not. To be honest, I've met so many people and been through so much in the last few days that I'm not even sure where to start. But if you're going to hang around me for an extended period of time, there's some things you should know."

Gaby leaned forward, her expression intent. "Whatever you can tell me that will help my parents, I'm all for it."

I gnawed at my bottom lip for a few seconds before nodding hesitantly. Then without further introduction, I told her *everything*: how I died and then reawakened when I met Joshua; how I fought off the wraiths when Eli sent them after Jillian; how I narrowly missed entrapment in the netherworld at the hands of the demons. I explained how ineffectual my attempts to reenter the netherworld had been since that dark night. Then I told her about all the things that I'd experienced in the last few days: Eli's warning; the bizarre dreams; the brief sighting of a handful of demons at the club.

I left out only one detail: what the Quarter ghosts had said about using a middleman to hand me over to the demons.

Despite my better judgment, I'd started to like Gaby. Maybe even trust her, on some level. But I couldn't be one hundred percent sure she wouldn't trade me to the darkness the second I dropped my guard. After all, it didn't escape my attention that the pirate had said "she" when referring to their intermediary.

By the time I'd finished my story, the sun had already shifted in the sky and the warm glow of late afternoon filtered through the trees. Gaby, who'd sat quietly while I talked, now leaned back against our park bench. She released a long sigh and began twisting a curl of her Afro around her index finger.

"Wow," she muttered. "And I thought my afterlife was eventful."

I snorted softly in agreement. Then, smiling just a tiny bit, I said, "Dude, you have no idea."

Gaby laughed and once again wrapped me in a half hug. Then she let me go, leaping to her feet. Still rapidly twisting her hair around one finger, she began to pace just as I had.

"So, how do we do it?" she mused. "How do we reopen the netherworld? I mean, without tracking down Eli or the demons and basically asking them for an extra house key."

I sighed and lifted my hands uselessly in the air.

"I wasn't kidding when I said I've had no luck at all. I stood at that river for *hours* every day, with no results. So what's the point? And besides, what are we going to do? Hitchhike back to Oklahoma to try again?"

Gaby shook her head. "We don't need to. You said it yourself: all the different parts of the netherworld are connected, according to the redheaded girl in your dreams. If we can get into one of those—what did she call it?—portals, then maybe we'd have access to all of them."

"It's an interesting theory. But where do we find another portal?" I asked.

She frowned, and her eyes flicked over my shoulder, to the south. "Actually . . . I have a pretty good idea," she murmured.

Abruptly, she lunged forward, grabbing my hand and yanking me to my feet. "Come on," she demanded, and began to hurry down the alley with me in tow.

"Where are we going?" I cried, stumbling behind her.

"You'll see when we get there," she called back over her shoulder.

"Why do I feel like you're always dragging me all over New Orleans?" I grumbled. Gaby laughed loudly.

"Because I *am* dragging you all over New Orleans."

Once she realized I would come along without duress, she released my hand and continued to walk briskly out of the park. I nearly had to run to keep pace with her as we moved west on the city sidewalks, back toward the Quarter.

I didn't ask her any questions; I didn't say anything at all. But when I saw a familiar awning up ahead, I slowed to a stop. After a few steps Gaby noticed that I no longer followed her. So she reversed course and crossed back to me.

"Amelia," she said impatiently, "it's, like, almost three o'clock. They've definitely gone home by now."

Without taking my eyes off Café du Monde, I nodded. "Yeah, probably. It's just . . . you know . . ."

"Yeah, I know." Her tone was surprisingly soft. Kind.

She gave me a brief moment to compose myself and then tugged gently on the sleeve of my jacket, urging me forward again. With a small breath for courage, I hurried alongside her, keeping my eyes glued to the sidewalk as I moved past the café. Even the beguiling scent of chicory couldn't entice me to look inside.

A few blocks away, Gaby slowed to round the corner of Decatur and Toulouse Streets. I followed her south on Toulouse, passing a tall building full of retail stores and crossing over a steep footbridge. At the bottom of the bridge, however, I skidded to a stop.

There in front of me, just behind a small building constructed to look like a lighthouse, stood the netherworld pavilion.

Or at least something that looked almost identical to it.

Through the open walls of the structure, I saw the gray water of the Mississippi River moving lazily past the Quarter. Underneath its roof, I could make out the shadowed angles of metal girders.

But the roof itself bore little similarity to the one in the netherworld. While the dark pavilion had a purplish, almost transparent ceiling, this structure's roof resembled that of Café du Monde, with its cheerful green-and-white stripes.

"The pavilion?" I whispered to Gaby.

"Not a pavilion, exactly," she said. "This is the entrance to the Toulouse Street Wharf, where all the old steamboats used to dock. The only boat still running from this wharf is the *Natchez*, though. When you described your dreams to me, I thought about this place. What do you think? Is it a match?"

Slowly, I nodded. "Yeah, this is pretty close. Not as bone-chilling creepy. But still . . ."

Gaby stared at the wharf with a thoughtful frown.

"Maybe this place is our portal into the netherworld. The dark pavilion going out over the water, the river that looks like an ocean from the right angle—it all fits the bill. We could always come back here tonight, to find out . . ."

When I shivered slightly, Gaby reached over and gave my hand a quick, reassuring squeeze. "But we don't have to do this if you don't want to," she added.

Of course, I didn't miss the disappointment in her voice. Still feeling a little unnerved, I shook my head.

"No, we need to try, and tonight's as good a time as any. But remember: we still have the problem of *how* to open it."

"I know." She sighed, leaning back against the rail of the footbridge. "I'm at a total loss. Part of me is tempted to walk right up to the Mayhew Seers and ask them to join me in some type of magical priestess-Seer council or something. But since we just got your heart to start beating again, we probably don't want to go break it one more time by letting you see Joshua. . . ."

Gaby hadn't even finished speaking before I jerked upright. My head whipped around toward her.

"Say that again?" I demanded.

She frowned. "We don't want you all mopey and pathetic tonight?"

"No, the other part. About my heartbeats," I urged.

"Um, that we just got it to start beating again?" she offered, obviously confused. "Or at least the resurrection spell makes it *act* like it's beating. I don't think it's actually pumping blood or anything. Maybe. I'm not exactly cutting myself to find out."

For the first time in hours, I flashed her a genuine, broad grin.

"Gabrielle Callioux, you're a genius."

"Of course I am," she gloated, and then frowned. "But would you mind telling me why?"

My grin widened. "In my experience, a ghost only hears a heartbeat when someone nearby is dying. That's how Eli tracked his other victims—how he knew the exact moment to take them into the netherworld. If *he* could hear dying heartbeats, don't you think other supernatural beings can? Say, for instance—"

"The demons," Gaby breathed. All at once she sounded excited. "You think if we trick them into thinking we're dying, they'll send one of their minions to take us into the netherworld."

"Exactly. But . . . there's still a big problem. When the redheaded girl gave me that vision of myself transforming, my heartbeat sounded pretty strong. That means we've probably got to find a way to make our heartbeats more sluggish. Make them sound like they're slowing down. And I obviously have no idea how to do that."

"But I *do*," Gaby said, beaming. "Marie has this off-limits potion that makes you seem like you're dead. She calls it zombie juice, but I know for a fact that it doesn't have the same effects as the stuff in Haiti: the trances, the deathlike stasis, and so on. It just slows the heart rate *way* down. It's still risky, of course. But since we're already dead . . ."

As she trailed off, I felt a little frisson of fear. But I shrugged it off and finished her sentence: "Since we're already dead, what's the worst that could happen?"

Gaby snickered nervously. "Totally. Other than blinking completely out of existence, right?"

"Right," I answered, placing my hands on my hips in an effort to look brave. Fearless.

For a full minute Gaby and I traded anxious, uncertain glances. Then she crossed over to me and threaded her arm through the crook of my elbow.

"Come on, Amelia," she said, flashing me a wicked grin. "Let me show you how to plunder a Voodoo priestess's secret stash."

Chapter
TWENTY-SIX

The outside of the Conjure Café looked just as shady today. Perhaps more so, when I gave myself time to think about its back room and what I planned to do there. As I stared up at the dirty front window—its grime so thick, it didn't even reflect the pinkish light from the sunset—I forced myself to flicker invisible. That precaution hardly eased my fears.

Gaby noticed my reluctant frown and nudged me with her elbow.

"Don't be such a wuss. We agreed to do this incognito,

remember? So as long as you don't freak out and go all visible on me, we should be fine."

"Sure. Fine."

I nodded mechanically and rubbed my palms on the thighs of my skinny-jeans. Why my hands chose *now* to start sweating again, I couldn't say. Gaby threw another glance my way and then, with a confident smile, opened the door of the Conjure for both of us to go inside.

Tonight, the restaurant had a few patrons: desolate-looking folks, faces sagging and eyes cast down to their unappetizing dinners. Not a single person glanced up when we entered, despite the fact that the door must have appeared to open on its own.

As I walked down the center aisle of the Conjure, I looked down at their food. Although their dinners smelled revolting, my stomach still churned with hunger. I felt it strongly enough that a nearby plate—covered in something that resembled a cross between lasagna and meat loaf—didn't look *that* bad. Now I really regretted dropping that second beignet at Café du Monde.

Feeling a bit disgusted with myself, I lowered my head and followed Gaby to the back of the restaurant, where she pulled aside the curtain to Marie's sanctuary. We ducked into the room, and Gaby let the curtain fall shut behind us.

As it closed, the limited light in the room all but

vanished. Tonight, no candelabra glowed, no incense burned. However impossible it seemed, the place was even creepier without the candlelight and tendrils of smoke.

After my eyes adjusted to the dark, I tucked my hands into my tiny jean pockets—something to do besides wring them, I supposed.

"Where's Marie?" I murmured softly.

I could just make out Gaby frowning into the darkness.

"Actually," she whispered, "that's a great question. She always lights candles and does a few spells before midnight mass. So . . . she *should* be here."

"Well, then," I said, rocking forward onto the toes of my boots nervously, "let's get what we need and hightail it before she comes back."

"Fair enough."

I could barely see Gaby's form as she crept across the room and slipped into the opposite doorway. In the pitch-black, she almost disappeared. Something about her disappearing trick bothered me. Frowning, I pulled one hand from its pocket and stared down at the muted quality of my own skin.

Then it hit me: we didn't glow in the dark anymore. While other ghosts shared that soft, eerie glow, Gaby and I looked like living people when the lights went out.

Just another ghostly power lost.

I shifted uncomfortably as Gaby rummaged around in Marie's secret-potion room. Something about our current mission felt wrong—something other than the theft and the very real risk of ingesting "zombie juice" in order to attract demons.

In fact, I sensed something wrong about this space, in particular. I could almost smell it in the dank air: tangy and bitter, like fear.

I'd leaned forward, about to tell Gaby to hurry up already, when I heard a soft groan somewhere behind me. I spun around, trying to find the source of the sound; but I couldn't see anything in the blackness.

The groan repeated, so I took a few blind steps backward.

"Gaby, someone's out here."

I fumbled behind me for a light switch, a flashlight, *anything.* Over the sounds of my floundering, I could hear ragged breathing from the corner nearest to me.

"Seriously, Gaby," I hissed. "Get out here and help me."

Cursing wildly, Gaby stumbled out of the tiny back room and started groping noisily along Marie's shelving. She must have found whatever she sought, because I heard a sizzle and then smelled the stinging scent of sulfur. Suddenly, candlelight flooded the room.

Gaby grabbed a lit candelabrum and held it up beside

me. When she did so, the glow of the flames fell into the corner of the room, and we both gasped.

A body lay crumpled in the corner. If not for the rasping breaths, punctuated by near-inaudible groans, I would have thought it was a corpse. But Gaby knew who it was on sight.

"Marie!" she cried, dropping beside the body and grasping at it. Of course, Gaby's hands passed over Marie without touching her. One of the many perks of being Risen.

Gaby growled in frustration. In the dim light, I saw her flicker out of and then into focus; going visible.

"Marie," she called out again, snapping her fingers next to the old woman's ears. "Marie, wake up."

Feeling incredibly unhelpful, I willed myself visible and then kneeled beside Gaby as she continued snapping. At that moment, Marie's head lolled back, just enough to reveal her face.

Her dark skin looked waxen, her cheeks sagged, and her eyes were bloodshot, unfocused.

Studying her closely, I frowned. For some reason, this hunched, sick old woman reminded me of someone. Maybe just because of their similar ages. Or maybe because of how fast they'd both deteriorated. Something about Marie's current state, and Ruth's appearance last night, itched at me. . . .

"Gaby," I murmured, lost in thought, "how would you go about drugging someone?"

Gaby's head snapped toward me, and her eyes widened in surprise. After a beat, she turned back to Marie and leaned close to the old woman's face. Gaby pulled in a sharp breath through her nose and then sat back on her heels.

"How is that possible?" she muttered, before jumping to her feet and bounding over to one of the well-stocked shelves. There, she sifted through items until she grabbed a small brown bottle, uncorked it, and took a deep sniff of its contents.

"Serpentwood. Holy hell. This stuff is a serious sedative. Mix a little bit of it with wine and it makes the drinker dizzy, confused—you name it. Marie never uses this crap, but over half the bottle is gone now." Gaby's eyes darted to Marie's slouched form and then back to me. "How did you know?"

I pressed my hands to my knees and stood. "Because I think someone's doing the same thing to Joshua's grandmother. And I'm pretty sure I know who."

Gaby raised one eyebrow in question, and I grimaced.

"Annabel Comeaux. Joshua's cousin. She may or may not be working with this Alex guy they've all been hanging out with, but . . . everything points to just her right now."

Gaby's eyebrow arched higher. "I find it hard to

believe that someone would poison their own grand-mother. And what about Marie? I heard Marie say she didn't even know the girl."

"But Annabel knows *her*. She's the one who told Joshua that Marie could help me. And . . . there's something else. Something I didn't want to tell you earlier."

I hesitated, studying Gaby one more time. Looking for some indefinable trait that meant I could trust her. Unsure if I'd actually found anything, I continued haltingly.

"Last night, when the Faders tried to take me, they wanted to give me to . . . an intermediary. Someone who would use me to secure their freedom. From the demons. And . . . they called the intermediary 'she.'"

Gaby frowned deeply.

"O-kay," she said slowly, reminding me—painfully—of Joshua. "You didn't tell me this earlier because . . . ?"

"Because I wasn't sure whether you weren't the one who was trying to trade me to the demons," I said, shame seeping into my voice. "And I *still* don't know for sure. But you didn't even know Ruth before you met me, so . . ."

As I trailed off, I saw hurt glimmer in Gaby's eyes. But she recovered quickly and shook her head. "It still doesn't make sense. Why would Annabel hurt her grand-mother?"

"I don't know," I said, shaking my head as well. "But

I'm betting Ruth would *strongly* disapprove of a Seer working with demons. I know for a fact that Ruth would do anything within her power to stop something like that."

"So would Marie," Gaby said, looking back at the collapsed form in the corner. "Maybe Marie helped Annabel, and then found out what she was planning to do."

"That's what I think too. But that still doesn't explain why Annabel told Joshua to bring me here."

Gaby bit her lip. "I don't know. I think we need to find a Mayhew, fast. Before we leave, though, let's make sure someone knows that Marie is sick."

"Absolutely. We shouldn't leave her like this."

I crossed over to the entrance, more than ready to let someone know and then get out of this place. But before I drew the curtain aside, I noticed Gaby pull another jar off the shelves. She dumped its contents into an incense burner, struck a match, and dropped the flame into the burner.

"Hawthorne," she explained quietly. "To protect Marie."

I pulled one corner of my mouth back. "I'd tell you that I don't believe in that stuff, but I guess I'm living proof otherwise. Well . . . sort of living."

"Amen," Gaby murmured, either to me or to the

Hawthorne offering. Then she turned away from it and hurried past me, obviously trying not to throw backward glances at Marie's huddled body.

Once we reached the relative brightness of the café, Gaby stormed over to the attendant, who still stood behind the counter flipping through what looked like an outdated *TV Guide*. Gaby cleared her throat, just once. When he didn't look up, she slapped her hands on the counter and shouted:

"Hey! Jackass!"

That certainly got his attention. His head shot up from the guide; and, after his eyes widened in momentary surprise, he scowled.

"What do you want?" he mumbled, no more pleasant today than yesterday.

"Marie's in the back, and she's really sick," Gaby said curtly. "Call an ambulance." Obviously unconvinced, the attendant sneered at Gaby. "Oh yeah? And just who the hell are you?"

"Mother freaking Teresa," she snapped. "What do you care? Now get back there and help her before she dies and you lose your cut of the weekly profits."

Finally, the threat of losing his paycheck seemed to break through his apathy. With a begrudging sigh, he turned to tromp over to the back room. At the same time, Gaby caught my gaze.

"Let's get out of here," she said through clenched teeth, "before he calls the cops on us."

I couldn't have agreed more.

I tried not to run out of the café, and I could tell that Gaby also struggled to keep a calm pace. The moment we stepped onto the outside curb, however, we both instinctively flickered invisible again.

Eyes wide with fear, confusion, I turned to face her.

"What's next?" I whispered, although I already knew the answer.

"What's next," Gaby said, "is a visit to the Mayhew family."

By the time Gaby and I crossed from Royal onto Ursulines, I wondered whether the entire population of New Orleans—living and dead—could hear my heart racing. Given the fact that I was now some kind of rare supernatural being, maybe my heart's pace would set it glowing again.

I struggled to keep my face impassive, expressionless. But every now and then my hands moved of their own accord, straying from my pockets to smooth my hair or straighten the hem of my tank.

It was stupid, with lives and afterlives in jeopardy, but I couldn't help feel uncontrollably nervous about staying invisible around Joshua again. It seemed like an impossible task, considering my current mental state.

While Gaby and I walked, I gave myself a quick pep talk. I could do this. I could follow the plan upon which we'd decided: while Gaby warned the Mayhews about Ruth's condition, I would find Annabel and confront her, reason with her if I could. I would *not* allow Joshua to witness that conversation if I could help it. I'd hurt him too much—hurt myself too much—to put him through *that*.

So many of the decisions I'd made this week revolved around my desire to protect him and the other people I loved. Although I certainly didn't love Ruth Mayhew, I couldn't let her suffer on my account, either. Not if my suspicions about her illness and who'd caused it were correct.

But as Gaby and I approached the Mayhews' town house, my heart sank. Once again, no lights glowed from the windows; everything appeared shut tight. We'd missed them.

Then I remembered: today was Christmas Eve. The Mayhews always ate dinner at a fancy restaurant the night before Christmas.

I turned toward Gaby. "They're not here. I forgot; they eat Christmas Eve dinner at one of the restaurants in the Quarter. You think they might be at Felix's place? What was it called—Anthony's?"

"Antoine's," she answered, shaking her head. "But there are, like, a bazillion restaurants open tonight. There's no guarantee we'll find them, even if we go to every single one."

I groaned in frustration and looked up at the house. Then I peered more closely at it.

There, at the drawing-room window, I could see the faintest glow seeping between the slats of the shutters.

"Gaby, I think someone's actually home," I hissed. Without waiting for her response, I stalked over to the front window. I prepared to kneel beside it so that I could try to peek through the slats when my feet made a strange, crunching sound against the concrete. I looked down and then took an involuntary step backward, away from the substance that had made the noise.

Gray Voodoo dust.

Thick clumps of it, looking like someone had sprinkled it without taking the time to crumble it properly. A patch of dust ran all along the base of the window and then extended unevenly across the front stoop and the base of the dining-room window.

The line hadn't been there last night while I'd waited for Joshua to sneak away from his family gathering. So someone must have sprinkled the dust recently. Judging by its shaky pattern and the intermittent breaks in the trail, someone with unsteady hands had poured it.

Maybe someone who'd been drugged.

Whoever had placed this dust on the ground, its power no longer affected me. My feet had crossed it effortlessly when I crouched to kneel. Taking advantage of this new ability, I placed my hands against the shutters and leaned close to the window.

"Ruth?" I called out loudly, fighting the urge to whisper. "Are you in there? If you are, I know that you're sick. I'm here to help; I promise."

"Amelia, look," Gaby whispered, waving me over to the front door.

Apparently the Voodoo dust didn't affect her, either, since she'd obviously crossed the line too. Facing the door, Gaby pressed one finger against the wood, and the door moved slightly inward. I pressed myself up and walked over to her.

"Someone left it open," she hissed.

We exchanged reluctant looks and then, together, pushed the door open farther.

Inside, the foyer was almost completely black except for the glow from a single candle on a small side table. But even in the dark I could see the outline of a figure sprawled across the entry rug. When it groaned, I released an enormous sigh of relief.

"She's still alive," I breathed, dropping beside Ruth's collapsed form.

"This is so not a good night for the elderly," Gaby murmured. "Should I call an ambulance or what?"

"Ambulance. Definitely," I said, nodding. "I think I saw a telephone in the corner of the drawing room."

Gaby crossed behind me, and soon I heard her muted voice as she spoke with an emergency service. Listening to her speak, I had another thought.

"Hey, Gaby," I called out. "Is there a pen and paper nearby?"

"Um, maybe. Why?"

"I need you to write down Joshua's cell phone number and call him next. Tell him the family needs to get home, fast."

Gaby hesitated before responding, "You sure you want me to do that?"

I bit my lip, wavering. Then I answered, "Yeah, I'm sure."

I called out Joshua's phone number, struggling a bit with the sequence since I'd never had a reason—or the ability—to call it before tonight. Then, with a distinct sense of déjà vu, I willed myself visible and leaned in close to Ruth.

"Mrs. Mayhew. Ruth," I whispered. "Can you hear me?"

She must have been in better shape than Marie, because her eyes fluttered open. Then, through labored gasps, she spoke.

"You . . . came to finish this?"

"No!" I cried softly. Immediately, I felt offended, but I forced myself to continue. "No, Mrs. Mayhew, I'm trying to help you. We think you've been poisoned—we're calling an ambulance right now."

"W-we?"

"My friend Gaby and me."

"Ghosts," she hissed.

"Yes," I said defensively. "Good ones, who wouldn't poison you. In fact, we're so good, we're going to wait for the ambulance to arrive. Then we're going to wait until your family gets home so we can tell them what happened. Then I'm going to kick the crap out of your granddaughter for needlessly complicating my afterlife."

Ruth shook her head, obviously confused by my rant. She reached up a shaky hand and tried to grab my arm. But of course her hand slid away without touching me.

"Not her. Him."

Although her voice faltered, her eyes were suddenly clear. For the first time in days, she appeared lucid. Sharp, like the Ruth Mayhew I knew and feared.

"Him," she repeated, obviously struggling. "He's been . . . giving me . . . herbs. For . . . my headache."

For some reason, my ears began to ring. From dread, perhaps. Or from realization.

"Alex?" I whispered.

Ruth nodded and then sank back to the floor from the effort.

So Alex *was* involved.

Whatever they'd planned for me tonight, Alex and Annabel clearly wanted both the Seer and Voodoo factions weakened, so much so that they'd drugged their leaders past the point of stupor and into danger. This wasn't just a bad sign for Marie and Ruth—it was a bad sign for *me*.

I absently ran a hand over Ruth, trying to comfort her in some way without being able to touch her. Then I looked up at Gaby, who now leaned in the doorway of the drawing room, finished with her phone calls. Her expression told me she had no idea what to do next, either.

"Maybe we should get out of here?" she suggested. "Or at least go invisible before the paramedics show up?"

"Maybe," I hedged, tossing another worried glance at Ruth, who appeared to have slipped back into unconsciousness.

Still feeling that inexplicable urge to soothe her, I reached out one tentative hand and let it hover above her. I felt unsure. Lost.

From the first moment Ruth saw me, she hated me— probably still did, right now. Despite all that, I couldn't leave her here unattended. At least Marie had someone waiting with her until an ambulance arrived. . . .

I had just turned back to Gaby, ready to suggest that we wait a few minutes longer, when something tugged roughly at my core. It yanked me backward, toward the door, just at the moment the edges of my vision started to blur. I shook my head, trying to fight both sensations, but they just grew stronger: tugging so hard that I could barely stay upright, blurring so much that I felt the sudden rush of a headache pounding at my temples.

"Amelia?"

Gaby's frightened voice sounded faraway, muffled by distance. Which made absolutely no sense, considering the fact that she stood only a few feet away from me.

"Amelia, what's happening to you? You're . . . fading," she seemed to whisper.

"I'm what?"

I could hardly speak, hardly concentrate through the headache. I forced my neck into an arch and tried to lock eyes with Gaby. But before I could do so, black flooded my vision completely.

I blinked rapidly against the darkness, and, strangely, the effort worked.

My vision began to refocus—hazy at first and then clearer, until finally I could see just as well as I had before the headache.

But in that brief interim a few things had changed.

Before, the narrow halls and low ceilings of the Mayhews' town house had surrounded me. Now I kneeled outside, staring up at a partially enclosed structure that looked an awful lot like the Toulouse Street Wharf.

Then there was the issue of my company. Gaby had disappeared, as had Ruth Mayhew. In their place, a small group of people faced me: Hayley, Drew, Jillian, Annabel . . . and Alex.

Grinning widely, he took one step forward. "Merry Christmas, Amelia. And welcome to the séance."

Chapter TWENTY-SEVEN

Before I even processed what he said, I'd bolted upward and retreated back across the small footbridge leading to Toulouse. Alex mirrored my movements, walking forward as I edged backward.

Behind him, the young Seers stood motionless. Except . . .

All four of them appeared to sway on their feet, as if they were trying to stay vertical during an earthquake. Keeping most of my attention on Alex, I tried to study them more closely from the corner of my eye.

Each of them—Hayley, Drew, Annabel, Jillian—looked dazed; bleary-eyed and unfocused. On the ground, just to the right of Drew, I could see a wine bottle tipped onto its side. Just one bottle, though, which bothered me. After all, the young Seers seemed way too drunk for only one bottle of wine shared among the four of them.

Alex caught me staring at them, and his smile widened. In a voice far calmer than I actually felt, I said, "You drugged them, too, didn't you?"

He nodded slowly, still pacing closer to me. "That was the last part of our summoning ritual—the part they didn't know about. Well, *one* of the parts they didn't know about."

A corner of my mouth twisted in confusion. "Why drug people who are part of your plan . . . whatever your plan is?"

"They've been helping me," Alex explained in an amiable tone. "But none of them really knew why, or what for. Jillian spied on you in Wilburton, especially when you'd go visit the river. She also told the Quarter ghosts where to find you on your first night here, while I performed a few spells to sabotage your materializations. But *Jillian* thought I was helping you find some new friends so you'd leave her brother alone. When you didn't join those ghosts immediately, I moved on to Annabel, who sent Joshua to the Conjure Café at my suggestion. But Annabel just wanted to help him help you. After that, Hayley negotiated with the Quarter ghosts for your capture, but she stupidly thought it was a staged exercise in her Seer training—just practice in speaking to ghosts, not an actual attempt to trap you. And Drew—well, he's relatively useless. But I needed his strength for the summoning spell tonight."

"That's . . . what pulled me here tonight," I said haltingly. "Isn't it?"

He nodded, chuckling. "They think we were calling you back, for Joshua. Because he's been *so sad* since you left."

He said the words "so sad" in a singsong tone, mocking Joshua. Mocking me. Perhaps I should have responded with something biting, but I'd temporarily fallen mute.

A chill shuddered its way down my arms. Obviously, I'd suspected Annabel's involvement. But *all* of them? Jillian guiding the Faders to Jackson Square, where Alex must have redirected me; Hayley inadvertently acting as the Faders' intermediary; Annabel sending me to Marie for . . . what, I wasn't sure yet.

If none of the young Seers meant to harm me, then what exactly was going on? When I demanded that Alex tell me as much, he chuckled again.

"Jillian followed you today, Amelia, to this very spot.

Even though you learned how to hide yourself from us, Jillian's learned to *listen*, too, just like the rest of them. And you know what she overheard? Your plans to open a place I also want to enter very, very badly."

I frowned, shaking my head fiercely. "The . . . the netherworld? I don't even know how to enter it, and I've been trying for months. Besides, I think you have to be *dead* to do that."

Alex had been staring absently at the swaying, disoriented Seers. But when he heard my last statement, his head whipped back toward me. The scant moonlight fell across his face and made it look bleached and gaunt, like a skull.

"That's a small price to pay," he whispered, "for what I want."

I couldn't help but gasp. "You *want* to die?"

He merely flashed me a wide smile in response.

It was a ghastly, freakish expression, devoid of humor and warmth. Smiling like that, he really *did* resemble a skeleton.

A strangled noise wormed its way out of my lips. "You're *insane*," I hissed.

He let out a slithery sort of laugh. "I'm also a descendant of Delphine LaLaurie, and those two traits have gone hand in hand for over a century."

"Who did you just say you were?"

Something about his ancestor's name bothered me. Something familiar . . .

Alex wandered casually back to the other Seers, who still swayed drunkenly on their feet. As he walked, he pressed his hand on their shoulders, pushing them downward. One by one, they dropped messily into seated positions on the concrete, which I could see had been lined with Voodoo dust. Part of their summoning ritual, probably.

While I watched him, Alex began to speak blandly, as if he were recounting a dull piece of history.

"In the eighteen hundreds," he said, "a wealthy Quarter woman named Delphine LaLaurie tortured and murdered many of her slaves. But before that happened, she had several daughters. I'm descended from one of them."

"And?" I said, struggling to keep my voice steady. The more calmly he spoke, the edgier I felt.

"*And*," he emphasized, "there are certain things that she passed on to her heirs. Most historians don't know this, but Delphine heard voices. Voices that told her terrible things and drove her mad. Doctors would label it schizophrenia today; but I know better, especially since I hear them myself. Have, ever since I was a child. That's why it's been so easy to teach these little Seers to hear them, too."

"The voices of the dead," I stated flatly. "Delphine heard them, and so do you."

Alex snapped his fingers, grinning. "You're a smart cookie, Amelia. Couple that with your special talents, and it's no wonder they want you."

"'They'?" I asked, though I already knew the answer.

"The ones I want to serve. The ones who talk to me, sometimes, when the ghosts are quiet."

"Demons?" I breathed. "They . . . speak to you? And you want to *serve* them?"

"Of course I do. They're the only family I have."

"But I thought you said—"

"I did," he snapped, his smile gone. "I did have a family. And the *minute* I showed my genetic inheritance, they had me diagnosed as a schizophrenic and shipped off to a 'home.' Just like my grandfather, great-grandmother, and on and on for generations in one long line of heart-warming family betrayal."

When he finished, he laughed almost giddily, as if he'd just told a joke.

If I didn't previously grasp the danger of this situation, I certainly did now. Not only had Alex tricked and drugged the other Seers—not only did he want to work for the most evil things I'd ever met—but he was also certifiable. I had to keep him distracted while I tried to think of some way to help the drugged Seers.

"That must have pissed you off," I murmured, moving

a centimeter closer to him on the footbridge. "When your family betrayed you like that."

His smile returned in the form of a smirk.

"That description doesn't do it justice, Amelia. The only reason I stayed focused, and determined, was because of the encouragement I got from the voices. The voices were my only comfort—my only family—for years. They promised things would be better one day; they told me stories about what I was destined to do. Because of them I'm the first LaLaurie to trick the doctors into thinking I took my meds and got better. I even got the home to release me in time to go to college. At the voices' command, I moved back to New Orleans and enrolled at Tulane. I used a fake name for a while, trying to get back to my roots, while I made a few sacrifices to the darkness. I even tried to kill *myself* for them, but they just weren't ready for me yet. That changed, though, when I met Ms. Comeaux here."

Alex paused to jerk Annabel's head back roughly by her hair and then let it flop forward. Although she didn't react, the movement looked like it hurt, and I winced for her.

"And what about Annabel is so special?" I asked.

"Her? Nothing." He laughed. "Aside from possessing a gift that I thought could help me open the dark world without killing myself."

I sneered. "What, your *'family'* didn't teach you the

secret handshake to get inside?"

Alex shrugged, obviously not bothered by my tone. "Those I want to serve require sacrifice. Effort. That's why I swallowed my pride and tried to break into the Seers' coven here. But of course, every Seer freaked out the second I started hinting at what I wanted. So I had to try a different route. I introduced myself to the newest member—Ruth Mayhew—and worked her connections to a group of young, untrained Seers so that I could put my own coven together."

"And you told them you were *helping* ghosts," I said. "So that *they* would accidentally open the netherworld for you."

Alex made a slight clicking noise with his tongue and winked at me. "You got it. Nothing like telling a group of inactive, malcontent Seers that their boring elders are the bad guys and that they can be the good guys. It worked like magic. Except for one small part: these useless idiots couldn't open a barn door much less the netherworld."

"So why torture them like this?" I gestured to the line of Seers at his feet. "Why keep them around at all?"

Alex smiled darkly and pointed a long, thin finger at me. He didn't say anything, but I caught his meaning well enough.

"Me," I concluded. "You wanted them to help you get me."

"Exactly. When Jillian told Annabel about what you did the night you saved her, Annabel told me. Then I told the voices. I guess it goes without saying that they were very excited by that news. It seems as though you'd avoided them once before; it seems as though they want you even more, now."

I felt a very real wave of nausea roll over me, but I fought it. I swallowed hard, shoving all of my internal shrieks of warning and fear to a back corner of my brain so that I could keep Alex talking.

But as I tried to come up with a distracting topic, my mind kept blanking. Like I was taking some kind of test for which I'd studied so hard that I'd started to forget the answers. Finally, I settled on something inane to ask him.

"So you . . . so you said you changed your name for a while. Alexander Etienne is, what? A real name? A fake one?"

"That's the name I was born with—the name I've been using with all of you. But in college I starting going by my middle name, and the last name of my ancestors. In college, I went by—"

"Kade LaLaurie."

The groaned name startled me, and I spun around to see whoever had spoken. To my surprise, I saw Gaby standing behind me. I had no idea how she'd found me, but I felt a huge surge of relief that she had.

But Gaby didn't look relieved to see me. She didn't look at me at all. Instead, she stared past me to Alex. Her eyes were wide, her mouth rigidly set, her fists balled at her sides.

"Gaby?" I whispered. "You know him?"

Still without looking at me, she nodded. "Oh, I know him. He's my ex-boyfriend. The one who killed me and my parents. The one who should be dead."

Chapter TWENTY-EIGHT

W hen Alex—Kade?—laughed loudly, my gaze whipped back up to his.

But Alex wasn't looking at me, either. Instead, he'd locked his eyes on Gaby's. As he stared at her, his grin became even crueler, if that was possible.

"Missed you too, babe," he taunted. From the corner of my eye, I saw her shiver.

"How the hell are you alive," she growled. "And why the hell are you here?"

Alex laughed again and started to pace behind the

young Seers, who still sat dazed on the concrete. As he strolled, he patted each of them roughly on the head like he was playing some bizarre game of duck, duck, goose.

"I'm alive," he explained, "the same way Felix is still alive; despite my best attempt to die and take all of you with me, I survived. That's the 'how.' And the 'why' is because you and your parents just weren't a good enough sacrifice to satisfy the darkness."

Suddenly, Gaby's frozen exterior melted. Before I had time to stop her, she'd lunged forward, racing across the footbridge toward Alex as if she intended to tackle him and claw his eyes out.

Alex's amused expression didn't change. When Gaby had only a few feet left to cross, he reached calmly inside his jacket, pulled something out, and pointed it at her.

The second I saw moonlight glinting off the silvery object, I screamed.

"Stop! Gaby, stop!"

Thankfully, Gaby obeyed. She skidded to a stop a mere foot from Alex, her eyes now trained on the gun in his hand.

I raised both of my hands in a gesture of surrender and hurried to Gaby's side. I'd just grabbed her arm to restrain her from doing anything reckless when she shook her head and smiled, looking as though she'd just come out of a trance.

"Can't kill me twice, Kade," she purred at Alex. "So who's the gun for?"

Despite the fact that Gaby had just blown a major hole in his defense plan, Alex flashed her a serene, close-lipped smile.

"It's for her," he whispered.

Then, holding his arm straight, he swung the gun toward me, just for a second, before pointing it downward.

At Jillian.

My entire body went cold. Before I'd even formed the words in my mind, I heard them snarling their way out of my mouth.

"Point that gun somewhere else or I swear I'll find a way to grant your wish and kill you myself."

Alex locked his cold eyes onto mine. With his free hand, he reached across and cocked the gun. Then he used it to gesture significantly at Jillian.

"Correct me if I wrong," he said, "but I think I've got the upper hand here. I guess you could *try* to wrestle the gun out of my hands and shoot me yourself. But you can't even touch living people now, so that might be a little difficult."

I gritted my teeth. "How do you know that?"

Keeping the gun trained on Jillian, he broke eye contact with me and gazed over at Gaby. "Oh," he murmured,

"I've kept pretty close tabs on my sweet ex-girlfriend. I mean, can you blame me? Just look at her."

"You bastard," Gaby swore. "You never loved me at all, did you?"

Alex faked a sad face. "No, babe. I didn't. But I *did* love your history: granddaughter of one of the most powerful Voodoo Raisers in history. Too good to be true, really. I bet you didn't know your gifts were as inheritable as mine."

"My what?" Gaby whispered, looking simultaneously confused and horrified.

Seeing her expression, Alex laughed. "God, Gabrielle, really? You didn't honestly think you came up with that resurrection spell all on your own, did you? Voodoo is in your blood—the spells you found at the Conjure weren't Marie's; they were created by your own grandfather. It's your birthright to raise the dead. Why do you think I choose *you* to sacrifice to the darkness? The dark spirits wanted your gifts, even if those powers were still latent when you died."

"So you . . . you really were trying to kill me."

For the first time since I'd met her, Gaby's lip quivered. Alex, however, remained unaffected by her show of emotion.

"Of course I was trying to kill you—and I succeeded. But Felix woke you from the death-fog before I could finish what I'd started. I changed back to my old name to protect myself and reenrolled at school. But I still spent two years stalking you, trying to get you alone so that when I either killed myself or got the Seers to reopen the netherworld, I could take you into the darkness with me. I even sent the Quarter ghosts after you once; but, unsurprisingly, they failed. Still, I've got to give it to you—you really helped me out by Raising yourself. Without the ability to dematerialize at will, you're a much easier target."

"So why didn't you just do it then?" Gaby spat. "Why not capture me yourself and get it over with?"

Alex sighed, sounding as though Gaby had brought up a sore subject.

"Like I said, it wasn't as easy as I thought it would be. The spirits were getting restless. Then, right around the time you transformed, Jillian began to call Annabel to talk about Amelia. After that, the voices demanded that I get them *both* of you. Which was just so much *work*. First, I tried to get Amelia to join the Quarter ghosts so that they could hand her over to the darkness themselves. Then I tried to get her to trust me, which obviously wasn't going to happen. So I just went ahead and set you two up with each other. I knew you couldn't resist making yourself a buddy, Gabrielle, after that failed encounter you had with the Quarter ghosts. And now, here you both are—two birds with one stone!"

As he finished, I gave Gaby a sidelong glance. Right now she looked too stricken to speak. So I sniffed imperiously and addressed Alex for the both of us.

"Well, thanks for confirming what your parents already knew: you're a demonic nutbag."

Finally, my words struck a raw chord. Glaring at me, Alex reached down and jerked Jillian up into his arms. Holding her against him with his gun-toting arm, he used his free hand to pull something out of his coat pocket.

I saw the glistening liquid inside the syringe, right before he plunged the needle into her arm.

"No!" I shrieked, but it was clearly too late.

"Oh, don't you worry," Alex sang, tossing the emptied syringe aside. "I'm not hurting her—I'm just raising the stakes."

Jillian's upper body flopped limply forward. As Alex hefted her up and across his gun-free arm, her head lolled backward upon his shoulder. She moaned softly, and her eyelids fluttered.

"What did you do to her?"

"I woke her up," he stated simply.

"She doesn't look very awake to me."

Alex's nasty grin returned. "Give her time."

As if to illustrate, he slid his arm aside and let Jillian

go. But just as she started to slump to the ground, he wrapped his fingers in her hair and yanked her to her feet. The pain must have sped up her awakening, because her eyes—now much clearer—darted around frantically. As she steadied herself, her gaze landed on Alex's crazed smile.

And the glint of his gun.

The second she saw that, Jillian grew very still—motionless except for the panicked rise and fall of her chest. I wanted to run to her, to jerk her away from him, but the gun hung in the air like an impassable barrier.

Alex gave her a quick appraisal. "Welcome to the party, Jillian. I was just telling the girls here about how you overheard them discussing how to open the netherworld by slowing their fake heartbeats. So . . . Amelia, Gabrielle, get to it."

"We don't even know if that will work," I said. "It was just something we were going to try to do to help our parents."

Gaby must have recovered, because she finally stirred beside me. "You remember my parents, don't you, Kade?" she snarled. "Those two really great people you killed?"

When Alex smirked, I snarled, too.

"Now that I think about it," I growled, "I don't care if it does work. Because we're not helping you."

Alex laughed and pulled Jillian closer. Without taking his eyes from mine, he pressed the barrel of the gun into her sternum. "One or both of you needs to slow your heartbeat now. Otherwise I'll just have to slow Jillian's."

For the briefest moment I thought about calling his bluff. Telling him to shoot at me and prove that the gun was loaded. But when a tiny squeak escaped Jillian's lips, I couldn't believe I'd even considered the idea.

Of course that gun was loaded. This boy had been plotting this moment for years; he wouldn't forget a tiny detail like that.

"Don't," I whispered, defeated. "Don't hurt her. I'll . . . I'll do it."

Gaby shot me a stunned look. "Amelia, we can't give him what he wants."

"We *have* to, Gaby. I have to. I can't let him hurt her."

Still pressing the gun to Jillian's chest, Alex seemed to swell with triumph. I kept my eyes locked on his and reached out one hand to Gaby.

"The zombie juice," I said softly. "I know you have it."

For a long second she didn't move. Then, with painful slowness, she reached into the pocket of her cape and removed a tiny bottle. I waited for her to press it into my palm. When she didn't, I turned to face her.

I found her eyes darting alternately between me and Alex. Her gaze lingered on him the longest, and I automatically knew why. After all, she'd loved him once. It must have hurt on a number of levels to see who he really was. To see the horrible thing he'd become.

And now he stood in front of her again, threatening not only our afterlives, but also the life of another young girl.

Gaby's eyes met mine again, and inexplicably, she nodded.

Then, in a flash, she uncorked the bottle with one thumb and slung back its entire contents.

I shrieked again, diving forward so that I could *shake* the liquid out of her, but she had already swallowed all of the zombie juice. She flung the empty bottle to the ground, and it shattered against the concrete.

"Why did you do that?" I cried, still shaking her shoulders violently despite the fact that the damage was already done.

Gaby kept her face stoic as she brushed my hands off of her.

"I'm not going to screw this up for you again, Amelia. Besides, this is my fight."

"No, this is *my* fight. The demons want me. They always have."

"I guess they want both of us," she said quietly. "Now shut up so we can hear what happens."

I opened my mouth to protest but then clamped it shut

instead. What *could* I say? How could I thank her for what she'd just done? Slowly, gently, I took one of her hands in mine and gave it a light squeeze.

Then we fell silent. Listening.

For a while nothing happened. The only sounds I could hear were my ragged breathing and Jillian's occasional whimper.

Then, suddenly, it began: a faint *thud, thud, thud* emanating from Gaby's rib cage. She heard it too, because her eyes widened and flickered down to her chest.

Alex apparently couldn't hear it. Behind me, he made a small, impatient sound.

"Well?" he demanded. "Is it happening?"

I didn't answer him. I just couldn't.

By now Gaby looked terrified, and for good reason. With each passing second, the thudding from her chest became louder. But despite the volume of the beats, the silent, empty spaces in between them grew longer.

If those silences continued to grow, then soon her heartbeats would stop altogether. And neither of us had any idea what would happen to her then. After all, how do the dead die?

Although I couldn't answer that question, I had a pretty good idea about what was happening to our surroundings. Although it was already a chilly night in the French Quarter, the air was growing colder. Almost unbearably so, to the point where my teeth began to chatter with each falling degree. Shadows started to lengthen and change, shifting from their normal grays to more livid, sinister purples.

"The dark world is opening," Gaby whispered, "isn't it?"

I simply nodded and tried not to shiver in the frigid wind. I sucked in another panicked breath; but before I had time to release it, I heard terrified cries coming from behind me.

I spun around and found the young Seers looking far more alert than they had a few seconds ago. By now Annabel had doubled over, moaning in pain, while Hayley and Drew fumbled closer together.

Shocked, I looked up at Alex. He hadn't moved, nor had he removed the gun from Jillian's chest.

"How did you wake them?" I demanded.

To my surprise, Alex shook his head. "I didn't. I only brought one syringe. I don't know what's woken them— maybe the cold."

It made a terrible sort of sense: the unnatural chill of the dark world would force them awake, force them to see this horrible place. That explanation, however, didn't fully pacify me.

"Let them go before everything shifts over," I demanded. "The demons just want Gaby and me—this isn't Jillian's fight, or theirs."

Alex shook his head again. "I have no power over that, Amelia. The voices said that if I found a way to open their world and bring you to them myself, they'd reward me by letting me inside. They must be letting in any living person who happens to be nearby."

Feeling another wave of terror, I glanced back at the young Seers. Although they were awake now, none of them looked like they were in any shape to get away. Not before the netherworld descended completely.

Still, I had to try. I let go of Gaby's hand and dropped down beside Annabel.

"Run," I whispered urgently. "Annabel, you have to run."

She turned her head, staring up at me with bleary eyes. "Amelia?" she croaked.

I realized, dizzily, that this was the first time she'd actually seen me. Hayley and Drew must have seen me too, because they repeated my name in a chorus of confused voices.

And at that moment, another confused voice repeated it as well.

"Amelia?"

My head shot up; and, in the span of one horrified second, my eyes met Joshua's.

Chapter
TWENTY-NINE

Joshua stood at the highest point of the footbridge, staring down in disbelief at the scene in front of him.

"Run!" I screamed, bolting up. "Joshua, you have to—"

But it was too late. Before I'd even finished my sentence, the world shimmered and changed.

All at once, frost spread in a glittering sheet across the landscape. The metal structure above the wharf groaned in protest as its roof dissolved and its girders turned lurid shades of red and purple. Even the footbridge changed, melting beneath Joshua until it disappeared—swallowed whole by a dune of cold, wet sand.

"Run," I whispered, finishing the useless command I'd tried to give Joshua before the darkness closed in on us.

I didn't know whether Joshua heard me or not. But when his eyes connected with mine, I saw a glimmer of understanding in them. Although he'd never seen it, Joshua had listened to me describe this place enough times to know where we were.

Alex obviously knew too.

"Yes!" he crowed, laughing giddily. "I'm home! I'm home."

I angled my body so that I could see him better. But the maniacal glow in his eyes made me recoil. The sheer joy of being here made him shiver uncontrollably. If he didn't look insane before, he certainly did now.

And I wasn't the only one who noticed.

Jillian also watched Alex's excited display closely. Taking advantage of his momentary distraction, she wriggled out of his grip. Unfortunately, she made a crucial mistake once free from Alex's grasp.

"Joshua!" she cried, stretching out one hand to her brother, who was more than an arm's length away.

In a flash, Alex grabbed a hank of her hair and jerked her back to him. Then, for extra measure, he lifted the gun into the air and brought the butt of it down—hard—onto her right temple. When she crumpled under the blow, Joshua screamed from the bridge.

I'd never heard him say such a foul word. The odd thing was, I'd screamed the same word.

Joshua and I moved simultaneously, scrambling to rescue Jillian. But Alex anticipated that reaction. With both hands gripped to the gun, he pointed it directly at Joshua and stared me down.

"Tell him to stay back or he's dead," Alex told me. "You don't want his life to end in this place, do you?"

I froze.

"Joshua," I muttered, holding my palm up to him. "Joshua, honey, stay back."

He froze, too, although his mouth curled up in anger and frustration. I tried not to look at him, keeping most of my attention focused on Alex instead.

Moving slowly so that he wouldn't do anything retaliatory, I circled around, placing myself between Joshua and Alex. My eyes flickered down to Jillian—cowering on the ground, bleeding but thankfully still conscious—and then I looked back up at Alex.

"That was unnecessary," I said.

"Trust me, it wasn't. I think all of you are underestimating the fact that I'm in control."

"I know you are. And Gaby and I are staying, I swear. But at least let Joshua get Jillian," I pleaded. "At least let him take her and his cousins away from here."

Alex frowned, studying me. Then, unexpectedly, he nodded.

"Fine. Joshua can drag them a few feet back. But I'm not promising that the dark ones won't take them too. And . . . Jillian stays right here. As leverage."

"That's not fair."

Alex glared at me. "Life's not fair, Amelia. I know that better than anyone."

"Then show a little mercy, for God's sake."

While Alex and I argued, Joshua crept over to the young Seers and helped each of them half crawl, half stumble away across the sand. Although Alex didn't try to stop them, I could tell he watched them closely.

Someone else—someone Alex had temporarily forgotten about—unfroze too.

Apparently Gaby had recovered, because she now moved carefully, almost out of Alex's line of sight. As I emphasized the unfairness of the situation to Alex, I saw Gaby crouch next to Jillian, whisper in her ear, and then drop something into her open palm.

Midsentence, Alex finally noticed the exchange at his feet. Scowling, he pulled the gun away from Joshua and directed it down at Jillian again.

"Back off, Gabrielle. Or I *will* shoot the girl."

Gaby did as he said, sneering at him as she crawled away from Jillian. Once Gaby had moved far enough away, Alex shook his gun at Jillian.

"Stand up," he ordered her.

Still bleeding, Jillian rose shakily. She faced Alex but kept her eyes on the ground, like she couldn't bear to look at him. Unaware of her fear—or enthralled by it—Alex reached out to brush a strand of her hair away from the bloody mess at her temple. When she flinched, he laughed.

"Why?" she asked softly, finally staring up at him.

"Because you hated her the most," he whispered, "so you questioned me the least."

"But . . . I liked you."

Alex had just opened his mouth to answer when Jillian's expression abruptly changed.

With a feral shriek, she wrenched her hand upward, shoved something into his open mouth, and then sealed his lips by planting her palm against them. She dug her fingers into his cheeks, and he flailed, grabbing at her with one hand and waving the gun with the other. I saw him swallow reflexively, right before his gun went off.

After that, everything seemed to happen at once.

Alex, who I thought would recover and fire again, stumbled backward instead. For a moment he simply looked furious. Then, without warning, his eyes rolled backward and he began foaming at the mouth.

While strangled sounds ripped their way out of his throat, Jillian clambered backward toward her huddled family. Gaby, however, didn't move. Which was strange, considering the fact that blood had begun to soak through the middle of her cream-colored shirt.

She'd been shot.

I gasped, dropping beside her on the floor of the pavilion. "I thought you said we couldn't get hurt!" I cried out, my voice harsh with fear for her.

"Don't worry about me right now," she said, but I didn't listen. I clutched at her abdomen, trying to staunch the flow of blood with my hands. Yet Gaby managed to stay perfectly calm, swiping away my hands without taking her eyes off Alex.

"Seriously, Amelia, stop it. It doesn't hurt. Besides, you don't want to miss the show." She cocked her head toward the pavilion, and the corner of her lips lifted into a frightening smile.

Almost involuntarily, I followed her gaze to the pavilion into which Alex had stumbled.

Although he remained upright, Alex had fallen to his knees as he convulsed. In the still moments between convulsions, his cold gaze found Gaby's. He must have been conscious enough to see her smile, because his eyes momentarily widened before they rolled completely back in their sockets and he collapsed.

Suddenly, I could hear another heartbeat, thudding loudly and wildly: Alex's, I was certain. But his heart didn't get the chance to ease slowly into death like mine had. Instead, it stuttered more frantically, its individual beats growing indistinguishable until they became one long thud.

Then, abruptly, they stopped.

The following silence was almost palpable compared to the preceding frenzy. In the stillness, Alex didn't twitch or gasp. He didn't move at all.

He was dead, as far as I could tell.

Everyone—the living Seers, the dead Risen—held their breaths as we watched his motionless body. Then we sucked in a collective gasp when Alex sat back up.

Slowly, horrifyingly, he opened his eyes and glared at Gaby. He grabbed for his gun, which had dropped to the ground when he fell.

But now he couldn't seem to grip it. He frowned, turning away from Gaby to stare harder at the gun. He swiped his hand over it once, twice, and then growled in frustration.

Gaby barked out a brittle laugh. "Having a little trouble, Kade?"

His cold gray eyes bore into hers again. "Did you . . . kill me?"

Gaby's grin widened. She raised her hand and began twirling another small bottle in her fingers.

"Technically," she said, "Jillian killed you. But I'm the one who gave her the ground oleander seeds, so I guess you can blame me."

Alex screamed inarticulately and fumbled for the gun again, with no success.

Watching him, Gaby *tisk*ed several times.

"That gun isn't going to do you much good, Kade. Besides, you've already killed me twice." She paused, glancing down at her bloody shirt. "Well, sort of killed."

"Gaby?" I whispered, reaching hesitantly for her. By now I couldn't hear *either* of their heartbeats. "Gaby, what's happened to you?"

Keeping her eyes on Kade, Gaby lifted one shoulder in her usual flippant shrug. "Who knows? I feel numb again, so maybe I'm not Risen anymore. But that would be a small price to pay to condemn Kade to this hell."

"You want to condemn me, Gabrielle?" he snarled. "Then come condemn me."

"Gladly," she spat.

She suddenly wrenched out from under my hands and flew at Alex. He bolted up as well, meeting her mid-lunge. Within seconds the two of them had tangled together, snarling and clawing at each other's throats.

I leaped up too, ready to intervene in their fight. But then I hesitated.

I glanced back at the young Seers, who'd gathered around Joshua like he was their protector. Which, given their hazy mental state, he probably was.

Despite the fact that she still looked disoriented, I caught Annabel's eye. "Form a circle," I commanded her, "and do an exorcism on Alex. *Now*."

"I don't know how—," she started, but I cut her off.

"It doesn't matter. You're the oldest, and I know you've seen your grandmother perform an exorcism before. So you have to try."

When she frowned reluctantly, I took a threatening step in her direction.

Almost immediately, Annabel nodded in agreement. She began grabbing at the other Seers and arranging them in a circle on the sand. While Alex and Gaby shouted obscenities behind me, I watched as the Seers—including Joshua and Jillian—clasped one another's hands and started to mimic Annabel's chanting.

Somewhat satisfied, I turned back to the brawling ghosts. To my horror, I found Alex straddling Gaby, with his hands wrapped tightly around her throat.

"Let her go!" I screamed.

But a screeching noise from somewhere high above us drowned my voice. I gazed upward and felt my heart go cold.

Because a hundred black, birdlike shapes filled the bruised sky. And they'd started to dive right for us.

Chapter
THIRTY

I didn't have time to warn anyone before the black shapes descended, some dropping to the wet sand and some landing noisily inside the pavilion.

Within seconds of landing they transformed, shifting from indeterminate forms to humanlike figures with white-blond hair, sleek black clothing, and bloodless-pale faces.

They were glorious. Hideous. And each of them turned their black, pupilless eyes on me.

One of them—a male with a cleft chin and thick

jaw—broke rank and strode over to Gaby and Alex. The male placed one hand gently on Alex's shoulder and when Alex glanced up, gave the boy a sharp-toothed grin.

Instead of being horrified, as any sane person would be, Alex immediately rolled off Gaby and dropped at the creature's feet.

"Thank you," he mumbled, touching the hem of the creature's pants. "Thank you for allowing me inside. Thank you."

The creature smiled benignly down at Alex's show of gratitude. Then it affected a worried frown.

"Oh, child. It seems that you've gotten yourself killed."

Alex shook his head forcefully. "But not before I brought them here. Both of them, sir. For you."

"Ah, excellent," the creature murmured. He looked down at Gaby, who was still gasping and clutching at her throat, and then up at me. When his black, pupilless eyes locked onto mine, he smiled again.

"Truly excellent." He glanced back at his companions. "I believe one of you is here for this one?"

Another demon stepped out of the crowd and approached us casually, moving as though she had all the time in the world to claim her prize. When she came close enough for me to see her features—long white-blond hair, angular bone structure—I hissed in recognition.

It was one of the demons from High Bridge. The female who had swooped down like a Harpy and dragged Eli with her into the darkness below the bridge.

And now she was here for *me*.

"Well, hello again," she said pleasantly. "You're finally home with us, yes?"

"This isn't my home." My voice sounded far stronger than I felt.

The female demon laughed, and at first her laughter seemed beautiful—crystalline and sparkling. But listening to it made my ears ring painfully. When I clapped my hands over them, she laughed even harder.

"Please stop," I begged, nearly unable to hear my own voice.

To my surprise, she listened, and obeyed.

In fact, she was silent as the grave when she flew, lightning fast, to stand in front of me. Now only inches away, she flashed me a ghastly, needle-sharp smile. Then she *touched* me—wrapping her frozen, skeletal fingers around my wrist.

I tried to scream. But once again I didn't have time. I hadn't even opened my mouth when the fiery glow burst forth across my skin like a torch.

This was what the demons wanted; *this* was what they'd

hunted me down to claim.

But when the red-orange glow ignited, the female demon shrieked, dropping my arm and scuttling away from me like an insect. She ducked behind her companion, peering around him only to hiss angrily at me.

I should have felt relief that she'd let me go. And I did.

I also felt very, very confused.

After all, her companion from High Bridge hadn't feared my glow; he'd coveted it. So why on earth was *she* suddenly afraid of me?

Frowning, I stared down at my arm. There, where she'd gripped me, was a steaming handprint. It looked like she'd burned me, which didn't make any sense since I didn't hurt.

Then I realized: *I'd* hurt *her*. The handprint on my arm wasn't a scald—it was the spot where something icy cold had touched something fiery hot.

I peered back at the female demon and saw that she cradled her burned hand in the uninjured one. Her male companion cast a scornful glance in her direction and sighed.

"Stop cowering and take her," he commanded.

"You take her," she spat, "if you think it looks so easy."

He sighed again and shook Alex off his feet. The movement roused Alex from the thankful prayers he was still mumbling, and he stared reverently up at his new master.

"I assume you can touch her now, child?" the demon asked him. When Alex nodded, the demon gave him a stern look. "Then if you truly want to serve us, you'll take her."

Alex glanced back over his shoulder and flashed me an eager smile. In response, my glow flared brighter. Although Alex winced, his smile didn't falter.

Unlike the female demon—unlike Eli—Alex obviously wasn't afraid of me. He stared me down like prey, rising from his knees and stalking over to me with clenched fists.

I clenched my fists too, trying to think of how I would fight him. My pulse began to race as I came up blank. Could I burn him as I'd burned the demon? Could I hurt him as I'd once hurt Eli? Could I still act as a poltergeist and make this place quake?

Alex was stalking even closer, and I still hadn't come up with a reasonable solution. I raised my fists to the sides of my head and groaned in frustration. Abruptly, Alex froze in place and mimicked me, clutching his head and groaning even louder.

At first I thought he was trying to mock me, but the longer he moaned, the more I doubted it. His groans turned into yowls, and his face contorted in pain.

Something or someone was hurting Alexander Etienne.

I peered past him to his would-be masters, who were staring at us in disbelief and confusion. A few of them even started to hiss defensively. Over the sounds of their hissing and Alex's groaning, however, I heard another sound. A sound I'd forgotten to track since the demons arrived.

I spun back around to find that the young Seers still held hands, still chanted. Their murmurs had lost that initial edge of reluctance and were now coursing through the air with urgency. With strength.

Even better, the darkness around them had abated. Through the purple shadows of the netherworld, I could see a faint, ghostlike outline of the footbridge. And in the sand beneath the Seers, I could see traces of concrete, shifting like seaweed underwater.

Whatever spell the Seers wove, it hadn't just brought Alex to his knees—it had also torn through the veil of the netherworld. Maybe even weakened the magic that held this place together.

My head whipped back around to Alex and his masters, and I grinned in triumph. Although Alex continued to moan and whimper, the demons unfortunately looked far more composed now. They still hissed and spat in my direction, but one by one their glinting smiles returned. Watching me intently, they began to cluster together.

Gathering . . . for something.

"Gaby," I murmured, despite the fact that I held their full attention, regardless of my volume. "You need to get over here. *Now.*"

Still lying on her back where Alex had left her, Gaby rolled to one side, coughed, and then began to crawl slowly toward me. Without taking my eyes off the congregating demons, I crouched low and stretched out one arm to her.

"Just a little bit farther," I urged her. "Come on. . . ."

She'd crawled several feet, with only a few more to go, when the demons began to screech again. In a flash they shifted back into indeterminate shapes and launched up in the air like startled ravens. But as they climbed higher in the sky, I realized that they were anything but startled: they were arcing, curving back around for a swift, final descent.

"Gaby!" I cried, far past the point of urgency now. "Hurry, please."

I took my eyes off of her for a moment, casting a panicked glance over my shoulder at the Seers. They still chanted in their circle, unaware of the shrieking army above them. Thankfully, even more elements of the living world had grown stronger around them. By now the footbridge was fully visible, and I could see the vague outline of several buildings in the French Quarter.

The netherworld was thinning all around the Seers.

But not around me. Here it was as dark and bleak as ever.

I turned back to Gaby and then leaned forward to close the gap between us. She reached out to me and I grabbed her hand, pulling her close. We huddled together a few feet from Alex—who still gasped and moaned—and stared up in fear at the wounded sky.

After a heavy silence, Gaby cleared her throat.

"Hey, Amelia," she whispered hoarsely. "Do you know you're on fire?"

Despite everything, I laughed. "Yeah. I don't think it'll be much help right now, though."

From the corner of my eye, I saw her grin. She wrapped one arm around me and gave me a tight half hug. I read the gesture well enough: if we were going to be swept into the darkness, at least we would go together.

"Friends till the end," I whispered with a wry smile.

Gaby snorted. "God, you're corny."

I laughed again and moved to give her my own half hug. But suddenly, she slipped from my arm and began crawling backward across the dark sand like a crab.

Except . . . she wasn't crawling. She was being *pulled*.

Alex must have fought through the pain of his exorcism, because he now had his arms wrapped around

Gaby's shoulders as he dragged her across the sand. I scrambled to grab her legs, but she was struggling so hard against Alex that I couldn't hold on to her.

The three of us were a tangle of flailing limbs and shouted threats, but no matter how hard I fought, Alex appeared to be winning. Perhaps he felt emboldened by his masters since they were only seconds away from attack.

Everything seemed lost: Gaby, Joshua, the young Seers, my own afterlife.

The unfairness of it all—the eternal unfairness of this existence—seared me to my core. I threw back my head and screamed up at the night.

And at that moment my fiery glow literally *exploded*.

The fire was uncontrollable. Inescapable.

I wrenched my eyes closed, shutting out the impossibly bright light until I could sense through my eyelids that it had dimmed—at least, enough for me to reopen my eyes.

The dark beach looked as though an atom bomb had gone off on it. Sand flew back in waves, showering against the pavilion, which rocked in the gale from the explosion. In an instant, the night seemed to turn to day, glowing brightly like a real beach in the sunshine.

The explosion had done another amazing thing too. Something I smelled, before I saw its source; it was a nasty chemical scent, like burning tar and singed hair.

Or singed feathers.

That's what the black bits of ash looked like as they fell around me: burned feathers, crisping and flaking all over the slate-colored sand. I looked up to the sky for their source and gasped.

Where a hundred bird-shaped demons had been, there were now less than twenty . . . and most of them had flown higher in the sky, away from this beach.

Away from *me*.

Their screeching sounded different now, more plaintive and wounded. The remaining demons gathered together in the sky and then shifted course, toward the black waters of the river.

To go home?

Was that possible? Were they actually retreating?

Another look around me suggested that the answer was yes. All along the beach and across the pavilion, images of the living world were filtering through the purples and reds. Even when my glow began to dim, I could still see the real Toulouse Street Wharf fighting its way through the veneer of the netherworld pavilion. I could see the concrete reappearing beneath me and the lights of the Mississippi River boardwalk shining through the darkness.

Gaby saw them too. She grinned up at me from Alex's

arms, her blue eyes radiant in the gloom that still surrounded her.

"It's closing again," she breathed happily.

"Yeah," I agreed as the boardwalk became more solid around me. "And you're in what looks like the very last patch of netherworld. So—"

"So let's speed this up," she finished, before digging one sharp elbow into Alex's ribs. He grunted from the blow and immediately released her so that he could clutch at his chest. Gaby took advantage of his moment of weakness to wrench away from him and scramble toward me.

She reached out one hand, ready for me to tug her to safety, when a shout made both of us pause.

"Gabrielle!"

Both of our heads whipped around toward the voice. From the corner of my eye, I saw Gaby's smile blossom when her brother crested the top of the footbridge, which was now fully visible.

Almost involuntarily, she swung her arm around, reaching for Felix instead of me.

And in that moment Alex pounced.

He wrapped one arm around her shoulders and tangled the other in her hair. With vicious force, he yanked her back into a diminishing shadow, which was folding in on itself so rapidly that they almost didn't fit into it.

Felix and I screamed at the same time, and I could hear his feet pounding the pavement as I dove forward.

But we were both too late.

As the murky portal constricted, I caught one last glimpse of Alex's twisted smile and Gaby's bright, horrified eyes. Then the dark patch closed entirely, lingering as a shadow for just a heartbeat before disappearing in the wind.

After that, everything was silent.

Only one sound disturbed the wharf: the ring of a nearby church bell, chiming twelve times and then echoing hollowly across the water.

Even when the bell stopped ringing, my hand still hung in the air, clawing at nothing.

After who knows how long, I slowly turned my head. Felix crouched beside me, his hand also grasping the void. He dropped his arm first, letting his palm smack loudly on the concrete. When I lowered my hand and placed it next to his, he kept his eyes downcast.

"How much did you see?" I whispered.

Felix shook his head like he was trying to clear it. "Just the end. Just the part where she . . ."

He trailed off, and I nodded. "So . . . you *do* know."

"I know."

We fell silent again. Like him, I turned to stare at the

ground, where I absently studied the cracks and imperfections in the concrete. Finally, I stirred.

"How did you know?" I asked him. "Where to find us, I mean?"

"Joshua," he stated flatly.

That answer surprised me. I frowned and glanced back up at Felix. He looked up, too; and when his electric blue eyes met mine, I felt a pang in my stomach. His eyes were so much like Gaby's.

"Joshua?" I repeated.

Felix sighed and ran one hand over his face before explaining.

"His family was eating at Antoine's when Gaby called him about . . . his grandmother, I think? After he got the call, Joshua freaked. He got up to leave and accidentally ran into me on his way out. I guess I look—
looked—enough like Gaby to send up a red flag, because he confronted me. I convinced him that Gaby and I hadn't exorcised you, and then we decided to go find his cousins—apparently they'd gotten permission to skip dinner to go to some 'party,' which turned out to be . . . this. I guess we're lucky his sister told him where they were really going, even if she didn't tell him what they were really *doing*. Anyway, we saw his cousins first, on the other side of the bridge. Joshua had just made it across when he disappeared into this weird shadow. And

then . . . well, you know the rest."

He finished weakly, hanging his head again. I didn't press him to tell me more, and he didn't ask me to detail the things he'd missed while waiting for us to reappear.

Which is why his next question surprised me so much.

"It was Kade, wasn't it?"

Gnawing on my lip, I nodded again, albeit more hesitantly this time. "His real name was Alexander Etienne. He was a Seer. And insane."

"No surprise there," Felix muttered.

The corner of my mouth lifted into what was probably a harsh smile.

"Well, you'll be happy to know that she killed him. Even if he did take her, she at least got the chance to exact *some* revenge."

Felix continued to stare at the ground. "Was it . . . a painful death? For Kade?"

"Looked like it, yeah."

"Good," Felix growled.

It was the first real emotion he'd shown. But his fierce expression disappeared almost as quickly as it had arrived—replaced once more by a blank mask. As I watched him recompose himself, I heard murmurs behind us coming from the direction of the Seers. I craned my head, looking over Felix's shoulder at the base of the footbridge.

The first pair of eyes I caught were Joshua's. Before I could read the thoughts in them, they darted away, toward Jillian. I followed his gaze and saw her struggling to help Annabel to her feet. Although Annabel looked rough, Jillian looked rougher—dirty and exhausted and bloody. Next to them, Hayley and Drew helped each other stand. Once all of them were upright, they turned unsteadily to face me.

I stared back at them blankly, until I realized: they were looking to me for instruction. For guidance.

I shook my head, mystified. Could these people make *any* decisions without a leader?

"Go home," I told them softly, knowing that they could probably hear me across this short distance. "Go home now."

Accepting my command without question, Annabel nodded. Then she pulled away from Jillian to join Hayley and Drew in propping up one another. Without a second glance at me, Annabel wrapped her arms around the other two Seers and they hobbled off together, disappearing over the footbridge and back into the Quarter.

Jillian waited until they'd vanished to stumble over to her brother. She kept her head bowed—either exhausted or contrite, I couldn't tell.

At first Joshua gave her a cold glare as she approached. But once she'd made it within arm's length, he pulled her in for a brief but fierce hug. After that, the two of them looked back at Felix and me.

"What do you want to do, Amelia?" Joshua asked quietly.

I glanced at Felix, then at Jillian, and then, finally, at Joshua. So softly I almost couldn't hear myself, I said:

"I want to go home."

Chapter
THIRTY-ONE

The four of us moved quickly down Decatur, trying to avoid the large crowds pouring out of midnight mass at the cathedral by Jackson Square. Once we reached the Lower Pontalba, Joshua and Jillian waited outside while Felix led me into the building.

Together, Felix and I walked in silence up the dark stairwell, down the narrow hallway leading to the apartment, and into the living room. There he clicked on a few lamps and then wordlessly signaled me to follow him out of the room.

When we passed the slipcovered couch—the place where Gaby had told me what I'd become—a hard lump formed in my throat. I tried to swallow it away as we moved toward Gaby's bedroom.

Inside, the room already felt colder. Emptier. I flipped on the overhead light and leaned against one of the bed-posts while Felix crossed over to the closet. He opened the doors and, even from here, I could see the top of the clothing pile on the floor. It was disorienting. To think that I'd stood here with Gaby only this morning—it felt like an entire lifetime ago.

After a few minutes the closet light went dark and Felix stepped out of it, carrying a brown-and-gold-checked overnight bag.

"Here," he said roughly, handing it to me. "Gaby would want you to stay fashionable. Besides, I don't think a few items of clothing and some shoes are going to make much difference."

I took the bag from him without protest, but in the few seconds when it touched both our hands, I hesitated.

"I can stay," I said softly, "if you want."

For a moment, emotion glimmered in Felix's eyes: sad-ness, regret, assent, uncertainty. Too much for someone to handle all at once. He closed his eyes, shutting those thoughts off from me, and shook his head.

"I'm not staying here, either. I only lived in this place to make Gaby happy. Now that she's really . . . Now I think I'll take my buddies up on their offer to be their fourth roommate. Anyway, it's safer to just get out of this apartment, right?"

"Right," I said with a humorless laugh. "Getting arrested for squatting would be—"

"The perfect end to a great couple of years," he finished, giving me a smile that seemed far more broken than bitter. We fell silent again, neither of us sure how to follow that statement.

Finally, I nodded in the direction of the disastrous closet. "So, should we clean this place up?"

"Nah, don't worry about it. I'll pick everything up before I leave. You should just go ahead and get back to the Mayhews."

"But, Felix, this is a lot for one person to clean—"

"Don't worry about it," he interrupted quickly, shaking his head. "Besides, I think I just need some . . . time. Alone."

I didn't imagine the crack in his voice when he said the word "alone." I didn't want to think about why that word had a particular significance to him now. I tucked my bottom lip between my teeth, nodded, and said, "I understand."

Without thinking, I reached out to give Felix's hand

a comforting squeeze. But I withdrew before we made that numb noncontact again. After all, he didn't need a reminder of the barrier between us—a barrier that existed because of his sister's magic.

Magic that didn't exist anymore. Not in this world.

Shouldering the overnight bag, I stepped aside so that Felix could lead me into the hallway. I tossed one last glance at the bedroom before he shut off the light, plunging it into darkness and out of my life forever.

Again, Felix and I remained silent as he walked me to the entrance of the apartment; but when we reached the front door, I paused.

He looked away from me, ducked his head, and began fumbling in his coat pockets. He pulled out a wadded-up restaurant receipt and a pen emblazoned with the word "Antoine's." Using his hand as a flat surface, Felix scribbled something on the back of the receipt and then handed it to me.

"My cell phone number," he explained. "In case you ever need to reach me."

"Thanks," I said, tucking the paper into my own pocket. Then I lowered my head, frowning as I studied the rounded toes of my boots. Finally, I looked up, caught Felix's gaze, and held it.

"Just so you know," I whispered, "in the end she was my friend."

Felix nodded, answering me in a heavy, raw voice.

"Just so you know, you were her friend too."

After that there was nothing more to say.

Felix pulled back the door for me, keeping it open so I'd have some light while I descended the stairs. At the bottom of the stairwell, I took a final glance up at him. But I couldn't see anything except a tiny glow of light high above me.

I sighed quietly and then pushed open the door that led outside. I rejoined the Mayhews and, without saying a word to one another, we moved in unison back out to Decatur.

On our walk to Ursulines, Joshua stayed on my right side. I tried not to look at him, since I had no idea what I would say or do once I did. Jillian walked on my left, and from that vantage point I could see the nasty cut where Alex hit her with the gun. It looked painful, jagging its way along her temple and into her hairline. A gory mess still covered her cheek. Jillian hadn't wiped it clean, probably because she just couldn't seem to stop apologizing to me.

Most of our exchanges started with her proclaiming "I didn't mean for anyone to get hurt." Then I answered with a quiet "I know."

Or Jillian tried the following route: "All I wanted was for my brother to be happier. To live his life like a normal guy."

To that, I again answered, "I know."

During these brief conversations, Joshua stayed quiet, even when I quickly explained my new state of being. Every now and then he would point out a less-crowded path along the sidewalk, where late-night revelers stumbled along singing Christmas carols and toasting each other from plastic cups. Otherwise, Joshua remained completely silent. He only spoke once we'd turned onto the much quieter Ursulines Avenue.

"We need to think up some excuse to get Amelia home with us," he murmured. "*Before* we leave for Oklahoma."

"I can just go invisible again. Maybe just hang out somewhere out of the way . . ."

"I think I've got it covered," Jillian said. "Just let me do the talking."

She hurried the few remaining feet to the Mayhews' town house; but before she could knock on the door, I called out to her.

"Jillian, wait."

I jogged over, unzipping my overnight bag with one hand. Reaching into the opening, I tugged out the first piece of fabric I could grasp. Then I stretched out my hand to offer Jillian a bundle of pink silk.

"Unless it's part of your plan," I said, "you'd better wipe off all that blood."

She gingerly touched the cut at her temple and withdrew blood-coated fingertips.

"Gross," she muttered. With her clean hand, she took the fabric from me. She'd nearly brought it to her head when she paused and stared wide-eyed at the silk.

"Am I crazy," she asked, "or does that label say Dior?"

I shrugged. "Just think of it as the world's most expensive compress."

Jillian cringed, but after another moment's hesitation, she pressed the fabric to her temple. She held it there for a while, making sure the blood flow had been completely staunched, and then started to dab the mess clean. While she did so, she smiled at me.

It was a macabre sort of image: a pretty young girl holding a bloody shirt to her head and smiling. Although the sight was odd, it was also one of the few times I'd seen Jillian smile genuinely. And she smiled at *me*. Even in this strange moment, I couldn't help but feel that she and I had just reached some kind of milestone.

"Thanks," she said, wiping away the last traces of blood. I don't think I imagined the many layers to that one word: a thank-you for the compress, sure, but also for saving her life. Again.

She wadded up the fabric and then looked up at me. "Don't suppose you want this back, do you?"

I held up both hands. "It's all yours, Jillian. But maybe you should just stash it somewhere for now?"

"Good idea." She wiped off her hands and then tossed

the ruined silk into the alley next to the house. Looking far more presentable now, she walked over to the front door and knocked. While we waited for someone to answer it, I allowed myself a covert peek at Joshua.

In the darkness, I couldn't see his eyes. But I could tell he'd given me a sidelong glance too. I saw his hand flex toward me, just once, before the front door burst open and a riot of noise from inside the house poured into the street.

Rebecca Mayhew stood in the doorway, looking almost as frantic as the crowd of people rushing around in all directions behind her. For a second she seemed baffled by our presence—particularly mine. But then she shook her head and pulled Jillian in for an enormous hug.

"Your grandmother is in the hospital," Rebecca murmured into her daughter's long hair.

"I know," Jillian said, her voice muffled against her mother's shoulder. "Joshua told me."

Rebecca released Jillian so that she could breathe, but then wrapped one arm tightly around her daughter again. With Jillian thus secured, Rebecca raked her free hand through her black hair and looked back into the house. Now that her children were safe, she was obviously torn about what to do or who to help next.

"Mom," Jillian said, trying to regain her mother's attention. "What exactly happened to Grandma Ruth?"

Rebecca looked back at her daughter and sighed wearily.

"Well, apparently, your grandmother took some herbal supplements to get rid of her headache. But I guess she just made things worse, since whatever she took is pretty toxic. Thank God she was conscious enough tonight to realize that something was wrong and she needed to call an ambulance. She must have given Joshua's cell number to that female EMT—that's how we knew to come home from Antoine's and why Joshua went to find all of you at that party."

Beside me, Joshua squirmed uncomfortably. *Gaby* had called him, not an EMT. And his cousins hadn't gone to a party—they'd conducted a séance under the direction of the boy who had poisoned their grandmother. I knew Joshua well enough to sense how conflicted he felt: he was relieved that his mom didn't know the true story, just as much as he probably regretted the complex web of lies that we'd have to keep weaving.

Unaware of her son's dilemma, Rebecca continued explaining the official version of tonight's events. "Your dad's at the ER right now. The doctor told him Ruth should be fine in a few hours—she just needed lots of fluids and rest since she had to get her stomach pumped."

From the corner of my eye, I saw Joshua wince. At that moment I felt a fierce stab of regret that I hadn't plunged Alex—or Kade, or whoever he was—into the darkness myself. Now it was *my* hand flexing, toward Joshua's. But of course, I pulled it back to my side before we could touch. Before he even noticed what I'd done.

"So what's the plan?" he asked his mother.

"Your dad is going to bring Ruth home whenever they release her sometime tomorrow afternoon." Rebecca checked her watch and sighed again. "Actually, some-time today. When Ruth gets home, we'll do Christmas then. After that, I think the entire family has agreed that we're all going to go home early, the morning after Christmas, to give Ruth some quiet time to rest."

Both Joshua and Jillian nodded, relieved—I think—to just get home. Jillian's expression changed, however, when her eyes met mine.

"Mom," she said, still holding my gaze, "this is my really good friend Amelia. You remember me talking about her?"

Rebecca gave me a vague look that was a cross between a welcoming smile and a frown of uncertainty. "Amelia . . . Yes, your name sounds familiar."

Beside me, Joshua stifled a cough. He knew very well why my name sounded familiar—because he'd been whispering it inside her house for months. Luckily, Jillian kept a cooler head and continued with the fabrication.

"That party we were at tonight, Mom? It was at

Amelia's boyfriend's house. See, she's home-schooled in Wilburton, and she met her boyfriend online. He lives here, so her parents let her ride down here with some friends to visit him. But it turns out he's actually a total jerk, and the party . . . it didn't end so well—"

Rebecca didn't wait for her daughter to finish. She released Jillian and strode over to me, stopping less than a foot away and studying my face closer. Only when she crossed her arms did I think about how I must have looked: pale, gaunt cheeks; tangled hair; dirty couture clothing.

"Did someone try to hurt you, honey?" Rebecca asked, low enough that only Joshua and I could hear. I could just see Joshua's jaw clench, probably because he knew who'd tried to hurt me. I was weak enough to hope that Alex's actions toward me had made Joshua want to hurt him back.

I nodded slowly, fighting to keep my eyes forward, on Rebecca and not on her son. "Yes, ma'am," I whispered. I didn't have to lie, and for that I was grateful.

It looked as if Rebecca might reach out to touch me, and I flinched. That would have been the cherry on this already-strange sundae: the first time I meet the mother of the boy I love, I'm covered in cuts *and* she can't touch me. Not the first impression I'd dreamed of making.

Thankfully, Rebecca must have read my reaction as one of understandable shell shock. She gave me a close-lipped, sympathetic smile.

"Would you like a ride home with us, honey?" she asked softly.

"Yes, ma'am," I repeated. "I'd really appreciate it."

Rebecca jerked her head toward the door. "Jillian, why don't you take your friend upstairs and help her get cleaned up? Amelia, honey, you'll have to excuse the chaos inside—we're having a minor family crisis."

"I understand crisis, ma'am."

Her sharp eyes studied my clothes one more time. "Yes. Looks like you do."

With that settled, Rebecca nodded lightly and then turned to go back inside, giving Jillian's shoulder a gentle squeeze as she passed.

Once her mother had disappeared from view, Jillian caught my eye. "You can . . . stay in my room tonight. If you want."

She'd started to accept me a bit, but I still heard some lingering reluctance in her tone.

Before I could tell her that I'd just find a spare corner and go invisible, Joshua—who'd been silent this entire time—finally spoke.

"Amelia can take my bed. I'll sleep on the floor."

Jillian's eyes darted back and forth between Joshua and

me, like she was watching a tennis match. Which was ironic, actually, considering the fact that neither Joshua nor I seemed to breathe, much less move.

"Well," Jillian said, after an awkwardly long pause, "you kids have fun with *that* conversation. I'm calling dibs on the second-floor shower 'cause it's the biggest. So . . . good night."

She gave me one last meaningful look before ducking through the open doorway and into the house.

After she'd gone, the silence drew out like a knife. Joshua and I both stood rigid, motionless in the flickering light of the gas lamps. The air between us felt charged, but by what, I wasn't sure. Anger? Desire? Uncertainty?

Eventually, Joshua spoke. "The joke's on Jillian—the hot water went out this morning on the second floor, and *only* on the second floor."

"Should we tell her?" I asked. I took a sidelong glance, and saw the corner of his mouth lift slightly.

"And spoil the fun?" he said. "Shame on you, Amelia. I thought I knew you so well."

"Don't you?"

When Joshua didn't answer, I turned to find him watching me intently. Catching my lower lip between my teeth, I finally allowed myself to meet his gaze.

The second our eyes met, my poor, mixed-up heart did

a little flip. It had only been one day—albeit an incredibly long, afterlife-changing day—but I couldn't believe how much I'd missed his eyes.

We stared at each other for a long, quiet moment until Joshua gestured with one arm toward the door.

"The third-floor shower really is the best one in the house. *And* it works. Promise."

I couldn't help but groan happily. "A shower sounds amazing. You have no idea how badly I've missed those."

Joshua grinned broadly and waved one hand in front of his nose. "You have no idea how badly you need one after tonight."

"Hey." I laughed, and then fought the urge to give him a playful nudge.

After all, I couldn't nudge him, even if I tried. And besides, given the events of the past few days, it felt strange to laugh with him again. Not wrong, necessarily. Just strange.

"So," I said quietly, fidgeting with the edge of my tank. Flattening the hem against my thighs although that might have been the only portion of the tank that had survived tonight unscathed.

Joshua noticed my anxious movements, and his grin widened. "So . . . upstairs?"

"Definitely," I said, nodding with a confidence I didn't actually feel.

As I followed him into the house, I didn't know whether to feel relief or regret about how we were interacting right now: calm; normal; without any discussion of the wild few days we'd just had. Was that a good thing? Bad? My mouth twisted in frustration as I walked behind him in the foyer. I was so lost in thought, I almost didn't look into the crowded dining room.

But at the last second I turned and saw Annabel sitting at the head of the dining table, flanked by Drew and Hayley. Annabel had her head in her hands, massaging her temples in an effort to get rid of what must have been a wicked serpentwood hangover. The moment our eyes met, she frowned miserably. Drew and Hayley followed her gaze; and when they saw me, their expressions mirrored Annabel's.

For a second I thought about storming over to them and delivering some whispered rebuke about how stupid they'd been to trust Alex. But I just couldn't bring myself to blame them. Nor did I have the energy to rush over and wrap them in a forgiving hug, either. So instead, I gave the group a very slight nod and moved on through the foyer, toward the stairs that Joshua had already started to ascend.

By the time he and I hit the second landing, my thighs stung from the effort of the climb. Too much adrenaline burned tonight, too much running and fighting had left me absolutely spent. Wiped of almost every last drop of energy.

When we finally made it to the third floor, I leaned heavily against the wall outside the bathroom door. Joshua moved around me to turn the doorknob, but I placed my hand on the wood just above his.

"That's okay, I'll do it."

He paused and then lifted one eyebrow, staring intently at me. "So . . . it's true?"

I released a ragged sigh. I expected this conversation—in fact, I *wanted* to have it—but I wasn't sure I had the strength to discuss everything right now.

"It's true. I'll tell you everything, if you want."

Fortunately, Joshua shook his head no. "Later," he offered. "After you've had time to rest."

"Thank you," I said, sighing in relief. "Just give me a chance to take a shower and change. Then we can talk."

He nodded, moving away from the door to go toward the stairs. Before he descended them, Joshua looked back at me.

"Amelia?" he called, so quietly I almost couldn't hear him. Despite his hushed tone, and despite my crushing exhaustion, the sound of my name on his lips still made my heart wrench.

"Yes?" I whispered back.

Joshua opened his mouth, about to say something,

then shut it and shook his head. "Never mind," he whispered. "Enjoy your shower."

Without a backward glance, he took the stairs two steps at a time, as if he needed to get away from me. Fast.

Watching him, I frowned.

Normally, I wouldn't have let him go. I would have run after him, confessed everything in a jumbled rush, and then waited breathlessly for his answer.

But tonight it took every ounce of my energy to stay upright long enough to twist the knob and push the door open with one shoulder. I dropped my overnight bag in the hallway, closed the door behind me, and turned to face the tiny, white-tiled room.

Inside, the bathroom smelled pleasantly of soap and lavender. I took a deep breath of the scent and felt my muscles relax for the first time in hours. Then I pushed back the shower curtain and groaned. Staring blankly at the bath fixtures, I couldn't remember which was hot or cold, and they weren't labeled. I gave up and began spinning the knobs ineptly until the hottest combination of water came pouring out of the faucet. Then I switched it to the shower spout and stepped back as steam began to fill the bathroom.

For a while I just stood in the steam, letting it envelop me. In the small mirror over the sink, I watched as my reflection—dirty face, matted hair, wide green eyes—slowly vanished. Once the wet fog had completely erased my image, I undressed, easing out of the tall boots (still in decent shape, thank goodness) and the skinny-jeans. I took off the white tank last, laying it gently on top of the pile of discarded clothes. Staring down at its careful beading, its delicate fabric, I felt something clench inside me; and I looked away quickly, back to the steaming shower.

I drew aside the curtain and stepped into the tub, where scalding hot water waited. When I moved under the spray, the heat stung my skin and began to redden it almost immediately. Even so, I luxuriated in the water, running my hands across my face and through my hair. Washing away that day, that week.

That decade.

In the roar of the shower, I almost couldn't hear myself think. If I concentrated hard enough on the pressure of the water—the burn of it—I could nearly block out those agonizing words of fault and grief that my brain had started to whisper to me. I kept my eyes shut tight in the hope that sheer force and blistering hot water could protect me from my own thoughts.

Some time later I pulled back the curtain and prepared to step out of the tub. But even through the fog, I caught the tiniest glimpse of that white tank, cast off and dirty. The thing that had clenched inside me earlier returned in full force, writhing and twisting until I dropped to the floor of the tub, breathless.

There I sat, for God knows how much longer, sobbing uncontrollably in the hot water.

Mourning Gabrielle Callioux.

Mourning my friend.

Chapter
THIRTY-TWO

L ong after the water turned cold and the steam evaporated, I wrapped myself in one of the spare robes and stepped out of the bathroom, carrying a pile of dirty clothes in one hand and lifting up my overnight bag with the other. I shifted everything to one arm so that I could open a nearby door, where the stairwell to Joshua's attic bedroom waited.

I'd expected to find the room empty. But after I climbed the stairs and entered the attic, I found Joshua lying on the bed, reading a thick paperback book in the dim glow of the bedside lamp. His eyes caught mine, and he set the book aside.

"Feel better?"

"Sort of," I said, my voice thick from all the crying.

Judging by the glint of worry in his eyes, Joshua didn't miss the significance of my tone. But instead of pressing the issue, he gave me an intentionally casual smile.

"You know," he mused, "it's still weird to see you wear anything but your dress."

I glanced down at the robe and then forced a weak smile. "Actually, the dress sort of . . . disintegrated. I'm sure there are some pieces left, if you want me to hunt them down for you."

Still smiling, Joshua pushed himself up and gestured for me to join him. After dropping my bag and clothes in the corner, I gathered my robe into one hand and sat on the edge of the bed next to his feet.

Once I'd settled, Joshua's expression grew serious again. For a second he just studied me, taking in my puffy, red-ringed eyes and my drawn face. Then he turned back to the bedside table and grabbed something I hadn't noticed before: a plate heaped high with food.

It was love at first sight: tomatoes and peppers and onions, swimming in a thick sauce around crawfish and rice. The rich, tangy scent of the food wafted toward me, and my hand moved of its own accord, reaching automatically for the plate. Joshua laughed at my enthusiasm and hurried to pass me the plate and a spoon.

"My dad's étouffée, left over from last night. I thought you might need it."

Lifting a spoonful of the mixture to my mouth, I tried not to moan. "I don't think I've ever needed *anything* so badly."

Joshua laughed again and settled against the pillows, watching as I attempted to eat like a human instead of gobble directly from the plate.

Once I'd devoured more than half the étouffée, he reached back to his night table for one last item and placed it next to me on the bed. I set aside my plate and took his new offering eagerly, unwrapping the layers of paper towel that surrounded it. When I saw what the towel held, however, I dropped it onto my lap.

There, in the middle of the paper, lay a single powder-coated beignet.

I must have stared down at it for too long, because eventually Joshua cleared his throat.

"Not hungry anymore?" he asked.

My head jerked upward. I thought I'd finished all my crying in the shower, by myself. But to my humiliation, my eyes welled with tears the minute they met Joshua's.

Immediately, he looked stricken. "Hey, it's okay," he murmured gently.

He shifted forward, reaching out to comfort me; but I shied away from his touch. Seeing this reaction, Joshua frowned.

"You don't want me to touch you anymore, do you?"

"No. Yes. But that's not the point. It's just—"

"Are you saying we shouldn't, because of everything that happened?" he interrupted.

"No," I repeated, feeling frustrated by my sudden inability to express myself. "That's not it at all. It's just that . . . I can't . . . you can't . . ."

"I *can't* touch you anymore?" he finished.

A tear trailed down my cheek, and I wiped it away with the back of my hand. "Bingo," I said miserably. "You can't. No living person can. That's part of what I've become. I can do all kinds of things now: eat, sleep, change clothes. I can even touch stuff. Just not living people. It's like I've regressed or something."

Both of Joshua's eyebrows rose. "But what about the fire?" he asked. "The sparks, when we touch?"

"No sparks. Not anymore."

Joshua sank down onto the bed. He raked one hand through his hair and then dropped it to the bedspread, where he traced absent circles with one finger.

After a few quiet seconds of tracing, he looked back up at me and asked, "That's what happened to you at the St. Louis Number One, isn't it? That's why you broke up with me?"

I grimaced. "Yes and no. At the St. Louis, Gaby transformed me without my permission. But I didn't find that out until after I . . . until after we . . ."

I trailed off, unsure of how to finish that statement. When Joshua realized what I meant, hurt flooded his eyes. "So if you didn't know you were changing, then why *did* you break up with me, Amelia?"

I hung my head, ashamed. "I wanted to keep you safe from what ended up happening anyway."

"What does that mean, Amelia?"

"It means I failed. I wanted to keep you and Jillian and everyone else I care about safe from the demons. I thought if I stayed away from *you*, then *you'd* stay off the demons' radar when they eventually came for me."

Joshua stirred uneasily beside me. "Why did you think they were coming for you in the first place? I thought they'd left you alone since Eli disappeared."

I sighed heavily and began rubbing my eyelids, mostly to avoid looking up at him. "I didn't want to tell you at the time because I thought it would just be too risky. But Eli reappeared on the night of the bonfire party. He warned me that the demons had decided to hunt me and that they were willing to hurt my loved ones, if they had to. I wasn't sure if he was telling the truth until I saw some demons at that club in the Quarter. I'd hoped that Gaby might be able to help me fight them, but after the ritual at the St. Louis, I realized that I was just delaying the inevitable and putting you in more danger in the process. So I . . . I ended it. And then screwed it all up tonight."

I was shocked when Joshua responded with a loud laugh. My eyes shot open, and I met his gaze, which was far softer than I'd expected it to be after a confession like that. Smiling again, he shifted closer to me on the bed.

"Amelia Elizabeth Ashley, I say this with affection, but you're totally crazy."

I laughed too, although I sounded tenser than Joshua. "Of course I'm crazy. But I'd love to hear *your* reason why."

Joshua smirked. "You broke up with me because you thought our relationship would put me at risk? Amelia, I'm a ghost-seeing descendant of exorcists who happens to be in love with—what?—the undead? My life blew past normal and safe a *long* time ago."

If I wasn't so incredibly flustered, I might have laughed. But instead, I couldn't focus on anything but one little four-letter word. Through all the fear and guilt and heartache, a real smile spread across my face.

"The proper term is Risen, actually—not undead. But are you? I mean, are you still . . . ?"

Joshua's own smile lifted higher. "Are you asking if I'm still in love with you? Despite the fact that you broke up with me because you're being chased by demons and rogue ghosts and evil Seers?"

"Yeah," I choked, taken aback by his frankness. "I guess I am."

Joshua unexpectedly ducked his head, once more scrutinizing the bedspread. For far too long he didn't say anything, and my pulse began to race uncomfortably. It outright stuttered when he looked up at me again.

"Amelia," he said roughly, "I'm not going to tell you I love you again. Not without something in return."

Suddenly, the entire world was a heart-stopping midnight blue. Before I even had time to think them, I whispered the four words that I'd been dying to say for the last three months:

"I love you, Joshua."

The moment those words left my mouth, I felt a huge whoosh of relief. One that made me wonder why I hadn't said that a long time ago. Joshua's answering grin told me that he shared my thoughts.

"Now, was that so hard?" he asked.

I grinned back, so widely my cheeks ached. Not that I cared right now. "Yes," I teased him. "It was brutal. That's why I waited this long to say it."

With a low, sexy laugh, Joshua leaned so close I could smell his cologne; could feel the warmth of his breath on my skin. Every single one of my nerve endings began to hum happily.

"You know," he whispered, "this would be the perfect moment to kiss you."

"If only you could."

Joshua's expression shifted from seductive to fervent. "Oh, don't worry: I'll find a way. I swear."

I rolled my eyes playfully and leaned back, putting some space between us before I started to hyperventilate from our closeness.

"Just because I love you," I cautioned, "doesn't mean I'm ready to join in another one of your optimistic schemes. Not quite yet."

He tilted his head to one side. "How about this: the only scheme I want us to join in is the one where we both try to stay away from the demons. Especially since we're *all* on their radar now."

I cringed. "Like I said: because I failed to protect you guys."

"You didn't fail at anything," he said. "Even if I don't agree with it, you tried to do what you thought was right. It just so happens that the Mayhews and their friends tend to mess with your plans on a semiregular basis."

"And make things better for me," I amended. "Or at least *you* do. I guess since I've officially failed, I can admit that, right?"

"Right." He laughed. "But you do realize you're dodging the real issue? You still haven't told me whether you'll agree to let me fight the demons with you."

I shrugged and gave him a skeptical, sidelong glance. "We'll see. Maybe."

Joshua looked like he wanted to argue. But after a moment's consideration, he thought better of it. Without speaking, he reached behind him and grabbed the discarded book from the nightstand. He dropped it beside me, picked up my plate, and eased off the bed.

Now facing me, he flashed a wry, confident grin, and I melted a little inside.

"You'll give in," he said. "Eventually."

"We'll see," I repeated.

Joshua chuckled and then jerked his head toward the bed. "The book is for you."

My eyes flickered to the book's cover. *"The Uniform Commercial Code?"*

"The 2004 edition. It was my mom's, from when she used to practice law. Guess she must have left it here. It's not exactly fine literature, but it might come in handy on the off chance you have trouble sleeping. Now, I hope you don't mind if I go downstairs and have a nice, long chat with my cousins."

I placed the uneaten beignet on the nightstand and shook my head. "Don't be too hard on them. Alex fooled everybody, including . . . Gaby."

Joshua clearly noticed my hesitation, but he wisely

chose not to address it.

"We'll see," Joshua said, using my own phrase. "Will you be okay up here by yourself?"

A small, weary smile twitched at one corner of my mouth. "I bet I won't be conscious for more than ten minutes."

And I was right.

Only a few seconds after Joshua said good-bye and crept down the attic stairs, I collapsed sideways on top of the covers. A few seconds after *that*, I couldn't remember anything, except the two times I briefly awoke.

The first was when I rolled on top of the bulky *Uniform Commercial Code*, which I irreverently kicked to the floor before falling back asleep. The second time didn't occur until a muffled chorus of laughter stirred me from sleep.

At first I thought I'd dreamed the noise. But another round of raucous laughter made my eyes flutter open. Rolling to one side, I stared blearily at the golden-red light pouring in through the attic's tiny dormer window. The light seemed too intense for dawn, so I slowly pushed myself into a seated position. Over the edge of the bed, I could just see a pillow and a pallet of rumpled blankets on the floor.

Apparently, Joshua had made good on his promise to sleep separately from me.

I slid off the bed with an old-lady kind of groan and

then hobbled over to the window on stiff legs. There, I lifted onto my toes to peer outside.

The view surprised me: over the rooftops and through the narrow spaces between buildings, I could see the rich oranges and reds of sunset. Which couldn't possibly be right.

At that moment, more muffled laughter and shouting filtered through the stairwell. It sounded as though the entire Mayhew clan had gathered together somewhere far below me in the house.

My eyes darted between the window and the stairwell until the realization hit me: I'd slept through Christmas Day, and almost into the evening.

I frowned and sunk back onto my heels. I knew it was foolish, but I couldn't help feeling disappointed that I'd spent my first Christmas awake from the fog of death—my first Christmas with Joshua—in a comalike sleep. Sighing, I plodded back over to the bed and flopped down near the pillow.

That's when I noticed the bedside table.

Sitting on top of the *Uniform Commercial Code* (which someone must have retrieved from the floor and placed on the table) was a rectangular object, wrapped in metallic green paper. It didn't have a label or bow, but I instinctively recognized it as a Christmas present.

For me?

I picked it up, running my fingers across its slick wrapping. For a fleeting second I worried whether the gift actually belonged to someone else; maybe I was interfering with a present that Joshua had forgotten to carry downstairs. The worry passed, however, mostly because I couldn't resist the childish impulse to find out for myself.

I slipped my finger into an opening in the green wrapping and delicately pulled the paper apart so that it wouldn't tear. After a few minutes of careful maneuvering, I'd fully removed the paper and placed it beside me on the bedspread.

I turned the unwrapped gift over in my hands, momentarily stunned.

It was a leather-bound copy of one of my favorite books: Jane Austen's *Sense and Sensibility*. Incidentally, it was also one of the books lying on the top of a reading pile in my old bedroom, the one and only time Joshua and I entered my childhood home.

In life I'd read and reread my secondhand copy so many times that the cover had started to pull away from the binding. This book, however, was gorgeous: blue leather embossed with golden flowers and cursive script. It looked old too, but only in the expensive, collector's edition sort of way.

I opened the front cover and found a white card with Joshua's handwriting tucked inside. It simply read:

This should have been your Christmas present.

As I ran my thumb over the thick black letters, a slow smile spread across my face. Despite the words on the card, I couldn't bring myself to regret Joshua's first attempt at a Christmas present. After all, it had brought me to Gaby and Felix; it was also the reason I could now hold this book in my hands, feel its embossing under my fingertips, and smell the scent of its leather.

But with *this* gift, I suddenly felt connected to Joshua again. I could still touch an object that meant something to both of us.

As I continued to trace the outline of the book's title, I wondered whether I should get dressed and go downstairs to join the Mayhews for Christmas. Other than see Joshua again, there were a few things I'd love to do: formally forgive Joshua's cousins; officially meet his father; maybe see if Ruth would thank me for helping her, or at the very least not try to exorcise me this time. . . .

I'd very nearly pushed myself off the bed when I hesitated and then sunk back into the covers. After everything that had happened yesterday with the Mayhew family and me, I didn't feel comfortable intruding. Particularly on Christmas Day, when it sounded as if the whole family had put aside their worries to enjoy time with one another.

I didn't belong with them yet.

I still suspected that I never would, despite Joshua's

and my proclamations last night. But whether or not that suspicion was unfounded, I certainly wasn't part of this family tonight.

With a regretful sigh, I sprawled across the bed and wriggled back until the pillow felt comfortable again. Then I grabbed my Christmas present, lifted it above me, and opened the front cover.

Slowly, deliberately, I flipped the pages. I let each one glide over my fingers, listening to the slight crinkling noise they made under my touch. As I did so, my smile began to return.

I could touch pages again. I could *read* again. For the first time in more than a decade, I could do something I loved because of Joshua.

Because of Gaby.

Yesterday had been a nightmare, as had so many days before that. And later I would face Ruth and the young Seers. I would spend ten hours in a car trying to pretend in front of Joshua's parents that I not only barely knew their son, but also didn't love him; I would go back to Oklahoma—to my home.

But tonight?

Tonight I would just rest.

ACKNOWLEDGMENTS

To my editor, Barbara Lalicki—someone once said that a good editor must see where a writer wants to go, understand why she isn't getting there, and explain the problem in a way that allows the writer to discover the path for herself. You have done all of this, and more. I am incredibly proud of this book, and I am even prouder to call you my friend.

To Katie McGee, Caroline Sun, Lindsey Blechman, Suzanne Daghlian, Kimberly VandeWater, Erin Fitzsimmons, and countless others at HarperTeen—you are my knights in shining armor. From exciting book trailers to gorgeous covers to shopping recommendations, you are tireless and gracious. I could not ask for a better team standing beside me on this journey.

To my agent, Catherine Drayton—you are my voice of reason (and humor) on this wild ride. I thank God you are only an email or a Skype visit away. Thank you, thank you, for still believing in and fighting for me.

To Lyndsey Blessing—your ability to negotiate foreign rights deals is truly humbling.

To the staff of InkWell Management—thank you for all of your hard work on my behalf. Because of you, I can call myself lucky!

To Phil Bacharach—thank you for introducing me to the world of TV interviews, and not laughing at me when I gave them.

To my parents, Karen and Dennis Stine—not only did you set an outstanding example of how to be a parent, but you also helped me survive when I became one myself.

To Jinx Hudson—grandmother extraordinaire, babysitter par excellence, and tireless publicist. You are not only my husband and son's family, but mine as well.

To Melissa Peters Allgood—you have kept me sane. Not an easy task. You don't need me to tell you that you are my sister in spirit, always.

To Kristen Buttram Beery—what you did for me, and for this book, can never be repaid. I love you dearly.

To Melissa Thompson and Mandy Haskins—you are my first readers, and my best.

To my dear friends Beth Prykryl, Krissy Carlson, Andi Newby, Tony Andre, Jason Brown, the YLD, and so many others—you keep doing it; you keep making me a better person. Why are you so awesome like that?

Finally, to my husband, Robert, and my son, Wyatt—you are the reason. You are my heart.